In 1771, **Johann Wolfgang von Goethe** (1749–1832) went to Strasbourg to study law. There, he had a love affair that later inspired the idyllic *Dichtung und Wahrheit* (1814). He then practiced law in Frankfurt, where he composed *The Sorrows of Young Werther* (1774). Goethe accepted an invitation from the Duke of Weimar in 1775 to join his court and for a decade held various official positions there. He spent 1787 in Italy, where he wrote *Iphigenie auf Tauris* and worked on the first part of *Faust* (1808). In 1791 Goethe was appointed director of the ducal theater, a position he held for twenty-two years. In 1806 Goethe married Christiane Vulpius, the mother of his four children. In the last year of his life, Goethe completed the second part of his masterpiece, *Faust*.

Marcelle Clements is a novelist and journalist who has contributed articles on culture, the arts, and politics to many national publications. She is the author of two books of nonfiction, *The Dog Is Us* and *The Improvised Woman*, and the novels *Rock Me* and *Midsummer*.

THE
SORROWS
OF YOUNG
WERTHER

AND SELECTED WRITINGS

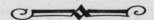

Johann Wolfgang von Goethe

Translated by
Catherine Hutter

With a New Introduction by
Marcelle Clements

SIGNET CLASSICS

SIGNET CLASSICS
Published by New American Library, a division of
Penguin Group (USA) Inc., 375 Hudson Street,
New York, New York 10014, USA
Penguin Group (Canada), 90 Eglinton Avenue East, Suite 700, Toronto,
Ontario M4P 2Y3, Canada (a division of Pearson Penguin Canada Inc.)
Penguin Books Ltd., 80 Strand, London WC2R 0RL, England
Penguin Ireland, 25 St. Stephen's Green, Dublin 2,
Ireland (a division of Penguin Books Ltd.)
Penguin Group (Australia), 250 Camberwell Road, Camberwell, Victoria 3124,
Australia (a division of Pearson Australia Group Pty. Ltd.)
Penguin Books India Pvt. Ltd., 11 Community Centre, Panchsheel Park,
New Delhi - 110 017, India
Penguin Group (NZ), cnr Airborne and Rosedale Roads, Albany,
Auckland 1310, New Zealand (a division of Pearson New Zealand Ltd.)
Penguin Books (South Africa) (Pty.) Ltd., 24 Sturdee Avenue,
Rosebank, Johannesburg 2196, South Africa

Penguin Books Ltd., Registered Offices:
80 Strand, London WC2R 0RL, England

Published by Signet Classics, an imprint of New American Library,
a division of Penguin Group (USA) Inc.

First Signet Classics Printing, August 1962
First Signet Classics Printing (Clements Introduction), July 2005
10 9 8 7 6 5 4 3 2

CONTENTS

INTRODUCTION

Like many novels that survive their authors and their era to become literary monuments *The Sorrows of Young Werther* is so heavily burdened by prestige and official responsibilities that we are surprised to discover it is only 130 pages long, the hastily written first novel of a very young author. Johann Wolfgang von Goethe was twenty-four years old when *The Sorrows of Young Werther* was published in 1774. "I wrote *Werther* in four weeks," he tells us in his memoirs,[1] "without ever making a plan of the whole or previously putting any of it down on paper." The result was a slim book that told an old story: A beautiful youth, who seems to carry some sort of sadness within him, encounters a beautiful maiden. He is entranced by her, but she is promised to another. He kills himself.

From the very start, the notoriety of *The Sorrows of Young Werther* flooded its relationship with the reader; that is, long before it became clear that it would be one of Western Civilization's Great Books, the forerunner of the modern psychological novel and the apogee of the Sturm und Drang movement. It has never been possible to read *The Sorrows of Young Werther* without the interference of its reputation: It never got that grace period between publication and the moment when fame distorts the relationship between a book and its readers, before the critics speak and the word of mouth builds, before the climb in sales and, eventually, if all goes well, the ascension, the awards, the new editions, the translations, the place in the canon. Immediately upon publication, its success was so immense that its

[1]Excerpts from Goethe's autobiography *My Life: Poetry and Truth* follow *The Sorrows of Young Werther*, starting on page 132 of this volume.

trajectory as a cultural artifact rivaled its interest as a literary creation. It was an instant bestseller in Germany, France and England and was quickly translated into every European language. It was reprinted, pirated, imitated, stolen from. It was retold or continued in thousands of poems, stories, novels, plays, ballets, musical pieces, paintings and prints. Then came the proto-pop products and happenings: There were Werther memorial processions, Werther clubs, Werther china figurines (the first literary action figures?), Werther waxworks, eau de Werther. Images of Werther and of his inamorata, Lotte, materialized on articles of clothing and household implements, ". . . on fans and gloves, on breadboxes and jewelry, on delicate Messen porcelain."[2]

If further evidence was required of the reading public's limitless craving for all things Werther—or *Wertherfieber* (Werther fever), as it became known—there was also a fashion for Werther-style *liebestod,* or love suicide. Picturesque young Wertherians, dressed in blue jackets and yellow vests just as Werther had been (because these items had been touched by Lotte and "rendered sacred"), leaped into rivers and drowned, a copy of *The Sorrows of Young Werther* in their pockets. Others shot themselves in the head as Werther had, while sitting at their writing desks on which copies of the book lay open. There is debate as to whether there was an epidemic of such deaths or a trickle, but today psychologists still refer to copycat suicide as "the Werther Effect."[3]

A novel about outsize desire, self-destruction and the need to flee urban civilization can be supposed to exert many types of bad influence on youthful enthusiasts, so it is difficult to imagine which of those themes was considered most dangerous but, in any event, the book was soon banned in several European cities—in some cases for as long as fifty years. There were German towns in which,

[2]Stuart P. Atkins, *The Testament of Werther in Poetry and Drama*, Harvard University Press, 1949.
[3]The term, coined in the 1970s by sociologist David P. Phillips, refers to suicides that mimic those described in the media. Werther's is probably still the most famous suicide in fiction, but statistics for copycat *liebestod* were not available to Dr. Phillips and his team. Instead, they began by studying the response to the huge number of media accounts of Marilyn Monroe's death, an apt pairing.

for good measure, the blue-and-yellow outfit was banned as well. Naturally, such obstacles only intensified the Werther craze, and Wertherians became legion. Among the best known was Napoléon, who said he brought *Werther* along on his Egyptian campaign, tucked in an inside pocket, next to his heart. In 1806—thirty years after *Werther*'s publication—while visiting Germany for a congress, the Emperor summoned its author for an audience and told him that he had read the novel seven times. Unfortunately, he had disliked the ending, and then proceeded to offer Johann von Goethe some advice about plotting.

The influence of *The Sorrows of Young Werther* on other writers was incalculable and enduring. Many fiction writers have included references to Werther in their work, sometimes distancing their hero, sometimes pointing out a telling identification. (In the latter category, the most moving may well be Mary Wollstonecraft Shelley's Frankenstein, who wept upon reading of Werther's death. ". . . A more divine being than I had ever beheld or imagined," the monster tells us.) There has been a prodigious amount of criticism and commentary written about it, and Young Werther and his sorrows are as present in Roland Barthes' exquisite modern musings on the nature of love as they were in Carlyle's manly reflections on literary history two hundred years earlier. Many passages became so well known that they were referred to by date—as in the May 10 letter, in which Werther's oneness with nature becomes clear to the reader: "I throw myself down among the tall grass by the trickling stream. . . ." Others are simply referred to by name, like the famous "bread scene," in which Werther first encounters Lotte giving some children their meal in the shade of two magnificent linden trees.[4]

Why did so many of Goethe's contemporaries want to

---

[4]William Makepeace Thackeray's contribution to the commemoration of this passage begins as follows:

> Werther had a love for Charlotte
> Such as words could never utter;
>   Would you know how first he met her?
> She was cutting bread and butter.

read a book whose ending they already knew? (In fact, not only did they know the ending, but they knew that Napoléon had disliked it!) And why should we? Why should we see Wertheriana (as it is actually called in some circles) as anything but a curiosity verging on the grotesque?

All of this reportage and gossip regarding *The Sorrows of Young Werther*'s publication and reception may seem to be frivolous to some, but the book's impact on the course of Western literature cannot be understood otherwise. *Werther* represented much more than a fashion: The colossal, unprecedented surge of youth-culture energy it produced was in itself a transformative phenomenon. When its themes, ideas, characters and style were disseminated all at once throughout Europe, they acted like an irresistible call to the artists who would become the Romantics and the young men and women of the emerging middle class who would be their audience. Because *Werther* tapped into a previously unknown but astoundingly widespread impulse to leave behind the prevailing Classicist aesthetic—the legacy of the enlightenment and its rationalism, materialism, its formality, pomp, and enforced dignity—a pan-European generation found its sensibility. The members of the establishment, which had suddenly become the old guard, disdained *Werther* as a *sentimental novel*, a much scorned genre, and they were appalled that this paltry work was the very first German book to become an international success. Before Goethe, no one would have assumed that anyone, let alone a German writer, could connect with such immediacy to readers of England, France, Italy and Spain and the German-speaking countries. It was finally understood that Goethe, who was both outside the French-English literary axis and tremendously knowledgeable about it, was a master of synthesis. In the view of many, he remains Germany's greatest author.

As if compacted in a time capsule, all the components of early Romanticism are contained within the pages of *The Sorrows of Young Werther*. Anyone with an interest in this era of fantastic transition can chart the territory: the awed passion for nature, even human nature, the will to access the unconscious, the celebration of imagination and transgression, the sense of the sublime, the transfiguration and exaltation of pain, martyrdom, the reverence for art and the worship of artists as the new heroes, of the rapturous, of the exultant, of the chaotic, of the dark.

Just as we cannot suspend our awareness of the stature of *The Sorrows of Young Werther*, we must accept the idea that, like someone about whom we've been told a great deal and who disappoints us when we meet at last, Werther may seem disconcerting when we finally encounter him in these pages. Expecting the prototype for the yet-to-be-born Romantic Hero, the precursor to Byron's tragic and masterful lover, who stands with wind in his hair, gazing out over a stormy sea, we find instead a chatty young lawyer taking a break in the country. Relieved to be alone, he has settled for the moment in a not particularly attractive town, which he never describes. Above all, he presents himself as someone who wants to stay calm. In his letters to a friend back home—although no one we know of has urged him to extend himself—he protests very loudly and insistently that he doesn't want to be disturbed. We soon suspect that roaming the countryside and inviting rapture by throwing himself down in the tall grass by the trickling stream are a bad strategy for him, if what he truly wants is to stay calm.

Even today, *The Sorrows of Young Werther* is often referred to as a tale of unrequited love. But this is a serious misreading of the book, as is apparent to anyone who scrutinizes the opening pages and notices that the young Werther's sorrows are already fully formed, his tragedy ordained by his character and his past experiences.

"I can't tell you how glad I am to have got away" is how he begins his very first letter. He is referring to his troubles back home, but is thereby announcing himself from the start as someone who can only flee what he cannot bear. He has no interest in seeming strong, impervious to temptation or disappointment. His is a very different type of masculinity. Like Hamlet, who was one of Goethe's inspirations, Werther is ambivalent, indecisive, inclined to brood about his torment rather than act to rid himself of it. He experiences himself as unformed, sometimes even amorphous—easily given to fantasies of merging with elements in his physical environment. And clearly, he is what the world would call "unwell." He doesn't need Lotte's love to disequilibrate him—he tells us, again and again, that he is unstable, so raw that he needs the "balm" of solitude. Alas, there isn't much for him to do, if he is to stay calm. Even reading is a problem, except for Homer in judicious doses. Other books are too agitating.

> My heart ferments sufficiently of itself. . . . Often do I strive to allay the burning fever of my blood; and you have never witnessed anything so unsteady, so uncertain, as my heart. But need I confess this to you, my dear friend, who have so often endured the anguish of witnessing my sudden transitions from sorrow to immoderate joy, and from sweet melancholy to violent passions? I treat my poor heart like a sick child, and gratify its every fancy. Do not mention this again: there are people who would censure me for it.

The entanglement with a threesome that will lead to his unbearable frustration is foreshadowed in the very first paragraph as Werther describes his chief reasons for leaving town.

> Poor Leonora! and yet I was not to blame. Was it my fault, that, whilst the peculiar charms of her sister afforded me an agreeable entertainment, a passion for me was engendered in her feeble heart?

He cues us to note the ambiguities of such relationships, when he adds,

> And yet am I wholly blameless? Did I not encourage her emotions? Did I not feel charmed at those truly genuine expressions of nature, which, though but little mirthful in reality, so often amused us? Did I not—but oh! what is man, that he dares so to accuse himself?

But for all his grasp of such contradictions, once caught in the triangle, Werther refuses to see that Lotte is seductive, nor how much he enjoys her subtle, playful sadism. Unlike her English and French predecessors, Richardson's

Pamela and Rousseau's Julie, Lotte often seems less virtuous than perverse in her refusal to respond to the unspoken but urgent desire of her would-be lover. Characterized not so much by goodness as by warmth, she's a more interesting character than the saintly damsels in distress.

Many critics—and even more readers—are persuaded that Lotte is moral, pure or, in other terms, passive, that she affectionately endures Werther's pathological passion. But with her allusions, her body language and, most clearly of all, with the language of the eyes, Goethe shows us how she arouses Werther. It is impossible not to see her as a tease or, more profoundly, as someone who is just as crazy as Werther. Eventually, Werther's ineffectual attempts to suppress his emotions, so much in evidence in the first few pages, cease completely. He doesn't even try to stop his feelings, only to restrain his behavior—to prevent himself from kissing, touching, taking. This has the effect of extraordinarily cranking up the sexual tension in his scenes with Lotte. The more she teases, the more Werther contains his longing, the more lascivious it seems.

Their relationship has long been crudely sentimentalized as an old-fashioned conflict of sin versus virtue, but a close reading of their exchanges will reveal an entirely different scenario—subtler, more complex and sensual and infinitely more psychologically authentic than the impossible cliché of monolithic male adulation of female perfection. At the beginning of their relationship, the reader can note how often Lotte would place her hand on Werther's arm, how close she sat to him, how she leaned against him, how she fed a bird from her own lips, kissed its beak and then passed it to Werther, instructing him to kiss it in turn. She really knows him, too. One evening at a ball, they escape from the crowd and go together to the open window. Lotte leans out as a soft rain falls, the passing storm still thundering at a distance. Moved by the beauty of the night, she turns to Werther, tears in her eyes, places her hand in his and says, "Klopstock!"

"At once," Werther writes his friend, "I remembered the magnificent ode which was in her thoughts: I felt oppressed with the weight of my sensations, and sank under them. It was more than I could bear. I bent over her hand, kissed it in a stream of delicious tears, and again looked up to her eyes."

From the start, Werther's fate is inscribed in his need to go mad with love and lust. He's had several rehearsals, and he knows. . . . His madness has only been waiting for that trigger—some equivalent of that exquisite moment of revelation under the linden trees—and now the tale can unfold. Goethe brilliantly demonstrates how Werther's attempts to dampen the roar of his love by tuning in to the louder cacophony of nature must be self-defeating. The more intense the emotion, the more complete the confusion, the more certain is the sacrifice of the self within the universe's endless energy. Nothing can emerge from this union with nature but limitless desire or death. Those are the terms, and whether we agree with them or not, by the time we have finished *The Sorrows of Young Werther*, we understand them thoroughly.

What of Albert? If Albert, Lotte's humorless fiancé, did not exist, the lovers, and the reader/voyeur, would have to invent him. Because he is often not at home, but always present in their minds, every glance stimulates. Every touch is inventoried, analyzed, nursed in memory.

Eventually, both are so sensitized to their own desire and each other's that they cannot permit themselves to touch at all or, in the final stages, even to look or speak. Because the give and take of lust is never verbalized, because it is never either consummated or ignored, it is constantly expressed. And then at last, as it must, the foreplay turns into fatal longing. The only other option would have been hate, and that's not what Goethe was interested in writing about. He would not have been so cruel to the lovers or, for that matter, to the reader. Werther must be sacrificed and his desire is so great that nothing will be commensurate but death. Lotte must be punished, and no punishment will suffice short of his death. And finally, Albert, stand-in for all of the reasonable, strong, humorless bourgeois father figures who always get the best of the child-artist, must get his due. It doesn't matter a bit that Albert has never really come to life for the reader. On the contrary, an essential element to the drama is the insignificance of Albert's presence. The more seductive Lotte is, the more tumescent

Werther becomes, the more it is not Albert but the reader who is the third in the threesome.

Goethe was so tremendously unsettled by the reaction to *The Sorrows of Young Werther* that he revised the original work and what we read now is based on a later, much subdued 1787 edition. The public response—certainly the suicides—scared him, and it also left him feeling insulted that his work had been so misunderstood.

> . . . Just as I felt relieved and lighthearted because I had succeeded in translating reality into poetry, my friends were confusing themselves that they had to turn poetry into reality, enact the novel and shoot themselves![5]

He was also maddened by the consequences of his sudden, extraordinary celebrity. Understandably, he found it difficult to work when so many people wanted to see him and to talk to him. Worse was the public's oppressive inquisitiveness about his own life. He hadn't imagined that "sympathizing, well-wishing souls were going to become such an unbearable nuisance. Instead of saying something nice about the book just as it was, all of them wanted to know how much of it was true!"[6] He certainly never denied that *Werther* was based to a certain extent on his experiences. On the contrary, in his memoirs, he explains that Lotte had been based on several girls he knew in his youth.

> This profusion of Lottes was a terrible nuisance because everyone who even looked at me wanted to know where the real one was. . . . I hoped I would soon be rid of these embarrassing inquiries, but unfortunately they pursued me throughout my entire life.[7]

Finally, he was led to bitter thoughts, and came to feel that ". . . the author and his public are separated by an immense abyss, both of them fortunately having no idea of its dimensions." Paradoxically, he found himself turning

[5] See "Reflections on Werther," page 149 in this volume.
[6] *Ibid*, page 152.
[7] *Ibid*, pages 153–54.

away from Romanticism and from the belief in the artist as a hero and in art as salvation. "Writing is a misuse of language," he would assert. "Reading alone quietly is a sad substitute for talk."

It is not *Werther* but the prose play *Faust* for which Goethe is now best remembered, but although he had already begun to conceptualize this vast, complex work, it would be a long time before *Wertherfieber* subsided enough for him to focus on new writing. Part I of *Faust* was not published until 1808; the monumental Part II was published posthumously. Eventually, he moved on to the drama, poetry and criticism that, together, made him known to the world as the Promethean creator who links the Age of Reason to the present, but for many years Goethe seems to have struggled to accept the origins of his fame.

> . . . [T]he greatest good fortune—or disaster—was the fact that everyone wanted to know more about the strange young author who had suddenly put in such a bold appearance. They demanded to see me and talk to me; those far away wanted to hear something about me. I therefore experienced a high degree of popularity that was sometimes pleasant, sometimes disagreeable, and always distracting. For plenty of unfinished work lay before me—in fact I had things planned that would take years to complete, even if I applied myself to them ardently. But I had been dragged out of my stillness, out of the twilight and darkness that alone favor the purity of creation, into the noise of daytime, where one loses oneself in others and becomes confused by sympathy as well as by coldness, by praise as well as by reproof.[8]

Decades after the publication, long after Goethe's ascent to the pantheon, he continued to speak and write with regret about *Werther*'s notoriety.

—MARCELLE CLEMENTS

[8]*Ibid*, pages 154–55.

TRANSLATOR'S NOTE

The purpose of this volume is to present *The Sorrows of Young Werther* in a new translation and to include a few of Goethe's writings that we feel go well with it in order to produce a book that is an entity at least in mood.

The effort was made to capture, however briefly, an aspect of Goethe's vast store of work that is rare in the great men of literature and even rarer in the artistic manifestations of our day, namely, his radiance. For this translator was left, after reading *Werther,* with an impression of the young man's capacity to enjoy life rather than of his inability to cope with it and with a memory of his strong sense of social justice rather than of his defeat by the laws of society. Goethe's attitude toward life, even in *The Sorrows of Young Werther,* is affirmative, and the "Reflections on Werther," taken from his memoirs, *Poetry and Truth* (*Dichtung und Wahrheit*), are included here not only to give the reader insight into how *Werther* came into being, how much of the novel is autobiographical and how much fiction, what the book did for the author and how it was received, but also to illuminate Goethe's approach to the negative aspects of life. Here he is clearly revealed as the man who said, "However it may be, life is good."

It was not difficult to find other examples of Goethe's deep love of women, of nature, of beauty in art and nature—in short, of life, for it is the mainspring of his work. The Sesenheim episode from *Poetry and Truth* is included for this reason, and two fairy tales: "The New Melusina," which is mentioned in the Sesenheim sequence, and "The Fairy Tale," in which Goethe disguises profound subject matter symbolically and happily. All are love stories. And we hope that the reader may find in them a type of heroine who has almost disappeared from the literature of our day—

the truly charming, well-balanced, blithe, unproblematical, and *living* girl.

The translator wishes to thank Beatrice Baumfeld for her invaluable help in compiling this volume and in keeping a watchful eye on the true and deeper meanings of words during the translation, and Professor Hermann J. Weigand for his illumination of various difficult passages.

—CATHERINE HUTTER

Whatever I could find concerning the story of poor Werther I have collected and present it to you herewith, in the belief that you will thank me for it. You will not want to deny his spirit and character your admiration and love, nor his fate your compassion. And you, my good man, who may feel a similar urge—take comfort in his suffering and let this book be your friend if, through fate or your own fault, you can find none better.

THE SORROWS OF YOUNG WERTHER

This is another one of those creatures whom, like the pelican, I have fed with the blood of my own heart . . . there were special circumstances close at hand, urgent, troubling me, and they resulted in the state of mind that produced Werther. I had lived, loved, and suffered much . . . that's what it was.

—GOETHE
TO ECKERMANN

BOOK ONE

May 4th, 1771

I can't tell you how glad I am to have got away. Dear friend, how strange is the human heart! I love you, we were inseparable—yet I can leave you and be content. I know you will forgive me. Were not all my attachments designed by fate to intimidate a heart like mine? Poor Leonore! But I was not to blame. Was it my fault that, while her headstrong sister charmed and amused me, a passion for me developed in poor Leonore's heart? Yet I ask myself—am I entirely blameless? Did I perhaps encourage her? Didn't I quite frankly enjoy her completely sincere and natural outbursts, which often made the two of us laugh, although there was really nothing laughable about them? Didn't I . . . oh, what is man made of that he may reproach himself? I shall do better in the future, my dear friend, I promise you. I shall stop dwelling on the petty wrongs of providence, as has been my wont. I intend to enjoy the present and let the past take care of itself. Of course, best of friends, you are right—there would be less misery in this world if man were not so ever-ready to recall past evils rather than put up with the indifferent present. God knows why he is thus constituted!

Please tell my mother that I am doing my best to straighten out her affairs and will give her news of them as soon as I can. I have spoken to my aunt and must say that I didn't find her to be the dreadful vehement woman with the kindest of hearts. I explained my mother's complaint concerning her share of the inheritance, which has been withheld. She gave me the reasons for it and the conditions under which she would be willing to hand over all of it, which is even more than we are asking. But I really don't

23

feel like reporting about it now. Just tell her that everything will be all right. And in the course of this little transaction, my dear friend, I discovered again that misunderstandings and inertia cause perhaps more to go wrong in this world than slyness and evil intent. In any case, the latter are rarer.

And, by the way, I feel very well here. The solitude in these blissful surroundings is balm to my soul, and with its abundance, the youthful season of spring cheers my heart, which is still inclined to shudder. Every tree, every hedge-row is a bouquet. It makes me wish I were a ladybug and could fly in and out of the sea of wondrous scents and find all my nourishment there.

The town itself is not attractive, but I find ample compensation in the indescribable beauties of nature surrounding it. That was what induced the late Count von M. to set his garden on one of the numerous hillsides that intersect here, forming the loveliest valleys. The garden is not elaborate, and the moment you walk into it you feel that it was designed by a sensitive heart rather than a scientific gardener, a heart that sought to find its enjoyment there. I have shed a few tears myself for the departed gentleman, in the little, broken-down summerhouse that used to be his favorite haunt and now is mine. Soon I will be master of the garden. The gardener seems to think well of me, though I have been here only a few days, and I will see to it that he enjoys working for me.

May 10th

My whole being is filled with a marvelous gaiety, like the sweet spring mornings that I enjoy with all my heart. I am alone and glad to be alive in surroundings such as these, which were created for a soul like mine. I am so happy, best of friends, and so utterly absorbed by the sensations of a peaceful existence that my work suffers from it. I couldn't draw now, not a line, yet was never a better painter. When the mists in my beloved valley steam all around me; when the sun rests on the surface of the impenetrable depths of my forest at noon and only single rays steal into the inner sanctum; when I lie in the tall grass beside a rushing brook and become aware of the remarkable diversity of a thousand little growing things on the ground, with all their peculiarities; when I can feel the teeming of a minute world amid the blades of grass and the innumerable, unfathomable shapes of worm and insect closer to my heart and can sense the presence of the Almighty, who in a state of continuous bliss bears and sustains us—then, my friend, when it grows light before my eyes and the world around me and the sky above come to rest wholly within my soul like a beloved, I am filled often with yearning and think, if only I could express it all on paper, everything that is housed so richly and warmly within me, so that it might be the mirror of my soul as my soul is the mirror of Infinite God . . . ah, my dear friend . . . but I am ruined by it. I succumb to its magnificence.

May 12th

I don't know whether deceptive spirits haunt these parts or whether it is the glowing fantasies of my heart that make everything around me seem so blissful. Just outside town there is a spring to which I feel mysteriously drawn, like Melusina and her sisters.[1] You walk down a short slope and at the bottom find yourself facing an archway from which about twenty steps descend to a place where clearest water gushes out of marble rock. The low wall that hems this spot in at the top, the tall trees all around it that conceal the coolness within, all suggest something mysterious. Not a day passes without my spending an hour there. Young girls come from town to fetch water, a simple and very necessary business—in days of old even the daughters of kings used to do it—and as I sit there, a patriarchal atmosphere comes to life all around me. I can see our forefathers meeting and courting at wells like this, and how good spirits hovered over all such places. Whoever can't feel with me has never refreshed himself at a cool spring after a long excursion on a hot summer's day.

NOTE: Numbered notes are by the translator and are printed on pp. 250–253. Goethe's notes, marked by asterisks, are set at the foot of the appropriate page.

May 13th

You ask whether you should send me books. Dear friend, I beg of you—don't. I have no wish to be influenced, encouraged, or inspired any more. My heart surges wildly enough without any outside influence. What I need is a lullaby, and I have found an abundance of them in my beloved Homer. How often I have to calm my rebellious blood! You have never known anything so wildly fluctuating as this heart of mine. But, dear friend, I don't have to tell you this—you, who have so often witnessed my transitions from grief to extravagant joy, from sweetest melancholy to pernicious passion. I coddle my heart like a sick child and give in to its every whim. But don't tell a soul. There are people who would condemn me for it.

May 15th

The simple folk here already know me and seem to be fond of me, especially the children. At first, when I made efforts to join them and ask questions about this and that, a few thought I was making fun of them and were quite rude. But I didn't let it bother me. I only felt keenly what I have noticed often—that persons of rank tend to keep their cold distance from the common man, as if they feared to lose something by such intimacy. And then, of course, there are those who shrink from all contact with simple people, and the tactless jokesters who talk down to them—they succeed only in making the poor souls more sharply aware than ever of their presumption. I know that we human beings were not created equal and cannot be, but I am of the opinion that he who keeps aloof from the so-called rabble in order to preserve the respect he feels is his due is just as reprehensible as the coward who hides from his enemies because he fears to be defeated by them.

Not long ago I came to the spring and found a young servant girl there. She had put her water jar on the lowest step and was looking around in the hope that a friend might come and help her place it on her head. I walked down the steps and faced her. "Would you like me to help you?" I asked. She blushed and replied, "Oh no, sir!" "Let's not stand on ceremony," I said. She adjusted the pad on her head, I helped her with her pitcher, she thanked me, and up she went!

May 17th

I have met all sorts of people but I have yet to find the right companionship. I don't know what my attractions are, but many people seem to like me and attach themselves to me. Then it pains me when our paths coincide for only a short way. You ask what the people are like here. All I can say is, as they are everywhere else. There is something coldly uniform about the human race. Most of them have to work for the greater part of their lives in order to live and the little freedom they have left frightens them to such an extent that they will stop at nothing to rid themselves of it. Oh, human destiny!

But really, they are good people. Sometimes, when I forget myself and indulge in a few of the pleasures still left to mankind and sit down at a prettily set table to enjoy myself with them quite naturally and sincerely; or when I arrange a drive or a dance at the appropriate time . . . things like that . . . it does me good. The only thing I must not think of is that I am possessed of other potentialities as well, all of them going to waste, and that I have to keep them carefully concealed. And oh, how this constricts my heart! Yet to be misunderstood is the miserable destiny of people like myself.

How I regret that the sweetheart of my youth is no more, how I deplore the fact that I ever knew her! If I had not known her, I could say: "You are a fool. You are looking for something that does not exist." But she was mine. I experienced the warmth of a heart and the nobility of a soul in whose presence I seemed to be more than I was because I was everything I possibly could be. Dear God, was there a facet of my soul then that was not alive? With her I could fully develop that wonderful feeling with which my heart embraces nature. Our relationship was a constant interplay of the most subtle perception, the keenest wit. Even its nuances, right down to occasional outbursts of mischievousness on her part, showed every indication of genius. And now! Alas, the years she was my senior took her to her grave before me. But I will never forget her—not her resolute mind nor her divine tolerance.

A few days ago I met a young man called V., an ingenuous fellow with a very pleasant face. He has just left the university and doesn't consider himself overly wise, yet thinks he knows more than most people. As far as I can make out, he seems to have been very diligent, in short, he is well informed. He had heard that I sketch a great deal and that I know Greek—staggering accomplishments in these parts—so he came to see me and unloaded his store of wisdom, everything from Batteux to Wood, and De Piles to Winckelmann; and assured me that he had read all of Sulzer's Theory (Part One) and owned a manuscript of Heyne's on "The Study of Antiquity." I let him talk.

I have also met another good fellow, the magistrate of this principality, a forthright, simple man. I have been told that it is perfectly delightful to see him with his children— he has nine! There is a lot of talk about his eldest daughter. He has asked me to visit them, and I shall do so as soon as I can. He resides in one of the Prince's hunting lodges, an hour and a half from here. He was given permission to move there after the death of his wife made it too painful for him to remain at his official residence in town.

Aside from these two, a few curious characters have crossed my path about whom everything is insufferable, especially their efforts to be friendly. Farewell! This letter should please you . . . it is strictly factual!

May 22nd

The illusion that life is but a dream has occurred to quite a few people, and I feel the same way about it. When I see the limitations imposed on man's powers of action and inquiry and observe how all his efficiency is aimed at nothing but the satisfaction of his needs, which in turn has but one purpose—to prolong his miserable existence—and when I see how all his reassurance on certain aspects of his inquiries is little more than a dreamy resignation, in that he chooses to bedaub the walls of his prison with motley figures and bright prospects—all this, William, makes me mute. I turn in upon myself and find a world there, again more in a spirit of presentiment and dour longing than dramatically or with vitality. Then everything grows hazy in my mind and I go on smiling dreamily at the world.

All learned schoolmasters and tutors are agreed that little children do not know what they want, but no one likes to admit that grown men stumble across this earth like children, not knowing whence they came nor whither they are going, and that a grown man can be just as poor at pursuing the higher aims of life and can be ruled, just like a child, by cookies, cake, and rod. To me all this is quite obvious.

I am perfectly willing to admit—because I know very well what your answer will be—that those people are happiest who live for the moment, like children dragging their dolls around with them, dressing and undressing them, eying the cupboard where Mama keeps the cookies with the greatest respect and, when at long last they get what they want, stuff their cheeks full, chew, swallow, and cry, "More!" Happy creatures! And they are lucky, also, who know how to give high-sounding names to their shabby professions, even to their passions, passing them off as great achievements that will benefit humanity. Any man is well off who can do that. But he who is humble knows very well where it all ends and can see how neatly every contented citizen prunes his little garden to suit his idea of Paradise, with what perseverance even the unhappy man bears his burden, and how all of them have but one thing on their minds—to see the sun shine for one short moment more. Believe me, such a man remains silent and learns how to create his own world by himself, and is happy—as they are—to be alive. And however confused he may be, he always carries in his heart a sweet feeling of freedom in the knowledge that he can leave his prison whenever he likes.

May 26th

You know my old habit of settling down in a place that suits me and of taking refuge there, however primitive it may be. Well, I have found such a spot here.

About an hour away there is a place called Wahlheim.*

---

*The reader need not take the trouble to look up the places that are mentioned here. It was considered necessary to change all real names that were found in the original manuscript.

Its location on the top of a hill is quite unusual, and if you take the footpath that leads to the village, you suddenly find yourself overlooking the entire valley. At the inn a good woman, who is pleasant and lively in spite of her advanced years, serves wine, beer, and coffee; but the crowning glory of the place are two linden trees that stretch their wide branches over the little green in front of the church, which is surrounded by cottages, barns and farmyards. I don't think I have ever before seen a place which was so secluded and in which I could feel so much at home. I have them bring a table and chair outside for me and there I sit, drinking coffee and reading Homer. When I came upon the place for the first time quite by chance on a beautiful afternoon, I found the spot deserted. Everyone was out in the fields. Only a boy, about four years old, was sitting on the grass, holding an infant of about six months pressed with both arms tightly to his chest between his feet, thereby forming a sort of armchair for the child. In spite of the alert way he was looking about him out of his dark eyes, he sat perfectly still. The sight amused me. I sat down on a plow that was standing nearby and began, with great enthusiasm, to sketch this little picture of brotherly devotion. I put in the fence, a barn door, and a few dilapidated wagon wheels—everything, just as it was—and found, after an hour had passed, that I had produced a very well-arranged and interesting drawing without really having contributed anything to it. This strengthened my decision to stick to nature in the future, for only nature is infinitely rich and capable of developing a great artist. There is much to be said for the advantage of rules and regulations, much the same things as can be said in praise of middle-class society—he who sticks to them will never produce anything that is bad or in poor taste, just as he who lets himself be molded by law, order, and prosperity will never become an intolerable neighbor or a striking scoundrel. On the other hand—and people can say what they like—rules and regulations ruin our true appreciation of nature and our powers to express it. Very well, say that I am being too harsh and that rules and regulations merely serve to curb us, cut down the rank vine, etc. Would you like me to give you an example? We can, for instance, apply what I have just said to love. A young man's heart belongs to a certain girl. He spends every hour of the day with her and expends all his strength and his entire fortune on assuring her at every moment that he is all hers. Along comes a Philistine, an official, let us say, and says to him, "My dear young man, to love is human, but you must love properly. Arrange your time more circumspectly into time for work, and spend only your hours of recreation with your sweetheart. Count your money and give her a present out of whatever remains after paying for the necessities of life . . . there is nothing to be said against that, only don't do it too often . . . for her birthday, let us say, or her nameday," etc. If the fellow obeys, you have a worthy young man and I would be willing to advise any Prince to let him head a committee. But as far as love is concerned, that's finished. And if he is an artist, the same applies to his art. Oh my dear friend, would you like to know why genius so rarely breaks its bonds, why it so seldom bursts upon us like a raging torrent to shatter our astounded souls? My friend, it is because of the sober gentlemen who reside on either side of the river, whose precious little summerhouses, tulip beds, and vegetable gardens would be ruined by it, and who know so well how to build dams and divert all such threatening danger in good time.

May 27th

I see that I was carried away by ecstasy, parable, and oratory and quite forgot to tell you more about the children. I must have sat for at least two hours, lost in contemplation of my work—the sketch I did yesterday will give you a somewhat fragmentary impression of it—when, with the approach of evening, a young woman came toward the children, who still hadn't moved. She was carrying a basket on her arm and called out to them from a distance, "My, what a good boy you are, Philip!" She nodded to me, I returned her greeting, rose, walked over to her, and asked if she was their mother. She said she was and, giving the older boy a bun, picked up the baby and kissed him in a very pretty display of motherly love. "I told Philip to hold the little one," she explained, "while I went to town with my older boy to get some white bread and sugar, and a small earthenware dish for the baby's porridge." I could see all the things she mentioned in her basket because the lid was up. "I want to make soup for my Hans this evening." Hans was the name of the youngest child. "My oldest boy, the rascal, broke the dish yesterday while he was quarreling with Philip over what was left of the cereal." I asked her where her oldest boy was, and she had just finished telling me that he was chasing a pair of geese in a nearby field, when he came running up to us with a hazel switch for his little brother. I went on chatting with the woman and learned that her husband had set out on a journey to Switzerland to claim an inheritance left him by a cousin. "They were going to cheat him of it," she explained. "They didn't reply to his letters so he had to go there himself. I hope nothing has happened to him. I have had no word from him since he left." I found it difficult to part from the woman. I gave each of the children a penny and gave her one for the little boy, so she could treat him to some white bread with his soup when she went to town again. Then we parted.

Let me tell you something, my dear fellow—when I no longer know how to contain myself, the sight of someone like that, who is content within the narrow confines of her existence, who knows how to get by from day to day, who, when she sees the leaves fall, thinks of nothing but that winter is coming . . . it stills the tumult in my heart.

Since that day, I have visited Wahlheim often. The children have grown accustomed to me. I give them my sugar when I drink my coffee and share my bread and butter and sour milk with them in the evening. Every Sunday they get their penny, and if I don't happen to be there after vespers, I leave word with the innkeeper to give it to them. They confide in me, all sorts of things, but what amuses me most is their wildness, and their simple outbursts of self-assertion when they are joined by other children from the village. It wasn't easy to convince their mother that they were not annoying me in the least.

May 30th

What I said the other day about painting is true also of poetry. It is simply that one should recognize and try to express only what is excellent, and that is saying a great deal in a few words. Today I experienced something that, simply told, could be a beautiful idyl, but what is poetry, episode, and idyl? Must it always be patchwork when we participate in a revelation of nature?

If you are expecting something very lofty and highly refined after this preamble, then you have been sadly misled again. Nothing more grandiose than a peasant lad produced this lively anticipation in me. I will tell the tale badly, as usual, and as usual you will say that I am exaggerating. It is Wahlheim again, always Wahlheim, where such unique things take place.

A group of people were taking coffee under the linden trees. They did not appeal to me, so I made up an excuse for not joining them. A peasant boy came out of one of the neighboring cottages and busied himself fixing the plow which I sketched a few days ago. I liked his appearance so I accosted him and asked him some questions about himself. We were soon on quite friendly terms, and, as is usual with this type of person, he began to confide in me. He told me that he was in the service of a widow and that he was being treated well there. He talked on and on about her, singing her praises, and it wasn't long before I realized that he was hopelessly in love with her. She was not young, he explained, and her first husband had treated her badly. She therefore did not want to marry again. From what he told it became quite clear how pretty and charming she was, and how much he wished that she would choose him to help her forget her first mistake. I would have to repeat what he said word for word really to convey to you his attraction to the woman, his love and devotion. Indeed, I would have to be a great poet to reproduce what he said, his attitude, the harmoniousness of his voice, the latest fire in his eyes, as spiritedly as I experienced them. But there are no words for the tenderness expressed by the man as a whole. Anything I might say would be clumsy in comparison. I was especially touched by his fear that I might come to the wrong conclusions about the relationship and doubt her propriety. It was charming to hear him speak of her appearance and figure, to which he was so strongly attracted although she was no longer young. I can recapture it only in the depths of my soul. Never in my life have I witnessed the driving forces of desire and passion so purely expressed. I will even go so far as to say that I have never seen them envisioned with so much chastity. Don't be vexed if I tell you that I catch fire myself when I recall his innocence and honesty. The thought of his loyalty and tenderness follows me everywhere, and I feel faint with desire myself, as if his passion had been contagious.

Of course I shall try to catch a glimpse of her as soon as possible, or rather, come to think of it, I don't think I shall. I'll do better to continue to visualize her through the eyes of her lover. Who knows . . . seen with my own, she might not look at all as I see her standing before me now, and why spoil the pretty picture?

June 16th

You want to know why I don't write? You ask me that, you who are supposed to be a learned man? You should know without a word from me that I am well and . . . oh, let's not beat about the bush. I have met someone who has touched my heart. I have . . . oh, I don't know what I have!

It is not going to be easy for me to tell you what happened chronologically—that I have met a most endearing creature. I am in high spirits and very happy, therefore no good at all for a factual accounting of affairs.

An angel? Rubbish! That is what every man calls his beloved, isn't it? Yet I am quite incapable of conveying to you how absolutely perfect she is and why she is so absolutely perfect. Let it suffice to say that she has captivated me.

She is naïve yet very sensible; she is kind yet firm, and tranquillity personified as she goes about her daily tasks.

And all I have just written is arrant nonsense and tiresome notions that really don't give you a single one of her traits. Some other time—no, not some other time but right now I am going to tell you about it. If I don't do it now, I never will. Because, to be quite frank, since I started writing to you I have put down my pen three times to see that my horse was saddled so that I could ride over to visit her. Although I swore to myself this morning that I would not go there today, I find myself constantly wandering over to the window to note how high the sun still stands in the sky.

There. Nothing to be done about it, I simply had to go
and see her, and here I am again, William. I shall have my
supper now and write to you. What joy it is to see her
surrounded by a swarm of charming, lively children, her
eight brothers and sisters!

If I go on like this, you won't know much more when I
am through than you did at the beginning. Very well, then,
listen. I will do my best to give you the full details.

I wrote to you not long ago that I had made the acquaintance of Magistrate S. and how he asked me to visit him
soon at his retreat, or rather, in his little private kingdom.
I didn't do anything about it at the time and might never
have gone if chance had not given me the opportunity to
discover what a treasure lay hidden in that quiet spot.

Some of our young people had arranged a dance in the
country, and I decided to go. I asked one of the young
ladies here—a nice, good-looking but rather insignificant
girl—to go with me, and it was agreed that I order a carriage for us and her cousin and that we pick up Charlotte
S. on the way. "You are going to meet a very pretty girl,"
my partner told me, as we drove through a clearing to the
lodge. "Watch out that you don't fall in love with her," her
cousin said. "And why shouldn't I fall in love with her?" I
wanted to know. "Because she is engaged," my partner
explained, "to a very worthy man who is away just now on
business. His father died and he has to attend to the settle-
ment of a quite considerable estate." The information did
not make much impression on me.

As we drove into the courtyard, the sun was low above
the hills. It was oppressive, and the women were afraid
that the leaden clouds gathering on the horizon presaged a
thunder storm. I pretended to know much more than I do
about the weather and succeeded in reassuring the ladies,
although I was beginning to wonder myself if our festivities
were not going to be upset.

I had already alighted from the carriage when a servant
girl, who had come to the gate, begged us to wait a moment, "Miss Lotte" would be out right away. I walked
across the courtyard toward the attractive house, and when
I had gone up the steps and through a doorway, I came
upon the most charming sight imaginable. Six children, from

about eleven to two, were swarming around a very pretty girl of medium height. She had on a simple white dress with pale pink bows on the sleeves and at her breast, and she was holding a loaf of black bread and cutting a slice for every one of her little ones, according to their ages and appetites. She gave each his share with the most enchanting graciousness, and the children cried out their "thank you's" to her absolutely at their ease, stretching out their little hands for their slice before she had even had a chance to cut it. Then they jumped off happily with their supper or, each according to his nature, walked away quietly in the direction of the courtyard to see the strange persons and the carriage in which their Lotte would soon drive away.

"I must apologize," she said, "that you had to come in for me and that I am keeping the ladies waiting, but dressing, and all the little household duties that had to be attended to before leaving, made me forget to give my children their supper, and they don't want anyone to give it to them but me."

I said something, a casual compliment, but all the while my whole being was absorbed with the sight of her, the sound of her voice, her behavior. When she ran into her room to fetch her gloves and fan, I barely had time to recover my composure. The little ones eyed me suspiciously with sidelong glances, and kept their distance. I went up to the youngest, the fairest child you could imagine. He drew away from me, but just then Lotte came out of her room and said, "Shake hands with your cousin, Louis," and the boy did, quite naturally, and I could not resist kissing him heartily in spite of his runny little nose. "Cousin?" I said, holding out my hand to take hers. "Do I merit being a relative?" "Oh," she said, with a bright smile, "we have so many cousins. It would be sad if you were the worst among them." As she was leaving, she told Sophie, the next oldest, a girl of about eleven, to take good care of the children and best greetings to her father on his return from his ride. She asked the children to obey their sister, Sophie, just as they would obey her, and a few said they would, but one bright little blonde girl of about six declared that it would not be like obeying her and "we should rather have you." The two oldest boys had climbed up on the box, and when I interceded, were given permission to drive with us as far as the forest if they promised not to tease one another and held on tight.

We had just settled down, and the women had finished greeting each other and exchanging the correct remarks about the others' clothes and hats and given the people they were going to meet a thorough going over, when Lotte asked the coachman to stop and let the boys off. They insisted on kissing her hand again, the older boy with a tenderness that seems to come naturally to boys of fifteen; the younger was much more impetuous and carefree about it. She sent her love to the little ones again, and we drove on.

The cousin asked whether Lotte had read the book she had sent her recently. "No," Lotte said, "I don't like it. You may have it back. I didn't like the one you sent me before that, either." When I asked her what the books were, and she told me, I was astonished.* Altogether, I found that everything she said displayed a resolute character, and with every word she spoke I could see some new attraction in her and a fresh radiance in her face, which soon seemed free of all constraint, because she saw that I understood her.

"When I was younger," she said, "all I liked to read was novels. I can't tell you how happy it used to make me when I could curl up in a corner on a Sunday and participate heart and soul in the joys and sorrows of some Miss Jenny[2] or other. I must say that I still like to read that sort of thing, but since I seldom have the opportunity to read, it must be something I can really enjoy. And I like those writers best who help me find my world again, where the sort of things happen that happen all around me, and the story is as interesting and sympathetic as my own life at home, which may not be paradise but is, on the whole, a source of quite inexplicable joy to me."

I did my best to hide the emotions her words aroused in

---

*We have found it necessary to suppress this part of the letter in order to give no cause for complaint, although actually no author could care very much about the opinion of one girl and a young, unstable man.

me. I didn't succeed very well because, when I heard her speak casually and very candidly about *The Vicar of Wakefield* and about ——* I was quite beside myself and told her all I knew of them and only after quite some time had passed, and Lotte turned suddenly to address the others, did I notice that they had been sitting there goggle-eyed, as if they weren't sitting there at all! The cousin looked down her nose at me several times, but I didn't care.

The conversation turned to the joy of dancing. "If a passion for dancing is sinful," Lotte said, "then I cheerfully admit to it. I don't know anything I would rather do than dance. When something is troubling me and I can sit down at my poor old piano—it needs tuning badly—and play a *contredanse,* everything is all right again."

I could not take my eyes off her dark eyes as she chattered; I could not look away from her animated mouth, her bonny cheeks; I was lost utterly in the infectious good spirits of everything she had to say, sometimes without even hearing the words with which she expressed it! That will give you some idea, since, after all, you know me well. In short, when we stopped in front of the pavilion I got out of the carriage like a dreamer, so lost in the twilit world around me that I scarcely noticed the music floating down to us from the illuminated ballroom.

The cousin and Lotte's partners, two gentlemen called Andran and N.N.—who can remember names?—met us at the entrance, appropriated their young ladies, and I led mine up the staircase.

One minuet followed another, and I asked one young lady after another to dance with me and it was always the most unattractive ones, of course, who would not end the figure. Lotte and her partner opened a quadrille, and you can imagine how delighted I was when the time came for them to start a figure with us. You should see her dance! She is so completely absorbed by motion, she dances with her whole heart, body, and soul. The result is harmony, so

---

*Here, too, the names of some authors have been omitted. Those of whom Lotte approved will surely know it in their hearts, if they have read this far, and the rest need not know anything about it.

carefree and natural, as if there were nothing to life but dancing, as if she never gave anything else a thought—and I am sure that in such moments everything else *is* gone from her mind.

I asked her for the second *contredanse*. She replied that she could give me the third and with the most engaging frankness assured me that she liked to dance the *allemande*. "It is customary here," she explained, "to dance the *allemande* with your escort. But my young man doesn't waltz very well and won't mind a bit if I relieve him of the obligation. Your partner can't waltz either and doesn't like to, so if you want to dance the *allemande* with me, why don't you ask my partner for permission, and I will go and speak to your young lady about it?" This was agreed upon and our partners entertained each other while Lotte and I danced.

So that is how it all began. For a while we were simply delighted with the interlacing of our arms as we danced together. How charming and fleeting was her every move! And when it was time for the waltz and the couples began revolving around each other like spheres there was quite a bit of confusion, at any rate, there was at first, because so few knew how to waltz. We were clever—we left the floor to the others, and when the clumsiest ones had had enough, we joined in and with Andran and his partner were the last couples on the floor. I can't recall ever having felt so light. I was transported! To hold the dearest creature in the world in my arms and fly through the room with her until everything around me was lost and . . . William, to be frank, I swore to myself then and there that the girl whom I loved and to whom I therefore had certain rights should never waltz with anyone but me, and if it should prove to be my downfall! Can you understand me?

We took a few turns around the ballroom to catch our breath, then she sat down. The oranges I had managed to procure for us—they were the last ones left—were most refreshing, except for the fact that I felt a stab in the region of my heart every time she graciously gave a piece to a greedy girl sitting next to her.

During the third quadrille, we were the second couple. As we danced down the row I was conscious of nothing but her arm in mine and the look on her face, which was so frankly suffused with the purest pleasure. We passed a woman who had attracted my attention before because of the kindly expression on a face no longer young. She looked at Lotte, lifted a warning finger and, as we flew by, said the name "Albert" twice, with emphasis.

"Who is Albert?" I asked. "If I may be so bold as to inquire."

Lotte was about to reply, when we had to separate for the figure eight, and I thought I could detect a certain reflectiveness in her features when our paths crossed again. "Why shouldn't you know?" she said as she gave me her hand for the promenade. "Albert is a good man, and I suppose you might say I am engaged to him." This, of course, should not have come as a surprise to me; the ladies had mentioned it on the way over. Still it came as a complete surprise because I had somehow not connected it with her, who had now become so precious to me. At any rate, it served only to confuse me utterly, I became involved with the wrong couple, the result was chaos, and it took a great deal of Lotte's presence of mind and a lot of pulling and readjusting to get all of us in orderly motion again.

The lightning, which had been noticeable on the horizon for some time—I had tried to assure everyone that it was only heat lightning—became more and more violent, and the rumbling of thunder began to drown out the music long before the dance was over. Three of the ladies left the dance floor, their partners followed them, the restlessness became general, and the music stopped.

If an accident or some disaster surprises us when we are enjoying ourselves, it naturally makes a stronger impression on us than usual, partly because of the contrast, which makes itself keenly felt, but also—and all the more strongly—because our sensibilities are open wide to all feeling and we can therefore be impressed more acutely. At any rate, I attribute the weird expressions and behavior of many of the women to this. The cleverest one very wisely sat down in a corner with her back to the window and held her hands over her ears; another fell on her knees in front of her and buried her head in the other's lap; a third pushed her way unceremoniously between the two and threw her arms around her sister, the tears streaming from her eyes. Many of the ladies begged to be taken home; others, who knew even less what they were doing, didn't have enough sense left to parry the impertinences of some of our young blades, who seemed anxious to intercept the prayers that rose to the lips of the frightened women and were actually meant for Heaven. A few of the gentlemen went downstairs to smoke their pipes in peace, and the rest were only too pleased to take advantage of the innkeeper's good suggestion to move into a room where the windows were shuttered and draped. All of us had scarcely assembled, when Lotte busied herself with making a circle of chairs, and as soon as everyone had sat down at her request, she suggested that we play a game.

I could see a few purse their lips and wriggle in happy anticipation of a smacking kiss as forfeit. "We are going to play numbers," she said. "Now listen carefully! I will go around the circle from right to left and you will count in the same direction. Each one must say the next number when it is his turn and you must count fast, fast as lightning. Whoever hesitates or says the wrong number gets a box on the ears. And we will count to a thousand."

What an amusing sight it was! She walked the circle with her arms outstretched. "One," said the first person she passed; the fellow next to him said, "Two"; the next girl, "Three"; and so on. Then she began to move faster, and someone missed . . . *ptch*! . . . a box on the ears. That made the fellow sitting next to him laugh . . . *ptch*! . . . he got one, too. And faster and faster. I was boxed on the ears twice, and with secret delight felt that she had boxed my ears harder than any of the others. General laughter and commotion broke up the game before she could count to a thousand.

The storm was over. Those who wished to be alone withdrew, and I followed Lotte into the dance hall. On the way she said, "The game made them forget all about the weather." I couldn't think of anything to say, and she went on, "I was terribly frightened but as I pretended to be brave to encourage the others, I suddenly felt courageous."

We walked over to the window. It was still thundering in the distance, the blessed rain was falling on the land, and a most refreshing scent rose up to us with a rush of warm air. She stood there, leaning on her elbows, her gaze penetrating the countryside; she looked up at the sky, at me, and I could see tears in her eyes. She laid her hand on mine and said, "Klopstock." I knew at once of what she was thinking—his magnificent ode[4]—and was lost in the emotions that this one word aroused in me. I bent down and kissed her hand, and now there were tears in my eyes too as I looked into hers again. Oh, noble poet, if you could have seen the adoration in those eyes! I hope I need never have to hear your name, so oft profaned, spoken again by any other lips!

June 19th

I don't know how far I got in my last letter, all I know is that it was two o'clock when I finally went to bed and if I could have talked to you instead of having to write, I would probably have kept you up until dawn.

I don't think I have told you yet what happened on our way home from the dance and I don't really feel like writing about it today, but I will.

There was the most marvelous sunrise. The trees were wet, the fields refreshed, our chaperones nodding. . . . Lotte asked me if I didn't want to close my eyes, too. . . . I should not stand on ceremony with her. "As long as I can look into your eyes," I said, looking at her steadfastly, "there is no danger of my falling asleep." And we stayed awake, both of us, until we arrived at her gate. The maid opened the door softly, and in reply to her query assured Lotte that her father and the children were well and still asleep. Then I left her, with the request that I might see her again that very day. She agreed, and I rode over to see her. Since then sun, moon, and stars can do what they will—I haven't the faintest notion whether it is day or night. The world around me has vanished.

June 21st

I am experiencing the kind of happiness that God dispenses only to his saints. Whatever is yet to come, I shall never be able to say that I have not felt the great, the purest joy life can hold. You know my beloved Wahlheim. I have moved there bag and baggage. From Wahlheim I can be with Lotte in half an hour, in Wahlheim I can be myself and experience every happiness known to man.

Who would have thought, when I chose Wahlheim as a goal for my walks, that it lay so close to heaven? How often I have seen on my wanderings, sometimes from a hillside, sometimes from the opposite side of the river, the hunting lodge that now houses all my desires.

Dear William, I have given a great deal of thought to man's desire for expansion and his urge to explore and roam the face of the earth, and then again, I think about his inner impetus to surrender willingly to the restrictions imposed by life and to travel in the rut of routine living, never giving a thought to what goes on to right or left.

It is truly marvelous—when I came here first and looked down into the valley from this hilltop—how the entire region attracted me. There . . . a little forest land . . . oh, to lose oneself in its shade. . . . There, a mountaintop . . . oh, to see the panorama from it! The rolling hills and enchanting valleys . . . I yearned to lose myself in them.

I would hurry down, but return home without having found what I had hoped to find. Distance is like the future. A vast twilit entity lies before us, our perception is lost in it and becomes as blurred as our eyesight, and we yearn, ah, we yearn to surrender all of our Self and let ourselves be filled to the brim with a single, tremendous, magnificent emotion, but alas . . . when we hurry to the spot, when There becomes Here, everything is as it was before and we are left standing in our poverty and constraint, our souls longing for the balm that has eluded us. Thus the most restless vagabond yearns in the end to return to his native land and find in his cottage, in the arms of his wife, with his children around him, and in the occupations that provide for them, the joys he sought vainly elsewhere.

When I ride out to Wahlheim in the morning with the rising sun and pick some sweet young peas in the garden behind the inn and string them and read a little Homer as I do so; when I then go into the small kitchen and get a pan and melt some butter and put the pan on the fire to cook them and cover them and sit down beside them to toss them a little every now and then—I can feel so vividly how Penelope's high-spirited suitors slaughtered oxen and swine and carved them up and roasted them. Nothing can fill me with such true, serene emotion as any features of ancient, primitive life like this. Thank God I know how to fit them into my life without conceit. Oh, how thankful I am that my heart can feel the simple, harmless joys of the man who brings to the table a head of cabbage he has grown himself, and in a single moment enjoys, not only the vegetable, but all the fine days and fresh mornings since he planted it, the mild evenings when he watered it, and the pleasure he felt while watching it grow.

June 29th

The day before yesterday the doctor from our town came out to the lodge and found me on the floor with several of Lotte's children on top of me, the rest teasing me. He saw me tickling them and succeeding generally in creating an uproar. The doctor is a dogmatic puppet, constantly repleating his cuffs as he talks and pulling out a loose thread here and there. Of course, he found my behavior undignified for a man of my intellect. I could tell by the way he turned up his nose at the whole thing. I didn't let it bother me, but as he went about his more sensible business, I rebuilt the children's house of cards, which they had toppled; whereupon he went about town telling everyone that the magistrate's children had always been wild, but now Werther was ruining them completely.

Yes, dear William, nothing is dearer to me than children. As I watch them and see in everything they do the seed of all the virtue and strength they will one day need, when I recognize future steadfastness and firmness in their present obstinacy, good humor and the ability to pass lightly over the perils on this earth in their mischief, everything so unspoiled, everything still whole—then I want to repeat the Golden Rule of the teacher of mankind: "Unless ye become as one of these . . ." And then, my good friend, we treat the little creatures, who are our equals, and whom we should use as models, as our inferiors. They are not supposed to have a will of their own. Why not? Don't we demand free will? What gives us the right to make such a decision? Because we are older and wiser? Dear God in Heaven, Thou dost look down upon old children and young children, and that's all there is to it! And Thy Divine Son told us long ago which of them pleaseth Thee more. But they believe in Him and don't hear Him, and that, too, is an old story. And they bring up their children to be like themselves and . . . farewell, William! I don't want to ramble on about it.

July 1st

My poor heart, which is worse off than many a heart wasting away on a sickbed, tells me what Lotte must mean to a sick person. She is going to spend a few days in town at the bedside of a worthy woman who, according to the doctor, is about to die. He wants Lotte at her side during the poor creature's final hours.

Last week I went with Lotte to visit the rector of St.——
a little town in the mountains about an hour away. We arrived there at four o'clock. Lotte took her two sisters with her. As we drove into the courtyard of the rectory, which lies in the shade of two tall walnut trees, the old man was sitting on a bench outside the door, and when he set eyes on Lotte he seemed to come to life. He forgot to use his knobby cane and rose to come forward to greet her without it. She ran to him and saw to it that he sat down again by the simple expedient of sitting down beside him herself. She brought him greetings from her father and made a fuss of his horrid, dirty little youngest boy, the joy of his old age. You should have seen her, how she kept the old man amused, raising her voice so that his deaf ears might hear her; how she talked about robust young people who had died quite suddenly and praised Karlsbad to the skies and his decision to spend his summers there from now on. She elaborated on how much better she thought he looked and remarked that he seemed to have more strength than when she had seen him last. Meanwhile I paid my respects to the vicar's wife.

The old man became more and more lively. Of course I had to admire the magnificent nut trees that were offering us such delightful shade, so he began, a little clumsy, to tell us their story.

"We don't know who planted the old one," he began. "Some say it was this clergyman, others say it was another.

But the younger tree over there is as old as my wife, fifty in October. Her father planted it in the morning of the day she was born . . . she was born toward evening. He was my predecessor here, and I can't tell you how much the tree meant to him. Naturally, it means just as much to me. My wife was sitting on a bench underneath it, twenty-seven years ago, when I walked into this yard for the first time, just a poor student."

Lotte asked after his daughter. She was told that the girl had gone out to the workers in the field with Herr Schmidt, and the old man went on with his story—how the vicar had become fond of him, then his daughter, too; how he had been curate first, then vicar. He was scarcely done when his young daughter came through the garden with the afore-mentioned Herr Schmidt. She greeted Lotte warmly, and, I must say, she was attractive—a lively brunette with an excellent figure who would have understood very well how to help anyone pass a short stay in the country. Her ad-mirer—Herr Schmidt quite obviously was just that—turned out to be a sensitive and quiet young man who did not seem to want to join in our conversation, although Lotte did her best to include him. What distressed me most about him was that I thought I could read in his expression that stub-bornness and ill humor, rather than any limitations of the mind, prevented him from expressing himself. Unfortu-nately, this became very obvious later when we went for a walk, for whenever Friederike happened to walk with Lotte or me, the young man's face—which was swarthy anyhow—darkened so visibly that Lotte plucked at my sleeve and gave me to understand I was paying too much attention to the girl. Now there is nothing that irritates me more than when people torment each other, especially when young people in the prime of their lives, who should be open to all joys, spoil the few good days they have with a dour mien and only find out too late that they have wasted something irretrievable. The whole thing rankled within me, and when we returned to the rectory toward evening and were seated around a table drinking milk, and the conversation turned to the joys and sorrows of life, I simply had to take over the conversation and hold forth against the moodiness of man.

"People often complain," I said, "that there are too few good days and too many bad ones, and as far as I can see, they do so unjustly. If we always kept our hearts wide open to receive the good things God has in store for us daily, we would soon have strength enough to bear the bad when they come."

"But our spirit is not ours to shape," the vicar's wife objected. "Think how much depends on our bodies. If we don't feel well everything seems out of joint."

I agreed with her. "So let us look upon moodiness as a sickness," I replied, "and ask ourselves if there be not a cure for it."

"That's a thought," Lotte said. "I for one believe that a great deal depends on us. I know that it does from my own experience. If something is bothering or depressing me, I get up and hum a few dance tunes, up and down the garden, and right away it is gone."

"That's just what I was trying to express," I said. "Ill humor is like indolence, because it is a form of indolence. Our natures tend toward it. But if we can muster the strength to pull ourselves together, work can be made easy and we can find true pleasure in activity."

Friederike was listening attentively, and now her young man interrupted me, declaring that one was not always in control of oneself, least of all of one's feelings.

"But what we are talking about," I explained, "is a disagreeable feeling, and everyone should be thankful to be rid of it. And no one knows how strong he is until he has tried. After all, if a man is ill, he goes to one doctor after another and puts up with any restrictions and the bitterest medicine to preserve his good health."

I noticed that the good old man was straining to hear what was being said so he could take part in the discussion. I therefore raised my voice and addressed him. "Our sermons speak out against so many vices," I said, "but I have never heard a word spoken from the pulpit against ill humor."*

---

*We now have an excellent sermon on this topic by Lavater, among those on the Book of Jonah.

"The preachers in the cities should see to that," the old man replied. "Our peasants are good-humored by nature. Still, it wouldn't do any harm from time to time, and it would certainly be a good lesson for my wife—and for the magistrate!"

Everyone laughed, and the old man joined in the laughter, until a fit of coughing put an end to the discussion for a while. The young man picked up the thread again. "You called ill humor a vice," he said. "Wouldn't you say that was exaggerating?"

"Not at all," I replied. "Anything that does harm to oneself or one's neighbor deserves to be called a vice. Isn't it sad enough that we cannot make each other happy? Must we rob one another of the pleasure every heart can sometimes provide for itself? Show me the person who is ill-humored yet good enough to bear it alone, without destroying the happiness around him. Isn't ill humor actually an inner annoyance with our own unworthiness, a dislike of ourselves, and isn't it somehow always connected with the envy that is egged on by our own foolish vanity? We see happy people whom we are not making happy, and we cannot bear it."

Lotte smiled at me because she could see how the topic touched me, and a tear in Friederike's eye spurred me on. "What wretches they are, those who take advantage of the power they have over the heart of another," I said, "and rob him of the simple joys within him! Not all the gifts in the world nor any favor can compensate for a moment of one's personal pleasure that has been made bitter by the envious ill temper of this tyrant of ours!"

My heart was full. Memories of things past brought the tears to my eyes too. "If only man would tell himself daily: you owe your friends nothing but to leave them their joys and increase their happiness by sharing it with them. Can you give them a little comfort when they are tormented by fear? And when the poor creature, whose soul you undermined in fairer days, is struggling with his last, fateful illness and lies there pitiful in his exhaustion, looking up at the sky, all feeling spent, the dew of death on his pale brow, and you stand by his deathbed like one damned, with the profound feeling that with everything in your power you can do nothing to help, and you are gripped by a dreadful fear and would give anything in the world if only you could imbue his perishing soul with one ounce of strength . . ."

As I spoke, the memory of such a scene overwhelmed me. I covered my face with my handkerchief and left the little group and was only able to control myself again when Lotte called out to me that we had to leave. On the way back, she scolded me for my too intense participation in all things going on around me and warned that it would lead to my ruination. I was, please, she begged, to think of myself. Angel! For you I have to live!

July 6th

She is with her dying friend constantly and is always the same: ever-present, ever lovely. Wherever her eyes fall, she eases pain and brings joy. Yesterday, she went for a walk with Marianne and little Amelia. I knew about it and met them, and all of us walked on together. About an hour and a half later we were approaching town again and we came to the spring that meant so much to me once and now means a thousand times more. Lotte sat down on the low stone wall, the rest of us stood around her. I looked about me, and the time that I was alone came to life again within me. 'Beloved spring,' I thought, 'since then I have not rested in thy cool aura. Sometimes, when hurrying by, I have not even given thee a glance.' I looked down and could see Amelia carefully carrying up a cup of water; I looked at Lotte and realized what she meant to me. Meanwhile, Amelia arrived with the cup and Marianne wanted to take it from her. "No," the child said, with the sweetest expression, "no . . . Lotte, you must drink first."

I was so entranced with the child's candor and goodness that I could express it in no other way than by picking her up and kissing her fervently, whereupon she immediately squealed and began to cry. "You shouldn't have done that," Lotte said.

I was abashed.

"Come, Melly," she said, taking the child by the hand and leading her down the steps. "Wash yourself in the fresh spring water quickly, and it won't matter at all." I stood there and watched the child rub her cheeks energetically with her little wet hands, so confident that the spring's miraculous powers would wash away all impurity, and she would not have to fear the shame of growing an ugly mustache. Lotte said that was enough, still the child went on scrubbing her cheeks as if more could only be better than little. William, I assure you that I never attended a baptism with more reverence, and when Lotte came up the steps again I longed to throw myself at her feet, as one throws oneself down before a prophet who has just washed his people clean of sin.

That evening my heart so overflowed with joy that I could not resist describing the event to a gentleman, a sensible fellow who, I was therefore sure, had a good understanding of human nature. But that was a mistake. He was of the opinion that Lotte was wrong—children should never be misled. Such nonsense could lead to innumerable errors and superstitions, and a child could not be protected from such things early enough in life. It occurred to me suddenly that only a week ago the man had had one of his children baptized, so I let it pass, but in my heart I remained true to my belief: we should treat children as God treats us when He lets us go our way in a transport of delightful illusions.

July 8th

William, we are children! Have you any idea how one can pine for a glance from one's beloved? We are children!

We visited Wahlheim—the ladies drove out—and on one of our walks I thought I could see in Lotte's eyes . . . I am a fool! Forgive me. But you should see those eyes.

I cannot write long. I am so sleepy my eyelids are drooping, but listen . . . the ladies were getting into the carriage. Young W., Selstadt, Andran, and I were standing beside it, chatting about nothing in particular. I tried to catch Lotte's eye. She was looking from one man to the other, but not at me, me, me, who alone stood there waiting for her glance. My heart was bidding her a thousand farewells, and she didn't even see me! The carriage passed us, and there were tears in my eyes. I looked after her and could see her bonnet as she leaned out and turned to look at—at whom? And that, in brief, describes my uncertainty, and my consolation. Perhaps she did look back at me. Perhaps. Good night. Oh William, what a child I am!

July 10th

You should see what an idiot I am when she is mentioned in public. And when someone asks how I like her! *Like* her? I can't abide the word. What kind of person could possibly "like" Lotte? What kind of person could possibly not be completely fulfilled by her? Like her! The other day someone asked me if I liked Ossian![5]

Frau M. is very ill. I pray for her as I share Lotte's anxiety. I see her only rarely, at the house of a friend, and today she told me something very strange.

Old M., it seems, is a miserly, avaricious fellow who has tormented his wife throughout their life together and forced her to live exceedingly modestly, but the good woman always managed somehow. The other day, when the doctor had declared that her last hour had come, she sent for her husband—Lotte was in the room—and addressed him thus:

"I have a confession to make that might prevent confusion and chagrin after my death. Until now I have kept house as frugally and properly as possible and I am sure you will forgive me for having deceived you these past thirty years. At the outset of our married life, you set aside a very modest sum for our household needs. As our mode of living expanded and business prospered, you could not be persuaded to increase my weekly household allowance to match our circumstances, in short—when we were most prosperous, you insisted that I manage on seven guilders a week. I accepted the seven guilders without demur and took the rest of what was needed out of our receipts, because I felt no one would ever suspect your wife of robbing the till. I never wasted any of it and would have gone to my rest happily now without mentioning it, were it not for the fact that whoever has to care for your household after me will not know how to manage, and you will insist, of course, that your wife always made do with the sum."

Lotte and I then spoke about the incredible fatuousness of a man who does not become suspicious when his wife manages on seven guilders a household that obviously betrays the fact that twice as much is being spent. But I have known people who accepted the widow's never-failing cruse of oil[6] without surprise.

July 13th

No, I am not deceived—I can read true sympathy in her dark eyes. Yes, I feel . . . and here I know I can trust my heart . . . that she . . . dare I, can I express heaven in a few words? That she loves me.

Loves me. And how precious I have become to myself, how I—I can say this to you, who have understanding for such emotions—how I worship at my own altar since I know that she loves me!

Is this presumption or fact, I ask myself? I don't know the man who, I fear, has a place in Lotte's heart, yet when she speaks of her betrothed with so much warmth and love, then I am a man degraded, robbed of his honor, title, and sword.

July 16th

Oh, how wildly my blood courses through my veins when, by chance, my hand touches hers or our feet touch under the table! I start away as if from a fire, a mysterious power draws me back, and I become dizzy . . . and in her artlessness and innocence she has no idea how much such little intimacies torment me. When she puts her hand in mine in the course of a conversation and, absorbed by what we are talking about, draws closer to me, and the heavenly breath from her lips touches mine . . . then I feel I must sink to the ground as if struck by lightning. William, if ever I should presume to take advantage of this heaven on earth, this trust in me . . you know what I mean. But I am not depraved. Weak, yes, weak God knows I am . . . and can this not be called depraved?

She is sacred to me. All lust is stilled in her presence. I can't explain how I feel when I am with her. It is as if every nerve in my body were possessed by my soul. There is a certain melody . . . she plays it on the piano like an angel, so simply yet with so much spirit. It is her favorite song, and I am restored from all pain, confusion, and vagaries with the first note.

Nothing that has ever been said about the magic power

of music seems improbable to me now. How that simple melody touches me! And how well she knows when she should play it, often at moments when I feel like blowing my brains out! Then all delusions and darkness within me are dispelled, and I breathe freely again.

July 18th

William, what is life worth without love? A magic lantern without light. All you have to do is put in the light, and it produces the loveliest colored pictures on a white wall. And if there is nothing more to it than these oh, so transient phantoms, always it denotes happiness when we stand in front of it like naïve boys and are enchanted by the magical visions. Today an unavoidable gathering prevented me from visiting Lotte. What could I do? I sent over my servant, if only to have someone about me who had been near her! The impatience with which I waited for him and the joy, when I saw him return, are indescribable! I would have liked to embrace and kiss him, but was, of course, too ashamed.

They say that when the stone of Bonona is exposed to the rays of the sun it attracts them and shines for a while into the night. That was how the boy affected me. The idea that she had looked at his face, at his cheeks, at the buttons on his waistcoat and the collar of his jacket, made every one of these things sacred and invaluable to me. At that point I wouldn't have let anyone have the boy for a thousand talers! I felt simply wonderful in his presence! Dear God, William, don't laugh at me! Do you suppose it is illusory to be so happy?

July 19th

I shall see her today! When I awaken in the morning and look blithely into the sunlight, I cry out, "I shall see her today!" And I don't have another wish for the next twenty-four hours. Everything—everything, I tell you—is lost in this one anticipation!

July 20th

I can't agree with you that I should go to —— with our ambassador. I don't like subordination, and we know only too well that the man is obnoxious. My mother, you say, would like to see me actively employed. I have to laugh. Am I not actively employed now, and does it make any difference, really, whether I am sorting peas or lentils? Everything on earth can be reduced to a triviality and the man who, to please another, wears himself out for money, honor, what you will, is a fool.

July 24th

I realize that it means a great deal to you that I do not neglect my sketching, so I would rather say nothing at all about it except confess that I have not done much work since I met Lotte.

I have never been happier. My appreciation of nature, down to the most insignificant stone or blade of grass, has never been more keen or profound, and yet . . . I don't know how to explain it to you. My powers of expression are weak and everything is so hazy in my mind that all contours seem to elude me. I tell myself that if I had clay or wax, I could shape them. And if this mood prevails, I shall certainly get hold of some clay and model it, even if all I turn out is a patty cake!

I have started three times to draw Lotte and three times made a complete mess of it. This irritates me, because only a short while ago I was quite a good portraitist. So I did a silhouette of her, and that will have to suffice.

July 26th

Yes, dear Lotte, I shall attend to everything, only please give me more errands to do and give them to me more often. And one more request: no more sand, please, on the little notes you write to me. Today I pressed your letter to my lips and felt the grains on my teeth.

July 26th

Every now and then I make up my mind to see her less often—as if anyone could possibly adhere to such a rule! Every day I give in to temptation and swear that tomorrow I will stay away, but when tomorrow comes, I of course find an absolutely irresistible reason for going to see her, and before I know it—there I am! Perhaps it is because she said the evening before, "Will you be coming tomorrow?" So who could stay away? Or she asked me to attend to something, and I tell myself that the only proper thing to do is go personally to inform her that it has been done. Or the day is so beautiful that I go to Wahlheim and, once I am there . . . well, after all, she is only half an hour away, I am too close to her aura . . . whoosh! and I am there.

My grandmother used to tell a fairy tale about the Magnet Mountain: the ships that came too close to it were robbed suddenly of all their metal, even the nails flew to the mountain, and the miserable sailors foundered in a crash of falling timber.

Albert has come back, and I shall leave. He might be the best, the most noble man in the world, and I would be glad to subordinate myself to him in any capacity whatsoever, but I would find it insufferable to see him take possession of so much perfection. To take possession . . . let it suffice, William . . . her betrothed has returned—a worthy, kindly man whom one simply has to like. Fortunately, I was not present when he arrived, it would have torn my heart to shreds. And he is an honorable man. Not once has he kissed Lotte in my presence. May God reward him for it! And I have to love him for the way he respects the girl. He seems to like me and I have the feeling that I have Lotte to thank for this rather than any impression of his own, because in things like that women have great intuition and they are right—it is always to their advantage to keep two admirers in harmony with each other, however rarely it may occur.

Meanwhile, I cannot help respecting Albert. His easy-going behavior contrasts strangely with my restlessness, which cannot be concealed. He is a man of strong feelings and knows what a treasure he has in Lotte. He seems to be a man of good spirits too, and you know that, as far as I am concerned, moroseness is a man's greatest vice. He apparently takes me for a sensible fellow, and my devotion to Lotte, my warm pleasure in everything in which she takes part, only increases his sense of triumph and makes him love her more. I have no idea whether or not he sometimes plagues her with little outbursts of jealousy—we will have to leave that point undecided—but if I were in his shoes, I don't think I would be entirely free of this base emotion.

Be that as it may, the joyous days with Lotte are over. What shall I call it? Folly? Delusion? It does need a name. The dilemma speaks for itself. I knew all I know now before he came; I knew that I had no claim to her and demanded none, or let us say, I did not desire her more than one simply has to desire anyone so altogether lovely. And now, idiot that I am, I stare wide-eyed with astonishment at my rival, who has come at last to take the girl away!

I grit my teeth and scoff at my misery and would scoff even more if anyone dared tell me to resign myself to the situation because there is nothing to be done about it. Just keep such straw men away from me! I tear through the woods and when I have gone as far as I can and find Lotte sitting beside Albert in the summerhouse in her little garden, I behave like an idiot and indulge in all sorts of absurdities. I don't even make sense! "For heaven's sake," she told me today, "please, I beg of you, no more scenes like the one in the garden last night. You are perfectly horrible when you are trying to be funny." Just between you and me: I watch out for the times when he is busy and then . . . whoosh, there I am and when I find her alone I feel perfectly wonderful!

August 8th

I assure you, dear William, that I did not mean you when I took those men to task who demand from us resignation to an unavoidable fate. It never occurred to me that you might be of the same opinion. And actually you are right. But, my good friend, in this world things can be settled with an either-or attitude only very rarely. Feelings and behavior overshadow each other with an effect as varied as the difference between hawk- and pug-nose. So you won't be offended with me, I hope, if I concede your entire argument and try to squeeze through between the either and the or!

You say that I must "either" have hope of winning Lotte "or" I must have none. Very well. In the first case I am to try to grasp the fulfillment of my wish and make my hopes come true; in the second I am to pull myself together and try to rid myself of this miserable emotion that must in the end utterly debilitate me. Dear William, you put it so well, and it is easily advised. But can you demand of an unfortu-

nate human who is dying by inches of an insidious disease
that he should end his misery with one knife thrust?
Wouldn't you rather say that his misfortune weakens him
to such an extent that it must rob him also of the courage
to rid himself of it?

Of course you might reply with an appropriate parable:
who would not rather sacrifice his right arm than lose his
life through hesitation and despair? I don't know. And don't
let us settle it with parables. Enough! Yes, William, sometimes I do have moments of surging courage to shake it all
off, and then . . . if only I knew whither . . . probably I
would go.

Evening

Today I came across my diary. I haven't written in it for
some time, and I was astonished to see how I got into all
this, step by step, with my eyes wide open; how clearly I
saw the whole thing and my condition, yet dealt with it
like a child. I see just as clearly today and note no sign of
improvement.

August 10th

I could be leading the best of happiest lives if I were not
such a fool. It would be hard to find more agreeable circumstances than those granted me now. But I am absolutely
sure that our hearts alone can give us happiness. To be
counted as a member of this charming family, to be loved
like a son by her father and like a father by the children,
and by Lotte! And then there is good, worthy Albert, who
does nothing to disturb my joy with moody behavior and
accepts me in a spirit of friendliness—even prefers me to
anyone else, after Lotte! William, it is a pleasure to listen
to us when we are out walking together and we talk about
Lotte. I don't think you will find anything in the whole wide
world more ridiculous than our relationship, and still my
eyes fill with tears when I think of it.

He talks to me about her good mother—how, on her
deathbed, she handed over house and children to Lotte,
who since then has been quite changed; how, through having to care for a household and face the more serious aspects of life, she has become a real mother, and not a

moment of her time passes without work or an act of love;
how, in spite of all this, her blitheness and vitality have
never forsaken her I wander along at his side, pick flowers,
arrange them carefully into a bouquet and . . . throw them
into the stream rushing by and look after them as they are
slowly sucked down. I do't know whether I wrote to you
that Albert intends to remain here, and that the Prince will
let him have a tidy little income because he is well liked at
court. I have rarely seen his equal when it comes to orderli-
ness and diligence in matters of business.

August 12th

Albert is the best man on earth . . . agreed! Yesterday I
had a strange experience with him. I went to see him, to
bid him farewell, for it had occurred to me that a ride up
into the mountains (I am writing to you from there now)
was just what I wanted to do. As I was pacing up and down
his room, I happened to see his pistols. "Lend me your
pistols for the trip," I said.

"By all means," he replied, "if you want to take the
trouble to load them. I only have them hanging around here
pro forma." As I took one down, he went on: "Since my
sense of caution played me such a nasty trick, I don't want
to have anything more to do with them."

I was anxious to hear the story. "I was in the country,
staying with a friend for about three months," he said. "I
had a brace of pistols with me, unloaded, and slept peacefully. On a rainy afternoon I was sitting there with nothing
much to do and, I don't know why, but it occurred to me
that we could be attacked; we might need the pistols and
could—you know how it is. I gave them to a servant to
clean and load. He fooled around with the girls, wanted to
frighten them. . . . God knows how it happened, but the
gun went off with the ramrod still in the barrel and shot the
ramrod into the thumb of one of the girls, smashing it. And
I had to listen to all the lamentations and pay the surgeon's
bill. Since then I leave the pistols unloaded. My dear fellow,
what is precaution? We can never learn all there is to know
about danger. To be sure . . ."

Now, you know, that I love this man very much, except
for his "to be sure," for isn't it obvious that every general-

ization admits of exceptions? But this fellow is full of such self-justification. When he thinks he has said something too hastily, or spoken a half-truth, or generalized too much, then you can't stop him from attaching limitations to what he has said, from modifying it, adding to it and subtracting from it, until at last nothing is left of the original idea!

In the end, Albert became so involved in what he was saying that I stopped listening and was soon lost in my own thoughts. Suddenly, with a rough, abrupt gesture, I pressed the mouth of the pistol against my forehead, just above the right eye.

"Shame on you!" Albert said, as he forced my hand down. "What on earth is the meaning of this?"

"It isn't loaded," I said.

"Even so . . . what was going on in your mind?" He sounded impatient. "I simply cannot imagine how a man could be so foolish as to shoot himself. The very idea disgusts me."

"Oh you people," I cried, "who, when you talk about anything must immediately declare: that is foolish, that is clever, that is good, that is bad! And what does it all amount to? Do you think you can uncover the vital circumstances of an action with your questions? Are you sure you know how to get at the heart of the matter: why did it happen? Why did it have to happen? If you were, you wouldn't be so hasty with your decisions."

"You will grant me, I am sure," Albert said, "that certain actions are vicious whatever the reason may be."

I shrugged and had to agree with him. "And yet, my dear fellow," I went on, "here too you will find your exceptions. To steal is a sin, true, but the poor man who steals to save himself and his dear ones from starvation, what does he deserve? Pity or punishment? Who will cast the first stone against the married man who, in his first fury, murders his faithless wife and her vile seducer? And what about the young girl who in a blissful hour loses herself in the irresistible delights of love? Even our laws, cold-blooded and pedantic as they are, can be moved to withhold punishment."

"That is something quite different," said Albert. "A man who lets himself be overwhelmed by passion can be considered out of his mind, and is treated like a drunkard or a madman."

"Oh you sensible people!" I cried, but I was smiling. "Passion. Inebriation. Madness. You respectable ones stand there so calmly, without any sense of participation. Upbraid the drunkard, abhor the madman, pass them by like the priest and thank God like the Pharisees that He did not make you as one of these! I have been drunk more than once, and my passion often borders on madness, and I regret neither. Because, in my own way, I have learned to understand that all exceptional people who created something great, something that seemed impossible, have to be decried as drunkards or madmen. And I find it intolerable, even in our daily life, to hear it said of almost everyone who manages to do something that is free, noble and unexpected: He is a drunkard, he is a fool. They should be ashamed of themselves, all these sober people! And the wise ones!"

"Now you are being fanciful again," Albert said. "You always exaggerate, and you are certainly wrong when you classify suicide—and suicide is what we are talking about— as any sort of great achievement, since it can be defined only as a sign of weakness. For it is certainly easier to die than to stand up to a life of torment."

I was about to break off the conversation, for nothing can so completely disconcert me as when a man presents me, who am talking from the heart, with an insignificant platitude. But I controlled myself because I had heard the same thing so often and let it vex me. Instead I said, with quite some vehemence, "You call it weakness? I beg of you, don't let yourself be misled by appearances. Would you call a nation groaning under the unbearable yoke of a tyrant weak if it revolts and breaks its chains? Or the man who, in his horror because his house is afire, musters sufficient strength to carry off burdens with ease which he could scarcely have budged when he was calm? Or the man who, enraged by insults, takes on six men and overpowers them? Would you call these men weak? And if exertion is strength, why should exaggeration be the opposite?"

Albert looked at me and said, "Don't be offended, but the examples you give don't seem to fit at all."

"That may be," I said. "I have often been told that my way of combining things borders on the absurd. Let us try and see if we can imagine in some other way how a person feels who shoots himself, thereby throwing off the burden of a life that is generally considered to be pleasant. Because we have the right to talk about a thing only when we can feel for it.

"Human nature," I continued, "has its limitations. It can bear joy and suffering, and pain to a certain degree, but perishes when this point is passed. Here there can therefore be no question of whether a man is strong or weak, but of whether he can endure his suffering, be it moral or physical. And I find it just as astonishing to say that a man who takes his own life is a coward, as it would be improper to call a man a coward who dies of a pernicious fever."

"Paradox! Paradox!" cried Albert.

"Not to the extent you would have it," I replied. "You must admit that we call it a fatal illness when Nature is attacked in a fashion that destroys a part of her powers and incapacitates the rest to such an extent that she cannot rise again and is incapable of restoring a normal flow of life. Well, my dear fellow, let us apply this precept to the spirit of man. Look at man, with all his limitations—how impressions affect him, how ideas take hold of him until finally a passion grows within him to such an extent that it robs him of his peace of mind and ruins him. The calm, sensible man overlooks the poor fellow's plight to no avail and encourages him with as little success, just as the healthy man, standing beside a sickbed, cannot imbue the invalid with any of his strength."

Albert found too much generalization in all this. I reminded him of a girl who had been found in the river, drowned, not long ago, and told him her story. She was a sweet young thing who had grown up in a world narrowed down by household duties and the regimentation of her daily chores. She knew no better pleasure nor could hope for anything more than a Sunday walk with girls like herself, in finery accumulated gradually, bit by bit. Perhaps she went dancing on our feast days or passed a few hours chatting with a neighbor, with all the liveliness of hearty participation in the cause of a quarrel or some other bit of gossip.

And then her passionate nature begins to feel more intimate needs and they are increased by the flattery of the men she meets. Slowly the little things that used to please her grow stale, until she at last meets a man to whom she is irresistibly attracted by a feeling hitherto unknown. Now she puts all her hopes in him, forgets the world around her, hears nothing, sees nothing, feels naught but him, longs only for him—he is her all. Unspoiled by the empty pleasures of fickle vanity, her desire has but one goal—to be his. In an eternal union with him she hopes to find all the happiness she lacks and enjoy all the pleasures she longs for. Promises, repeated over and over again, seem to assure the fulfillment of her hopes; bold embraces increase her desire and make her soul captive. With her consciousness dulled, she wavers in the anticipation of happiness and reaches the highest possible degree of tension. At last she stretches out her arms to grasp all she desires—and her lover leaves her. Petrified, out of her mind, she stands in front of an abyss. All is darkness around her, she has no comfort, nothing to hope for, because he, in whom she had her being, has left her. She doesn't see the wide world in front of her nor the many people who might make up for what she has lost. She feels alone, abandoned; and blindly, cornered by the horrible need in her heart, she jumps and drowns her torment in the embrace of death. And you see, Albert, that is the story of quite a few people, and tell me—would you not call it a sickness? Nature finds no way out of a labyrinth of confused and contradictory powers and has to die.

"What a wretch, the man who sees it happen and can say, 'Foolish girl! If only she had waited, if only she had let time take effect, her despair would have left her, another would have come forward to comfort her.' That is as if someone were to say, 'The fool! He died of a fever. Why didn't he wait until he regained his strength, until his physical condition improved and the tumult in his blood died down? Then everything would have turned out well and he would be alive today!' "

Albert, who still couldn't see the point, had a few things to say—among others, that I had spoken about a simple girl. But he could not understand how any sensible person, not so limited, with a broader outlook on life, could be excused for similar behavior.

"My friend!" I cried. "A man is a man, and the little bit of sense he may have plays little or no part at all when passion rages in him, and the limitations of humankind oppress him. And what is more—but no, we'll talk about it some other time," I concluded and reached for my hat. Oh, my heart was full, and we parted without having understood each other. And that is how it is in the world. It is not easy for men to understand each other.

August 15th

One thing is certain—nothing justifies a man's existence like being loved. I feel that Lotte would not like to lose me, and it never occurs to the children that I might not turn up every day. Today I went over to tune Lotte's piano, but never got around to doing it, because the little ones would not leave me alone. They wanted a fairy tale, and in the end, even Lotte asked me to tell them one. I cut their supper bread for them—now they are almost as willing to receive it from me as from Lotte—and I told them their favorite tale about the princess who is waited on by invisible hands. I learn a great deal when I do this sort of thing, I can assure you, and am astonished by what an impression it makes on them. Sometimes, when I have to invent an incident because I have forgotten how I told the story the first time, they tell me at once that last time it was different, so now I try to tell every tale in a sustained singsong tone. This has taught me that an author can harm his book if he publishes a second, changed version of his story, however improved it may be poetically. The first impression finds the reader willing, and a human being can be persuaded to believe in the most daring adventure, but it takes root immediately, and woe to him who tries to dig it up and eradicate it!

August 18th

Why does that which makes a man happy have to become the source of his misery?

My full, warm enjoyment of all living things that used to overwhelm me with so much delight and transform the

world around me into a paradise has been turned into unbearable torment, a demon who pursues me wherever I go.
When I used to look at the far-off hills across the river from
the crags that give me a full view of the fruitful valley below
and saw all things burgeoning around me: the mountains
opposite, overgrown with thick, tall trees; the valleys winding in the shade of the loveliest forests; the river flowing
gently between whispering reeds, mirroring the pretty
clouds moving slowly across the horizon in the light evening
breeze; when I heard the birds around me bringing the
woods to life with their song and saw millions of little gnats
swarming in the sun's red light; saw how its last tremulous
rays brought the humming beetles up out of the grass, and
all this whirring and buzzing around me made me more
aware suddenly of the ground beneath my feet, of the moss
wresting its nourishment out of the hard rock, of the brush
flourishing on arid, sandy slopes, revealing the innermost,
glowing, sacred life of nature itself—how warmly I used to
be able to embrace all this and feel like a god in its abundance! How the magnificent creatures of this infinite world
came to life in my soul! I was surrounded by titanic mountains, abysses lay at my feet, waterfalls tumbled down steep
slopes, rivers flowed beneath me, and forest and mountain
resounded with it all. And I could see unfathomable powers
working and creating in the bowels of the earth, generations
of divers creatures milling around above the ground, beneath the sky—all of it taking a thousand different shapes—
and the human beings seeking protection in their little
houses, settling down together and, in their way, ruling over
this wide world. He is a poor fool who has so little respect
for all this because he is so small!

From the forbidding mountain range, across the barren
plain untrodden by the foot of man, to the ends of the unknown seas, the spirit of the Eternal Creator can be felt rejoic-
ing over every grain of dust that comprehends Him *and lives*!
Oh, how often I used to yearn in those days to fly with the
wings of the crane above me to the shores of the limitless seas
and drink the surging joy of life from the foaming cup of
eternity and feel, with the restricted powers of my breast, one
single drop of the bliss of Him who created all this.

Dear brother, merely recalling hours such as these refreshes me; even the exertion of remembering those indescribable feelings, and the retelling of them, lifts me out of myself—but then I feel my dread condition doubly hard. Something has been drawn away from my soul like a curtain and the panorama of eternal life has been transformed before my eyes into the abyss of an eternally open grave. Who can say, "That's how it is!" when all things are transient and roll away with the passing storm, and one's powers so rarely suffice for one's span of life but are carried off in the torrent to sink and be dashed against the rocks? There is not a moment in which one is not a destroyer and has to be a destroyer. A harmless walk kills a thousand poor crawling things, one footstep smashes a laboriously built anthill and stamps a whole little world into an ignominious grave. The rare disasters of this world, the floods that wash away our villages, the earthquakes that swallow up our cities—they do not move me. My heart is undermined by the consuming power that lies hidden in the Allness of nature, which has created nothing, formed nothing, which has destroyed neither its neighbor nor itself. Surrounded by the heavens and the earth and the powerful web they weave between them, I reel with dread. I can see nothing but an eternally devouring, eternally regurgitating monster.

August 21st

I stretch out my arms for her in vain when, troubled by my dreams, I awaken in the morning; at night I vainly seek her in my bed when a happy, innocent dream has deceived me into imagining I am sitting beside her in a field and holding her hand and kissing her. Oh, when I feel for her, still half dazed with sleep, and wake myself with it—a flood of tears flows from my oppressed heart and I weep inconsolably into a dark, dreary future.

August 22nd

It is a tragedy, William. My creative powers have been reduced to a restless indolence. I cannot be idle, yet I cannot seem to do anything either. I have no imagination, no more feeling for nature, and reading has become repugnant to me. When we are robbed of ourselves, we are robbed of everything! I swear there are days when I wish I were a common laborer if only to have something to do that day, an impetus, some hope when I awaken in the morning. I often envy Albert when I see him up to his ears in legal papers and tell myself that I would feel wonderful if I were in his place. How many times it has occurred to me to write and tell you that I was going to ask the minister for that post at the embassy, that you assured me would be granted me! I think it would be, too. The minister has shown a liking for me for some time now and has been urging me to seek some sort of occupation. For an hour or two I can work up a measure of enthusiasm for it, but then, when I think it over again, I am reminded of the fable about the horse that, impatient with its freedom, permitted itself to be saddled and ridden to death. I don't know what to do. And isn't it possible, my dear friend, that my longing for a change in my circumstances is an innate impatience that will pursue me wherever I go?

August 28th

It is true—if my illness were not incurable, these people could cure it. Today is my birthday, and early in the morning, I received a little package from Albert. When I opened it, I at once saw one of the pink bows Lotte was wearing when I saw her for the first time, which I have begged her so often to give me. The package consisted of two slim duodecimo volumes, the small Wetstein Homer, an edition I have often tried to find so that I would not have to drag my heavy Ernesti edition with me on my walks. So there you are—they try to fulfill my every wish; they think of any little friendly favors they can do me that are worth a thousand times more to me than those dazzling gifts that make us feel ashamed of the donor's vanity. I have kissed the little bow a thousand times, and with every breath I inhale the bliss with which those few, happy, irretrievable days filled me. William, that is how it is and I am not complaining. The flowers of life are illusion. How many blossom and leave no trace, how few bear fruit, and what a small amount of this fruit ripens! And still there are enough left, and still—oh, dearest friend—can we neglect the ripened fruit or despise it, or let it rot without ever having enjoyed it?

Farewell. It is a marvelous summer. I often sit in the fruit trees in Lotte's orchard and with long shears cut the pears from the top of the tree. She stands below and takes them from me one by one as I hand them down to her.

August 30th

Miserable wretch! Aren't you a fool? Aren't you deceiving yourself? What is the meaning of this riotous, endless passion? There are no more prayers in me except prayers to her; my imagination can shape no other figure but hers; I see everything around me only in its relationship to her. And this results every now and then in a few happy hours, until I must tear myself away from her again. William, William, you have no idea what my heart often urges me to do! When I have sat beside her for two or three hours and have basked in the sight of her, in her behavior, in the heavenly expression she puts into everything she says—then slowly but surely all my sensibilities are stretched to the breaking point. It grows dark before my eyes, I can scarcely hear, it has me by the throat like an assassin. My wildly beating heart tries to give breath to my afflicted senses and succeeds only in confusing them further. . . . William, then I don't know where I am! And when my melancholy gets the better of me and Lotte grants me the miserable consolation of giving way to my anguish in a flood of tears, as happens sometimes—then I have to get away, out, out . . . and I wander disconsolately in the fields. At moments such as these I like to climb a steep mountain or hack my way through uncleared forest, through hedges that hurt me, through brambles that scratch me! Then I feel a little better. A little better. And when I lie down to rest on the way, exhausted and thirsty, or when in the dark of night, with the full moon shining above me, I sit down on the branch of a deformed tree to rest my sore feet for a moment and sleep in an enervating stillness into the dawn—William, a solitary cell, a hair shirt, and a crown of thorns would be balm for which my soul is pining. Adieu! I can see no end to this misery but the grave!

September 3rd

I must leave here. Thank you, William, for encouraging me in my feeble decision. For the last two weeks I have been going around with the idea of leaving. I must get away. She is in town again, staying with a friend. And Albert . . . and—I must get away!

September 10th

What a dreadful night! William, now I know I can bear anything. I shall not see her again. Oh, why can't I fall on your neck and, in tears and rapture, confide to you, best of friends, the tumultuous passion that is breaking my heart! Here I sit, breathless, trying to calm down, waiting for the dawn when the horses will stand saddled outside. But she sleeps peacefully and has no idea that she will never see me again. I have succeeded in freeing myself, William, and found the strength, in the course of a conversation that lasted two hours, *not* to betray what was on my mind. And oh, dear God, what a conversation!

Albert had promised me that he and Lotte would come out into the garden after supper. I stood on the terrace under the tall chestnuts and saw the sun set for the last time across the delightful valley and the gentle stream. How often I have stood there with her and watched that magnificent sight—and now . . . I walked up and down the path that was so dear to me. A mysterious attraction often drew me there, even before I knew Lotte, and how delighted we were in those early days of our friendship when we discovered that both of us were drawn to this spot, which is really one of the most romantic ones any gardener could possibly produce. First you have the wide view between the chestnuts. I seem to recall having written to you about it—how two lines of tall beeches finally wall it in, and the path is darkened by the adjoining shrubbery, until all ends in an enclosure that has a mysterious aura of loneliness. I can still feel the sense of seclusion I experienced when I entered it for the first time, one day at noon. Fleetingly I sensed then what a setting it would be one day for my bliss and pain.

I had languished for about half an hour in the bitter-sweet thought of reunion and separation when I heard the two of them coming up the terrace steps. I ran to meet them, and I shivered as I took her hand and kissed it. We reached the terrace just as the moon rose above the wooded hills. We talked about this and that and without noticing it, drew nearer to the gloomy enclosure. Lotte entered it and sat down; Albert sat on one side of her, I on the other. But I could not remain seated; I was much too restless. So I rose and stood in front of them, walked up and down, sat down again. I was in a miserable state. Lotte drew our attention to the beautiful effect of the moonlight. Beyond the beeches, it was illuminating the entire terrace for us, a marvelous sight, made all the more striking by the fact that we were sitting in profound darkness. We were silent, and after a little while she said, "I never walk in the moonlight, never, without being reminded of my dead. In the moonlight I am always filled with a sense of death and of the hereafter. We live on"—and now she spoke with glorious feeling—"but, Werther, do we meet again? Shall we recognize each other? What do you feel? What do you believe?"

"Lotte," I said, stretching out my hand to her, and my eyes were filled with tears, "we shall meet again. Here and there . . . we shall meet again." I could say no more. William, did she have to ask me that just when my heart was full of this dreadful separation?

"And I often wonder," she went on, "if our dear departed ones can see us. Do they know it, when all goes well with us, that we remember and love them? I can feel my mother with me always when I sit with her children . . . my children . . . in the quiet of evening, and they crowd around me as they used to crowd around her. Then, when I look up to heaven, my eyes filled with tears of longing, and wish that she could look down at us, if only for a moment, and see how I have kept the promise I made to her when she was dying . . . that I would be a mother to her children— oh, with what a wealth of feeling my heart cries out to her then, 'Forgive me, beloved, if I cannot be to them what you were, I do my best . . . I dress them and feed them and . . . oh, what more can we do than cherish and love one another? If you could see the harmony between us, oh my blessed mother, you would praise and thank the good Lord to whom you prayed for the well-being of your children with your last bitter tears.' "

That is what she said. But William, who can possibly repeat what she said? How can cold, dead letters express the heavenly revelation of her spirit? Albert interrupted her gently by saying, "Dear Lotte, you take these things too much to heart. I know that such ideas mean a great deal to you, but please . . ."

"Oh, Albert," she said, "I know you haven't forgotten the evenings when we sat at the little round table. . . . Papa was away and we had sent the little ones to bed. You often brought a good book with you, but seldom had the opportunity to read aloud from it because . . . oh, wasn't it worth more than anything to listen to her? What a wonderful spirit she had, what a beautiful, gentle soul she was—and never, never idle. God knows the tears I have shed, kneeling at my bedside and praying to God that He might make me like her."

"Lotte!" I cried, kneeling down beside her, and my tears fell on her hand as I took it in mine, "Lotte, the grace of God is upon you, and you are filled with the spirit of your mother."

"If only you had known her," she said, pressing my hand. "She deserved that you should have known her!"

It took my breath away. Never had anyone said anything so glorious to me.

"And she had to die in the prime of life," Lotte continued, "when her youngest son was not yet six months old. She was not ill for long. She was so calm, so resigned. Only when she saw her children did she feel pain, especially the baby. When the end was near, she said to me. 'Bring them up to me,' and I did as she asked. The younger ones, they didn't know . . . and the older ones, who didn't comprehend . . . they stood around her bed. She lifted her hand and prayed for them and kissed them one by one and sent them away again. Then she said to me, 'Be a mother to them.' I promised her I would and gave her my hand on it. 'You promise a great deal, my child,' she said. 'A mother's heart . . . a mother's eyes . . . your tears of gratitude have told me often that you know what they mean. Feel like that for your brothers and sisters, and for your father have the loyalty and obedience of a wife and you will be a comfort to him.' She asked after him. He had gone out, torn by his anguish, to hide his unbearable grief.

"Albert, you were in the room. She could hear someone walking up and down and asked you to come to her bedside, and she looked at you and me with her tranquil eyes, assured that we were happy and that we would be happy together."

Albert threw his arms around her neck and kissed her and cried, "We are! We are! And we shall be!" The quiet man had lost his composure and I—I didn't know I was alive.

"And this good woman is supposed to be gone from us," Lotte went on. "Dear God, Werther, when I think how one permits the dearest thing in life to be carried away, and no one feels it as keenly as the children. For a long, long time after it was all over they lamented—how the black men came and carried Mama away."

She rose, and it brought me back to my senses. I was shattered and remained seated, still holding her hand. "Let us go," she said. "It is late." She wanted to withdraw her hand, but I clung to it. "We shall meet again!" I cried. "We shall find each other, whatever shape or form we may have. We shall recognize each other. I will go," I added. "I will go willingly, but if I had to say goodbye forever, I could not bear it. Farewell, Lotte, farewell, Albert. We shall meet again."

"Tomorrow, I imagine," she said gaily. I could feel the word "tomorrow." She didn't know, as she drew her hand out of mine. . . .

They walked down the path in the moonlight. I stood up and watched them go. Then I threw myself on the ground and wept until I could weep no more after which I jumped to my feet and ran out onto the terrace. Below, in the shadows of the tall linden trees, I could see her white dress shimmering as the two moved toward the gate. I stretched out my arms . . . and it vanished.

BOOK TWO

October 20th, 1771

We arrived here yesterday. The ambassador is indisposed and will not be going out for a few days. If only he were not so unpleasant, things would be a great deal easier. But fate has many trials in store for me—I know it, I know it. However, let us not lose courage, for a light heart can bear all things. A light heart? I have to laugh. How could I write such words? Ah yes, a little lighter blood could make me the happiest man on earth! Come, come, Werther! How can you doubt your strength, your gifts, when others complacently parade their puny strength and talents? Dear God, who hath bestowed all this upon me, why didst Thou not withhold a half of it and give me instead faith in myself and a modest capacity for contentment?

Patience! Patience! Things will improve. Because I want to assure you, my dear friend, you are right. Since I spend my days among people again and observe what they do and how they live, I find it much easier to live with myself. Since we mortals happen to be so constituted that we compare everything with ourselves and ourselves with everything around us, our happiness and our misery have to lie in the things with which we compare ourselves. Nothing is therefore more dangerous than solitude. Our imagination, forced by its very nature to unfold, nourished by the fantastic visions of poetry, gives shape to a whole order of creatures of which we are the lowliest, and everything around us seems to be more glorious, everyone else more perfect. And all this happens quite naturally. We feel so often that there is a great deal lacking in us and that our neighbor possesses just what we lack and, for good measure, we proceed to read into him *our* finer attributes, adding a bit of idealistic comfort to boot, and with that have rounded out a perfectly happy, fortunate man who is actually a figment of our imagination. If, on the other hand, we can make up our minds to go about our daily tasks, resigned to our failings, and hardships, we often find that, in spite of our meanderings and procrastination, we have gone farther than quite a few others have gone with their sails unfurled and steering gear functioning. And, truly, it is a wonderful feeling when one manages somehow to keep up with one's fellow men, or better still, outpaces them.

November 26th

All things considered, I am beginning to find life quite tolerable here. The best part of it is that I am kept sufficiently busy, and the many different types and the fresh personalities create a colorful spectacle that distracts me. I have met Count C. and have to admire him more and more daily. He is a man of true intellect, never aloof just because he happens to be more discerning than most people. He radiates friendliness and affection. He took an interest in me when I had to transact some business with him and says that he noticed, with the first words we exchanged, that we understood each other and he could speak with me as he could not speak with anyone else. I can't praise his candor sufficiently. There is no truer, no greater pleasure imaginable than to enjoy the confidence of a truly great mind.

December 24th

The ambassador is causing me a lot of trouble. I saw it coming. He is the most punctilious fool imaginable, everything has to be done step by step—and long-winded! A man who is never satisfied with himself and can therefore never be satisfied. I like to work fast and let it go at that, but he is just as likely to return a paper to me and say, "It isn't bad but I would go over it again. One can always find a better word, a more precise specification . . ." Then I could tell him to go to the devil. No "ands" nor "buts," no conjunctions may be missing, and he is dead set against any inversions that sometimes slip out before I have caught them. And if I don't let one sentence follow the next in the same singsong rhythm, he can't follow the meaning at all. Really, working for such a man is misery!

Count von C.'s friendship is the only compensation. The other day he told me quite frankly how dissatisfied he was with my ambassador's procrastination and pedantry. People make things so difficult for themselves and for others; still, according to him, we have to resign ourselves to it, like a traveler who has to drive across a mountain. Of course the way would be easier and shorter if the mountain were not there, but the mountain *is* there and has to be crossed! I guess the old man notices too that the Count prefers my company, and that must annoy him; he never misses an opportunity to speak derogatively of the Count to me. I, of course, don't let it pass, which only serves to make matters worse. Yesterday he really made me lose my temper, because I knew he was also referring to me. When it was a question of business matters, he declared, the Count did well enough. Things came easily to him, and his style was good, but like all belletrists he lacked erudition! Then he gave me a look as much as to say, "Did that strike home?" But it didn't. I despise any man who can think and behave like that. I stood up to him and fought back, quite vehemently too. I said that the Count was a man who commanded respect, not only for his intellect but for his character as well. I had never known anyone, I said, who had succeeded so admirably in broadening his mind to include so many subjects and still be able to attend to the daily business of life. All of this was Greek to him, and I retired before I had to swallow any more of his *déraisonnement*.

And it is all your fault, all of you who talked me into this strait jacket and gave me such a song and dance about having something to do! If the man who plants his potatoes and drives his wagon to town to sell his grain isn't doing more than I am, I will gladly spend another ten years chained to the galleys as I am now!

And the glittering misery, the boredom of the perfectly horrible people I meet here! Their social aspirations! In their efforts to gain the slightest precedence they can't take their eyes off the next fellow. The most abject passions are displayed quite shamelessly. There is one woman, for instance, who can talk of nothing but her titles and her

estates. One doesn't have to know her to realize that she is
a complete fool who flatters herself with paltry titles and
has an inflated provincial pride. But the worst part of it is,
she is actually nothing more than the daughter of a local
magistrate. I cannot understand how people can be so insen-
sitive as to prostitute themselves in such a vulgar fashion.

Thus I notice daily, my dear friend, how foolish we are
when we judge others by ourselves. And since I am so pre-
occupied with myself, and my heart is so tempestuous, I
prefer to let others go their way—if only they would let me
go mine!

What irritates me most are the deplorable social conditions. I know as well as anyone else how necessary it is that
there be differences in rank, and how much this is to my
advantage. All I ask is that it should not stand in my way
when there is a small chance of my enjoying myself, or a
glimmer of hope that I may still know happiness on this
earth. A few days ago, while I was out walking, I made the
acquaintance of a Fräulein von B., a charming creature who
has somehow managed to remain natural in spite of the
formalities of life here. We enjoyed our conversation, and
when we parted I asked for permission to call on her. She
said that I might so unreservedly that I could scarcely wait
for the proper time to elapse until I could visit her. She is
not from these parts and lives with an aunt. I did not like
the looks of the old lady. I paid her a great deal of attention, almost everything I said was directed at her. But in
little less than half an hour I realized what the young lady
admitted later—that her dear aunt, with nothing but an inadequate fortune at her disposal and even less intellect,
finds sustenance solely in her lineage and security only behind the ramparts of her rank, which is her castle, and takes
pleasure in nothing but looking down her nose at the lower
classes. In her youth she was beautiful and frittered her life
away, at first by making many a young man miserable with
her capriciousness; later, in her maturer years, she was completely under the thumb of an old army officer who, in
return for having married her and a tolerable maintenance,
was her companion in her bronze age, and died. Now, in
her iron age, she finds herself alone and no one would pay
her any heed if her niece were not so kind.

January 8th 1772

How dreadful people are who have had nothing on their minds for years but formality, whose every effort and thought are bent toward moving one place higher up at table! And it is not because they have nothing better to do. Not at all! Important work piles up just because one is prevented from attending to it by a thousand vexations concerning rank and promotion. Last week there was a lot of such bickering on our sleigh ride and all the fun was spoiled.

If only the fools would realize that the seating doesn't really matter, that he who sits at the head of the table rarely plays the leading role. Many a king is ruled by his prime minister and many a minister by his secretary, and then who is first? I would say he who can see through all the others and has the forcefulness or cunning to use their powers and passions to further his own ends.

January 20th

I must write to you, dear Lotte, here in a humble peasant inn where I have taken shelter from a severe storm. When I am in that miserable little town of D., among strangers, with people who are totally alien to my heart, there isn't a moment, not one, when my heart bids me write to you. But now, in this lowly house, in this solitude and confinement, with hail and snow pelting against the little window of my room, my first thoughts go out to you. When I entered I was overwhelmed by a vision of you, by my memories, oh Lotte—such sacred, such heartfelt memories! Dear God, this is my first moment of happiness since I left!

If you could only see me, dearest—in a whirl of distraction, but how arid is my spirit! Not a heartfelt moment, not a blissful hour—nothing . . . nothing. Sometimes I feel as if I were standing in front of a peep show. I can see tiny men and horses maneuvering in front of me, and I ask myself if it is not an optical illusion. I join in the games, or rather, I should say that I let myself be manipulated like a puppet, and sometimes I touch my neighbor's wooden hand and withdraw mine in horror. In the evening I decide to enjoy the sunrise, but in the morning I don't bother to get up. During the day I look forward to an enjoyment of the moonlight, then at night I stay in my room. I don't know why I get up or why I go to bed! The leaven that used to set my life in motion is lacking; the stimulus that kept me wide awake late into the night and woke me in the morning is gone.

I have found only one sympathetic female here, a Fräulein von B. She is very like you, dear Lotte, if there can be any comparison. Oh, I can hear you say, "He is in a mood for paying a pretty compliment," and you would not be entirely wrong. For some time now I have been behaving myself, because that seems to be the only thing to do. I have become quite a wit. The ladies say no one knows how to sing their praises like Werther (and to fabricate like him, they usually add, for there is no other way of doing it, you understand?). But I wanted to speak of Fräulein von B. She is a soulful creature who looks one straight in the eye. Hers are blue. Her rank is a burden to her that satisfies none of her aspirations. She longs to get away from all the hollow confusion around her, and we dream-talk many an hour away in blissfully serene, pastoral surroundings. We talk about you. How often she has to worship at your altar—doesn't have to, does so willingly. She likes to hear me talk about you; she loves you.

Ah, if only I were sitting at your feet in our cozy little room, with our little darlings romping around us! If they were making too much noise I would gather them around me and tell them an eerie fairy story to calm them down.

The sun is setting magnificently behind a landscape glittering with snow. The storm has passed, and I—I have to lock myself in my cage again. Adieu. Is Albert with you? And how—oh, dear God, forgive me the question!

February 8th

For eight days now we have had the most terrible weather, and it does my heart good, because since I have been here we have not had a nice day that was not spoiled for me by someone. But if it rains and blusters, is chilly or thaws—ha! I tell myself that it can't get worse inside than out, or if you like, the other way round, and that suits me. But if I see the sun rise in the morning, promising a fine day, I say to myself, "There they have another treasure to do each other out of." There is nothing in this world, William, that

they would not like to do each other out of—health, good
repute, happiness, recreation—for the most part because
they are foolish, narrow-minded, and dull-witted. You can
listen to them with the best of open minds and come to no
other conclusion. Sometimes I feel like falling on my knees
and imploring them not to be so fanatically intent on cutting
each other's throats.

February 17th

I am afraid my ambassador and I are not going to be able
to put up with each other much longer. The man is impossible! His working habits and way of doing business are so
ridiculous that I simply cannot control myself and have to
contradict him; and often I do a thing the way I feel it
should be done, which of course never suits him. He complained about me at court the other day and the minister
reprimanded me—gently enough, but all the same, it was a
reprimand. I was about to hand in my resignation when I
received a personal letter from him that makes me want to
kneel down and worship this infinitely noble and wise
mind.* He rebukes me for being overly sensitive, yet respects my exaggerated ideas on effectiveness, influencing
others, and succeeding in business, as examples of youthful
high spirits and in no way tries to suppress them. All he
wants to do is tone them down and guide them into the
correct channels, where they may have the right effect. Now
I have the strength to carry on for another week and have
come to an understanding with myself. Peace of mind and
the ability to take pleasure in oneself are glorious things.
Dear friend, if only the treasure were not as fragile as it is
precious and beautiful!

February 20th

God bless you, my dear ones, and give you all the good
days He denies me!
I thank you, Albert, for having deceived me. I waited to

---

*Out of respect for this admirable man, this letter and one men-
tioned later are not included in this collection, in the belief that such
indiscretions would be inexcusable, however grateful the reader might
be.

be told the day of your wedding, and it was my intention, on that day, to go through the ceremony of taking the little silhouette I made of Lotte down from the wall and burying it with some other papers. Now you are united, and her picture is where it always has been. Very well, let it remain there. And why not? I know that I am with you too and have a place in Lotte's heart that does you no harm. I would go so far as to say second place and I want to hold onto it—must hold onto it! I think if she forgot me, I would go mad. Albert, all hell lies in the very thought! Farewell, Albert, farewell dear angel from heaven. Lotte, farewell.

March 15th

I have just had a very distressing experience that will drive me away from here. I am still foaming at the mouth! The devil take it! I can't get over it, and it is your fault—you, who egged me on and drove me and tormented me to take a post that doesn't suit me at all! So now I'm saddled with it and so are you! And don't tell me again that it is my exaggerated ideas that ruin everything! Here, my dear sir, is the whole unvarnished story, properly told, just as any historian would let you have it.

Count von C. is very fond of me. He singles me out— but you know all that. I have mentioned it a hundred times. I was invited to lunch there yesterday, and it happened to be the day on which the nobility from hereabout gathers at his house in the afternoon. I have never given them a thought, and it never occurred to me that we inferiors do not fit in. Very well. I lunched with the Count, and after lunch we walked up and down the great hall. I was conversing with him and Colonel B., who had joined us, when the time for the sociabilities drew near. Nothing was further from my mind. The first to enter was the oh, so honorable Lady von S. with her spouse and the little goose of a daughter the two of them managed to hatch—with her flat little chest and dear little waist laced tight—their aristocratic eyebrows raised, their noses turned up. Since I wholeheartedly detest the entire breed, I was anxious to take my leave and was only waiting for the Count to free himself from their miserable prattle, when my Fräulein von B. came in. The sight of her always cheers my heart a little, so I decided to stay and took up my stand behind her chair. It took me a little while to realize that she was not conversing with me as freely as usual; in fact, she was behaving toward me with quite some constraint. Then it was suddenly very noticeable. She couldn't be like all the rest of them, I thought, and was hurt and wanted to leave, but then I stayed on because I wanted so much to give her a chance to absolve herself. I couldn't believe her capable of such snobbery and still hoped to hear her speak a few pleasant words, and . . . oh, I don't know what! Meanwhile, the hall had become quite crowded. There was Baron F., decked out in the complete regalia of Franz I's coronation era, Privy Councilor R., here, in his official capacity, called Herr *von* R., with his deaf wife, etc. And let us not overlook S., shabbily dressed as usual. He mends his antiquated wardrobe with patches of new material. After that they came pouring in; I conversed with a few of my friends and found all of them rather laconic; but I could think of nothing and pay attention to no one but my friend, B. I didn't notice the ladies at the other end of the room whispering to each other and how this spread to the men and how Frau von S. went over to the Count and spoke to him (I found out all this later from Fräulein B.) until finally the Count drew me over to one of the windows. "You know what charming conditions prevail here," he said. "I notice that my guests are displeased to find you present. The last thing in the world I want—"

"Your Excellency," I interrupted him, "a thousand apologies. I should have noticed it myself long before this, and I know you will forgive my inconsistency—I wanted to take my leave some time ago but," I added, smiling as I bowed, "a devilish impulse held me back." The Count shook my hand with a pressure that indicated just how he felt about it. I slipped away quietly, got into my cabriolet, and drove to M. to see the sun set from the hill there and read Homer's glorious verses about Ulysses and the hospitable swineherd. And all that was well and good.

In the evening, I returned home for my supper. There were only a few people in the taproom; they had turned back the tablecloth and were playing at dice. Suddenly honest old Adelin came in, put his hat down on the table, and said softly, "You're in trouble, I hear." "I?" said I. "The

Count asked you to leave his party." "The devil take his party!" I said. "I was thankful to get out in the fresh air again." "I'm glad to see you're not taking it to heart," he said. "It only annoyed me because it's already all over town." And until then the whole thing hadn't bothered me a bit! But after that, of course, I felt that everyone who came in and looked at me was staring at me because of that. It was maddening!

And now, since everyone commiserates with me wherever I go and I am told that those who used to envy me are triumphing and saying, "There you can see how the presumptuous end, those who try to lift their insignificant heads too high and think they can go where they please and do as they like . . ." I could run a knife into my heart! Because people can say what they like about being independent— show me the man who can stand being raked over the coals by scoundrels when they have the advantages over him. When their talk is idle nonsense, ah, then it can be easily ignored.

March 16th

Everything conspires against me. Today I met Fräulein von B. on the promenade. I simply had to go up to her, and as soon as we had withdrawn a little from the others, I let her know how I felt about her behavior the other day. "Oh, Werther," she said fervently, "how could you interpret my behavior in such a fashion when you know what my feelings are? You have no idea how I suffered for you from the moment I entered the hall. I knew just what was going to happen. A hundred times it was on the tip of my tongue to tell you. I knew that the Von S.'s, and T., and their husbands, would rather have left early than stay at a gathering that included you, and that the Count could not afford to offend them . . . and now, all this fuss!"

"What do you mean, *Fräulein*?" I said, trying to hide my dismay, because everything Adelin had said the day before ran suddenly like wildfire through my veins. "You cannot imagine how dearly I have had to pay for my behavior already," the sweet creature replied, and there were tears in her eyes.

It was all I could do to control myself. I was on the point

of throwing myself at her feet. "You must explain yourself!" I cried. "I insist!"

The tears were coursing down her cheeks. I was beside myself. She didn't try to hide them from me as she dried her eyes. "You know my aunt," she said. "She was there and, oh, the expression in her eyes as she watched the whole thing! Werther, last night and this morning I have had to endure a lecture about my friendship with you and hear you degraded and could only half defend you. I dared do no more."

Every word she spoke with a stab in the heart. She didn't seem to realize at all how merciful it would have been to spare me all this, but went on to say how people would continue to talk about it, and what kind of people would gloat over it, and how it would amuse and delight them to see my arrogance and my poor opinion of others punished . . . I have been reproached for them often enough. To hear her tell me all this, William, with so much compassion in her voice . . . I was shattered and am still furious with myself. I wish someone would dare reproach me about the whole thing so that I could run a dagger through his heart. If only I could see blood, I know I would feel better. Oh, I have picked up a knife a hundred times with the intention of plunging it into my own heart! I have heard tell of a noble breed of stallions who, when they are overheated and run wild, instinctively bite open one of their veins to relieve themselves. I feel like that often. I would like to open the vein that would give me eternal freedom.

March 24th

I have asked to be relieved of my post and hope my resignation will be accepted. You will forgive me, I am sure, for not having first asked your permission. I simply had to get away, and I know all the things you would have said to persuade me to remain. Inform my mother of the fact gently. I can't help myself, and she will just have to put up with my not being able to help her either. I realize that she will be hurt when she sees the fine career her son had just embarked on, which was supposed to lead to Privy Councilor and Ambassador, suddenly stop, and back with the creature in its stall! Break the news to her in any way you like and come to some sort of agreement on the conditions under which I could possibly have and certainly should have stayed . . . enough! I am leaving, and so you may know where I am going. Prince —— is here and seems to find my company to his liking. He heard of my decision and has asked me to accompany him to his estate to spend the beautiful season of spring with him. He has promised that I will be entirely on my own, and since we understand each other up to a point, I intend to grasp the opportunity and accompany him.

April 19th
For your information:

Thank you for both letters. I did not reply because I left this letter unfinished until the time of my departure from court. I was afraid my mother might appeal to the minister and make it more difficult for me to go through with my plans. But now it is all over, and the time for my departure has come. I don't want to say how reluctant they were to let me go or what the minister wrote—you would only break out in renewed lamentations. The young duke gave me twenty-five ducats as a farewell gift, with a few words that moved me to tears, so my mother need not send me the money I asked for recently.

May 5th

Tomorrow I leave here, and since the place of my birth lies only six miles away, I want to visit it again and recall those happy, dreamlike days. I want to walk up to the gate through which my mother rode with me when she left that beloved, familiar place after my father's death to incarcerate herself in the unbearable town she lives in now. Adieu, William. I shall report on the trip.

May 9th

I undertook the journey to my former home with all the reverence of a pilgrim, and was gripped by a few quite unexpected emotions. I had the carriage stop beside the tall linden tree that stands about a quarter of an hour's drive from the city in the direction of S. I got out and told the postilion to drive on so that I might enjoy every memory on foot, vividly and renewed, according to the dictates of my heart. There I stood, under the tree that was once goal and limit of my walks as a boy, and how changed I was! In those days I longed with a happy ignorance to go out into the unknown world where I hoped to find so much nourishment for my heart, so much delight for my yearning soul. And now I have returned from the wide, wide world, oh my friend, with so many shattered hopes and ruined plans. Stretched out before me I saw the mountains that had been the objective of my longing a thousand times. I used to be able to sit there by the hour and yearn for those mountains and lose my whole being in the woods and valleys that presented themselves to me in such a pleasant twilit fashion. And then, when I had to return at a certain time, with what reluctance I used to leave the beloved spot!

I approached the town and greeted all the old familiar little houses, thought the new ones were repulsive, also all over innovations. I walked in at the gate and at once found myself again—all of me! Dear friend, I don't want to go into details. It was an enchanting experience, but would only fall flat in the telling.

I had decided to take lodgings on the market square next to our old house. On the way there, I noticed that our former schoolroom, where an honest old woman had crowded all our childhood together, had been turned into a general store. I recalled the restlessness, the tears, the dullness, and fear that I had experienced in that little room. I could not take a step that was not worthy of note. A pilgrim in the Holy Land would not find so many places with sacred memories, nor could his soul possibly be filled with more reverent emotions. One more example will suffice: I walked down river to a certain farm. It used to be a favorite walk of mine and a place where we boys tried to see how many times we could make a flat stone ricochet on the water. I could remember vividly how I used to stand sometimes and watch the water, with what a marvelous feeling of reverie I would follow its course, and in a highly adventurous spirit, imagine the regions into which it flowed, until I soon found that my imagination had gone as far as it could—still it had to go on and on until I was lost utterly in invisible distances.

Yes, my dear friend, that is how restrained yet happy our glorious ancestors were; their feelings and poetry were childlike. When Ulysses speaks of the boundless sea and the never-ending earth, it is so true, so human, so sincerely felt, so close and mysterious. Of what use is it to me that I can now recite with every schoolboy that the earth is round? A human being needs only a small plot of ground on which to be happy and even less to lie beneath.

So now here I am at the Prince's hunting lodge. Life with him is pleasant, and we get along well. He is honest and simple and surrounded by very odd people whom I can't even begin to understand! They don't seem to be rogues, yet they don't impress me as being honest, either. Sometimes I feel they are sincere, still I can't trust them. Another thing I regret is that he speaks often of things he has only heard or read about, and then from the other person's point of view, and he seems to value my mind and my various talents more than this heart of mine, of which I am so proud, for it is the source of all things—all strength, all bliss, all misery. The things I know, every man can know, but, oh, my heart is mine alone!

May 25th

I have had something on my mind that I did not want to mention to you until I had gone through with it. Now that nothing has come of it, it is just as well. I wanted to enlist and get into the fighting. My heart has been full of the idea for some time. It is the main reason why I came here with the Prince. He is a general in the service of ——. While out for a walk, I disclosed my intention. He advised me against it, and it must have been a caprice on my part rather than a sincere desire, for I heeded his argument.

June 11th

Say what you will—I cannot stay here any longer. What is there for me to do here? Time hangs heavy on my hands. The Prince sees to it that I am well cared for, as well as could possibly be, still I do not feel at home. He is a man of intellect, yet there is nothing extraordinary about his mind; being with him is no more entertaining than reading a good book. I shall stay another week, then I shall start wandering again. The best thing I have done here are a few sketches. The Prince has a certain amount of understanding for the arts and would be even better at it were he not fettered by distasteful scientific ideas and commonplace terminology. Sometimes it sets my teeth on edge when I point out nature and art to him with my heartfelt imagination, and he feels suddenly that he must do the correct thing and ruins everything with a platitude.

June 16th

Yes, I am a wanderer on this earth—a pilgrim. Are you anything more than that?

June 18th

You would like to know where I am heading? Let me inform you, confidentially . . . I have to stay here two weeks more, then, I tell myself, I want to visit the mines in ——. Of course there's nothing to it, really, but that I want to be near Lotte. And I have to laugh at my heart as I do its bidding.

July 29th

No, all is well, all is well just as it is. I . . . her husband! O God, Who didst make me as I am, hadst Thou but granted me this bliss, my whole life would have been a paean of praise to Thee! But I shall not remonstrate, and I beg Thee to forgive my tears and my vain desires. Lotte . . . my wife! If only I could say that I had held the most beloved creature under the sun in my arms! It makes me shudder, William, to think of Albert putting his arms around her slender waist.

And—do I dare say it? Why not, William? She would have been happier with me. He is not the man to fulfill all her desires. A certain lack of sensitivity, a lack . . . oh, put it any way you like . . . his heart does not respond to certain passages in a book over which Lotte's and mine would meet, and on a hundred other occasions . . . when we are talking about someone else's behavior . . . oh, my dear William, of course he loves her with all his heart, and love such as that merits all things!

A perfectly unbearable person interrupted me at this

point. I have dried my tears, I have been distracted, adieu, my friend!

August 4th

I am not the only one thus afflicted. All men suffer disappointments and are deceived in their expectations. I paid the good woman under the linden tree a visit. Her eldest boy ran to meet me. His cry of joy brought out his mother. She looked despondent. Her first words were, "Oh, my dear, good gentleman, my little Hans died." He was her youngest boy. I was speechless. "And my husband has returned from Switzerland with empty hands," she went on. "If it had not been for some kind people he would have had to beg his way home. On the way back he was stricken with a fever." What could I say? I gave her boy something. She asked me to accept a few apples, which I did, and left the sorrowful scene.

August 21st

Like the turning of a hand . . . things change with me just as quickly. Sometimes a happier outlook on life tries to struggle to the surface—alas, only for a moment. When I am lost in my dreams I can't help thinking—what if Albert were to die? You would . . . she would . . . and then I follow this phantasmagoria until it leads me to an abyss and I draw back trembling.

When I walk out of the gate, the way I drove when I went to fetch Lotte for the dance—how different things were then! All past, all over and done with! Not a trace left of that bygone world, not a heartbeat of my former emotions. I feel like a ghost who returns to the burnt-out, ruined castle he built when he was a virile prince, and furnished with all the treasure of a glorious life, and left hopefully to his beloved son.

September 3rd

Sometimes I simply cannot understand how she can love another, how she dare—since I love her alone, so deeply, so fully, and recognize nothing, know nothing, have nothing but her!

September 4th

Yes, I am right. That's how it is. As all nature tends toward autumn, it becomes autumn within me and all around me. My leaves turn yellow, as the leaves of the nearby trees fall to the ground. Didn't I write to you, shortly after I came here, about a peasant lad? I enquired about him in Wahl-heim the other day and was told that he had been dismissed and nobody seemed to know anything about him. Yesterday I met him quite by chance on his way to another village. I accosted him, and he told me his story, which touched me deeply, as you will readily understand when I repeat it to you. But why do I bother? Why don't I keep what frightens and hurts me to myself? Why must I sadden you, too? Why do I constantly give you the opportunity to pity and scold me? Very well . . . that, too, may be a part of my destiny.

At first the poor fellow answered my questions with a quiet sadness in which I thought I could detect a certain shyness, but soon he spoke with less reserve, as if he had suddenly recognized me and himself. He was quite frank about the mistakes he had made and told me his whole sad story. I wish I could pass on every word of it to you, for you to pass judgment on it. He admitted, with something akin to the zest and happiness of remembrance itself, how his passion for his mistress had grown stronger daily, until in the end he hadn't known what he was doing or saying or where to lay his poor head. He couldn't eat, drink, or sleep, he felt choked with emotion, he did things he wasn't sup-posed to do and what he was supposed to do he left undone. It was as if he were pursued by demons until, one day, when he knew that she was in one of the upstairs rooms, he went to her there—more than that, he was drawn to her. She wouldn't give in to him, so he tried to take her by force. He didn't know what came over him. As God was his witness, his intentions had always been honorable, and he had never longed for anything so much in his life as that she should marry him. After he had spoken on and on like this for a while, he became hesitant, like someone who has more on his mind but is afraid to speak out. At last he shyly confessed to the small intimacies she had allowed him and how close she had let him draw. He broke off several times to protest over and over again that he was not telling me all this to damage her reputation in any way . . . that was how he put it. He loved and respected her as much as ever; he had never talked about it before and was only telling me now to assure me that he was not a warped or unreasonable man. And here, good friend, I must repeat the old refrain I am constantly singing: if only I could put this man before you as I see him now! If only I could relate his story so you could feel how I share his fate—must share it! But enough—since you know me and my destiny only too well, you probably also know what attracts me to all unfortunate people, and to this man in particular.

On rereading this page, I see that I have forgotten to tell you the end of the story. It isn't difficult to guess. She rejected him. Her brother happened upon them. He had always hated the poor fellow and wished him out of the house because he feared his sister might marry again, and his children thereby lose the inheritance that he had high hopes would be theirs, because the woman is childless. The brother threw him out and noised the whole thing abroad to such an extent that she could not possibly have taken him back, even if she had wanted to. Then she took on another servant and it is rumored that she has had trouble with her brother about the new man too, but this time everyone feels sure she will marry him. My poor lad, however, is determined not to live to see it.

I have not exaggerated any of this or oversentimentalized it. I would go so far as to say that I have told it laconically—yes, laconically—and have tried to make it more commonplace by telling it in conventional terms.

Love, loyalty, and passion such as this are therefore no figments of my imagination. They live and can be found in all purity among a class of people we like to call uncultured and crude! We cultured ones—cultured until there is nothing left! Read my little tale with reverence, I beg of you! Today, as I write it down, all is quiet within me. You can see by my handwriting that I am not scribbling as I usually do. Read, my dear friend, and reflect that it is your friend's story too. Yes, it has happened to me, and the rest will happen to me too, and I am not nearly so well behaved or determined as that poor wretch, with whom I scarcely dare to compare myself.

September 5th

She wrote a little note to her husband, who is away on business. It started off with the words, "My best, my dearest one. Come home as soon as you can. I live in joyous anticipation of your return." Just then a friend came in with the news that, owing to certain circumstances, Albert would not be able to return as soon as expected. The little note was forgotten, and in the course of the evening I came across it. I read it and smiled, and she asked me why I was smiling. "What a divine gift our imagination is!" I said. "For a moment I imagined that it was written to me." She said nothing, but she seemed displeased by my behavior, and I was silenced.

September 6th

It was very difficult for me to decide to put aside the simple blue jacket in which I danced with Lotte for the first time, but it had become too threadbare. I have had one made exactly like it—collar and cuffs just alike, and the same yellow waistcoat and breeches. But it doesn't have quite the desired effect. I don't know . . . in time I suppose I shall grow fond of this suit, too.

September 12th

She was away for a few days. She left to fetch Albert. Today I walked into her room, she came to meet me, and I kissed her hand, my heart overflowing with joy. A canary flew from the mirror onto her shoulder. "My new friend," she said and coaxed him onto her hand. "I brought him for the children. He is such a darling. Look, when I give him bread, he flutters and picks it up so neatly. And he kisses me. Look!"

She held the little creature to her mouth, and it touched her beloved lips so sweetly, as if it could feel the bliss it was being granted.

"Let him kiss you too,' she said, stretching out her hand to me, with the bird on it. His little beak found its way from her mouth to mine, and the little peck it gave me was like a breath, a premonition of the delights of love.

"I wouldn't say that his kiss was entirely without desire," I said. "He seeks food, and the kiss leaves him unsatisfied."

"But he eats out of my mouth too," she said, and let him take a few crumbs from her lips. She was smiling, radiant with the joy of an innocent love. I turned away. She should not have done it. She should not incite my imagination with such exhibitions of heavenly innocence and bliss; she should not rouse my heart, which the indifference of life sometimes rocks to sleep. And yet, why not? She trusts me. She knows how much I love her.

September 15th

It is enough to drive one mad, William! To think that there are people who have no feeling at all for the few things on this earth that are of real value! Do you remember the walnut trees under which I sat with Lotte when he visited the good vicar in St. ——? Those magnificent trees that, God knows, always delighted me . . . how snug they made the rectory courtyard, how cool, and what marvelous branches they had! And the memories that went with them, back to the worthy vicar who had planted them so many years ago. The schoolmaster mentions his name often; he has it from his grandfather. What a good man he was, and his memory was sacred to me always under those trees. Let me tell you, there were tears in the schoolmaster's eyes yesterday when we spoke about how they had been cut down. Yes, cut down! The very idea drives me crazy! I could murder the dog who drove in the first ax. I, who would grieve if I had a pair of trees like that in my yard and had to see them die of old age . . . I have to see the thing happen! But, my dear friend, there is another side to it—human reaction. The whole village is grumbling about it, and I hope the vicar's wife will be made to feel, by a lack of butter and eggs and the dearth of other little friendly gestures, how she has wounded the town. Because it was done on the orders of the new clergyman's wife (our dear old man died), a gaunt, sickly woman who has every reason not to participate in the life going on around her because it wants no part of her. She is a crazy creature who pretends to be very learned, dabbles in new interpretations of the Scriptures, shrugs off Lavater's ecstasies, and occupies herself with the moral-critical reformation of Christianity that is currently fashionable. She is thoroughly unhealthy and

therefore knows naught of the joys on God's earth. Only a
person like that could have cut down my walnut trees! You
can see—I can't get over it! Just imagine—the falling leaves,
she says, messèd up her yard and made it dank. The trees
took away the light, and when the nuts were ripe, the boys
threw stones at them, and that made her nervous! I suppose
it disturbed her profound thoughts as she weighed the merits of Kennicott, Semler, and Michaelis. When I saw how
upset the villagers were, especially the older ones, I asked,
"Why did you let it happen?" "When the bailiff wants anything done," they said, "what can we do about it?" But I
can report on one act of justice: the bailiff and the vicar—
who wanted to see some gain from his wife's whim; they
don't usually fill his larder—thought they would divide the
profit of the trees between them. But the chamberlain got
wind of it and said, "It goes into our coffers!" According
to him, his office holds claim to that part of the parsonage
on which the trees stood and will sell them to the highest
bidder! There they lie. Oh, if I were Prince, I would see to
it that vicar's wife, bailiff, and chamberlain—prince? Ah
me, if I were prince, of what concern would the trees on
my land be to me.

October 10th

If only I can look into her dark eyes, then all is well with
me again. And do you know what grieves me? I don't think
Albert is as happy as he . . . hoped to be . . . as I thought
I was when . . .
I don't like all these pauses, but can't seem to express
myself in any other way at this point . . . and am expressing
myself clearly enough, I think, anyway.

October 12th

Ossian has replaced Homer in my heart, and what a world
it is into which this divine poet leads me! Oh, to wander
across the heath in a blustering wind storm, by the light of
a waning moon, as it conjures up the ghosts of our ancestors
in clouds of mist! Oh, to hear, above the rushing of a forest
stream, the half-fading groans of specters issuing from caves
in the hillside, and the keening maiden weeping herself into
her grave beside the four moss-clad, grass-o'-ergrown stones

of her noble, fallen hero—her beloved. When I see him—
the roving, hoary bard—seeking the footsteps of his forefathers on the wide moor only to find their gravestones; and
he looks up, lamenting, at the gentle star of eve about to
sink into the rolling sea and times gone by revive in his
heroic soul, times when a friendly light still guided the brave
man in his peril, and the moon cast its serene light on his
garlanded ship, sailing home victorious . . . when I can read
the profound sorrow on his brow and see this last, forsaken,
magnificent one reel exhausted to his grave, still finding a
melancholy yet glowing joy in the powerless presence of the
shades of his departed ones, and can hear him cry as he
looks down upon the cold earth and tall waving grasses,
"The wanderer will come, will come, who knew me in my
glory and will ask, 'Where is the bard, oh, where is Fingal's
admirable son?' His footsteps cross my grave and he asks
in vain for me on earth!" Ah my friend, then, like a noble
armiger, I would like to draw my sword and in a trice free
my liege lord from the agonizing torment of a life that is a
gradual death and send my own soul after the liberated
demigod!

October 19th
Oh, this void, this dreadful void in my breast! Often I
think—if just once I could press her to my heart, it would
be filled!

October 26th
Yes, I am growing certain, dear friend, more and more
certain, that the life of a human creature is a negligible
factor, a very negligible factor. A friend came to see Lotte,
I went into the next room to find a book—and couldn't
read. Then I picked up a pen to write. I could hear them
talking softly about unimportant things, new happenings in
town, a wedding, someone was ill, very ill . . . she has a
hard dry cough and every bone in her face shows, she faints
. . . "I wouldn't give a penny for her life," says Lotte's
friend. "I hear that N.N. is not well either," says Lotte.
"He's so bloated," says her friend. And my lively imagination carries me off to the bedside of these poor people. I
can see with what terrible resistance they turn their backs

on life, while she—William, my girl speaks about it the way
. . . the way one talks about such things . . . a stranger lies
dying. And when I look around me and see this room—
Lotte's clothes, Albert's papers, the pieces of furniture that
have by now become my good friends, even this inkwell
here—I think: see what you mean to this house. All in all,
your friends respect you; you are a joy to them; your heart
tells you that you could not do without them; and yet . . .
if you were to go now, if you were to leave this aura . . .
would they . . . and how long would it take them to fill the
gap your loss would tear into their destiny? How long? Oh,
man is so transient that he can be blotted out even where
he feels quite sure of his existence, where he leaves the only
true impression of his presence on earth—in the thoughts
and souls of his loved ones. From them, too, he must van-
ish—and so soon!

October 27th

Often I would tear my breast and bash my brains in because
we can mean so little to one another. Ah, the love, joy,
warmth, and ecstasy that I cannot contribute and will therefore never receive from anyone else! With a heart full of
joy I cannot make happy the man who stands before me,
helpless and cold.

October 27th. Evening.

I have so much, yet my feeling for her devours it all. I have
so much, yet without her all of it is nothing.

October 30th

A hundred times, at least, I have been on the point of
taking her in my arms. The good Lord knows what it means
to see so much graciousness passing to and fro before one's
eyes and not be allowed to grasp it, for grasping is the
most natural urge of mankind. Don't children try to grasp
anything they can think of? And I?

November 3rd

God knows, I go to bed often with the wish—yes, sometimes in the hope of not waking up again; then, in the morning, I open my eyes to the sun and am miserable. If only I

could be moody and put the blame on the weather, or on some third person, or on a project that has failed, then the unbearable burden of my ill humor would be only half mine. But alas, I know only too well that it is all my fault, my fault. Suffice it to say that the source of all misery is within me just as I formerly bore within myself the source of all bliss. Am I not still the same man who used to bask in such an abundance of emotion, whose every step led to a paradise, who had a heart that could embrace the whole world lovingly? But now this heart is dead, no ecstasy flows from it any more. My eyes are dry, and my mind, no longer laved by refreshing tears, describes fearful furrows on my brow. I suffer much, for I have lost what was my singular joy in life—the sacred, invigorating power with which I could create worlds around me. It is gone. When I look out my window at the far distant hills and see the morning sun breaking through the mists that lie upon them and flooding the peaceful meadows with its light, the gentle river winding toward me between leafless willows—when all magnificent nature stands still before my eyes like a glossy picture, and all this glory is incapable of pumping one ounce of bliss from heart to brain—then the whole poor fellow that I am become stands before God like an exhausted fountainhead, a leaky pail run dry. Often I have thrown myself on the ground and begged God to give me tears, as a plowman begs for rain when the sky is leaden above him and his parched earth.

But oh, I can feel it, God gives no rain or sunshine in answer to our tempestuous pleas, and those bygone days, the memory of which torments me now, why were they so blissful if not because I waited then in patience for His grace and received the bliss He chose to bestow upon me with a whole and deeply grateful heart?

November 8th

She reproached me for my excessiveness—but so sweetly! My excessiveness—that I sometimes let a glass of wine lead me to drink a bottle! "Don't do it," she said. "Think of Lotte." "Think!" I said. "Do you have to tell me that? I think—I don't think—you are in my mind constantly. Today I sat down where you got out of the carriage the other day . . ." She spoke hastily of something else to stop me from pursuing the topic further. My dear friend, I am done for! She can do with me what she will.

November 15th

Thank you, William, for your sympathy and well-meant advice, and don't worry, please. Let me suffer it through to the end. With all my weariness of spirit, I still have the strength left to persevere. I respect our religion, you know that. I feel that it is a staff for many a weary man and a comfort to him who is pining away. Only—can religion, must religion mean the same thing to every man? When you look at our vast world, you see thousands to whom it does not mean these things, thousands to whom it never will, whether it be preached to them or not. Must it therefore mean these things to me? Doesn't the son of God Himself say that those will be with Him whom His Father gives unto Him? But what if my Father wants to keep me for Himself, which is what my heart tells me? I beg of you, do not interpret this falsely, do not see ridicule in these innocent words. In them I lay my soul at your feet, or I would better have remained silent. I don't like to speak about things of which everyone else knows just as little as I do. What else is it but the fate of man to suffer his destined measure and drink his full cup to the end? And if the cup that the good Lord in heaven has put to his lips be too bitter, why should I put on airs and pretend that it is sweet? And why should I not feel ashamed in those dread moments when I tremble between being and not-being, when the past shines like a flash of lightning above the dark abyss of the future and everything around me sinks down, and the world comes to an end? Is mine not the voice of a man cowering within himself, a man who has lost himself, hurtling inexorably downhill, who must cry out from the innermost depths of his vainly struggling forces, "My God, my God, why hast Thou forsaken me?" And why should I be ashamed to thus cry out—why should I dread this moment since it was not even spared Him who can roll back the heavens like a cloth?

November 21st

She doesn't see, she doesn't feel, that she is preparing a poison that will destroy her and me, and with voluptuous delight I drink the cup she hands me to the last dregs, and to my ruination. What is the meaning of that kindly look that she so often—often? . . . no, not often, but sometimes gives me, the graciousness with which she sometimes accepts a chance expression of my feelings for her, the compassion for what I am enduring, that is written on her brow?

Yesterday, as I was leaving, she gave me her hand and said, "Adieu, dear Werther." Dear Werther! It was the first time she called me "dear" and I felt it to the core of me. I have repeated it to myself over and over again, and last night, when I was about to retire and was talking all sorts of things over in my mind, I suddenly said out loud, "Good night, dear Werther!" and had to laugh at myself.

November 22nd

I cannot pray: let her remain mine, yet often it seems to me that she is mine. I cannot pray: give her to me, for she belongs to another. Thus I mock my pain. Were I really to let myself go, a whole litany of antitheses would be the result.

November 24th

She knows how I suffer. Today her eyes looked deep into my heart. I found her alone. I said nothing, and she looked at me. And I no longer saw her loveliness nor the radiance of her wonderful spirit. All that had disappeared from before my eyes. Instead I had a far more glorious vision. I saw her face filled with an expression of the most intimate sympathy, the sweetest compassion.

Why couldn't I throw myself at her feet? Why couldn't I counter with an embrace and a thousand kisses? She escaped to the piano and sang to her own accompaniment in her sweet, low voice, and so melodiously. Never were her chaste lips more enchanting. It was as though they parted thirsty for the sweet tones that swelled forth from the instrument and only a furtive echo escaped them. Ah me, if only I could explain it to you! I offered no more resistance. I bowed my head and vowed that never would I presume to kiss those lips, o'er which celestial spirits hover . . . and yet . . . I want to kiss them. Ha! You see? That is what stands

before my soul like a bulkhead—such bliss, and then . . .
down, down, to atone for such a sin. . . . A sin?

November 26th

Sometimes I tell myself my fate is unique. Consider all other
men fortunate, I tell myself; no one has ever suffered like
you. Then I read a poet of ancient times, and it is as though
I were looking deep into my own heart. I have to suffer
much. Oh, has any human heart before me ever been so
wretched?

November 30th

It seems that I am not going to be permitted to recover, no
doubt about it. Wherever I go I encounter something that
upsets me utterly. Today—oh, fate, oh, humankind!

At noon I was walking along the river. I didn't feel like
eating. It was a dreary day. A raw wind was blowing down
from the mountains and gray rain clouds were rolling into
the valley. Ahead of me, I could see a man in a shabby
green coat, scrambling about among the rocks. I thought he
was gathering herbs. As I drew nearer, and he, hearing me,
turned around, I found myself looking into a most interesting face. Its main expression was a quiet sadness, otherwise
it betrayed nothing but candor and honesty. His black hair
was pinned up in two rolls; the rest hung in one thick braid
down his back. Since, judging by his dress, he seemed to
be a man of humble origin, I decided that he would not
take offense if I chose to comment on what he was doing,
so I asked him what he was looking for. With a deep sigh,
he replied, "I am looking for flowers, but can find none."

"This is not the season for them," I said, smiling.

"But there are so many flowers," he replied, moving
down to my level. "I have roses in my garden, and honey-
suckle, two kinds. My father gave me one. They grow like
weeds. I have been looking for them for two days and cannot find them. And outside there are always flowers, yellow
ones, blue and red ones—and centaury has such a pretty
blossom. I can't find any of them."

I could sense something mysterious, so I asked in a
roundabout way, "And what does he want to do with the
flowers?"

A bright, tremulous smile crossed his face. "If the gentleman won't give me away," he said, putting a finger to his lips, "I promised my sweetheart a bouquet."

"Now there's a good man!" I said.

"Oh, she has many other things," he replied. "She is rich."

"And yet she likes his nosegay," I said.

"Oh," he countered, "she has jewels and a crown."

"What is her name?"

"If the Netherlands would only pay me," he said, "it would make a changed man of me. Yes, yes, there was a time when I was very well off. Now that's all over and done with. Now I am . . ." He turned his moist eyes skyward to express the rest.

"So he was once a happy man?" I asked.

"Ah, if only I could be like that again," he replied. "How happy I used to feel in those days—so merry, like a fish in water."

"Henry!" cried an old woman who now came up the path. "Henry, where are you? We've been looking for you everywhere. Come and eat."

"Is that your son?" I asked, stepping forward.

"Indeed he is my poor son," she said. "God has given me a heavy cross to bear."

"How long has he been that way?" I asked.

"Quiet like that," she said, "he has been only for the past six months. God be thanked that he is as he is now. The year before, he was a raving maniac and they had to keep him chained in the madhouse. Now he does no harm, but he is always troubled, his kings and emperors on his mind. He was such a good, quiet lad who helped toward my support and could write a pretty hand, but suddenly he became despondent and fell into a violent fever, and from that into raving madness, and now he is as you see him. If I were to tell you, sir—"

I interrupted her flood of words with the question, "What sort of time was it that he praises so highly, when he was so happy, so content?"

"The fool," she cried, with a pitying smile. "He means the time he was deranged, the time he spent in the madhouse, when he didn't know what was going on around him—that's the time he is forever praising so highly."

It struck me like a thunderbolt. I pressed a coin into her hand and hurried away.

"So that was when you were happy!" I cried aloud, as I hastened back to town. "When you felt like a fish in water!" Oh dear God in heaven, hast Thou made it man's fate that he cannot be happy until he has found his reason and lost it again? Poor wretch! Yet how I envy him his dim mind, envy him pining away in his confusion. He goes out hopefully in the winter to pick flowers for his queen and grieves when he finds none and can't grasp when he finds none . . . and I? I go out without hope in my heart, with no purpose, and return home as I went. He can see the man he would be if only the Netherlands would pay him. Fortunate fellow! He can ascribe his lack of bliss to an earthly hindrance. He doesn't feel, he doesn't even know, that his misery lies in his destroyed heart, in his disordered mind—a fate from which all the kings on earth cannot save him!

The miserable wretch should perish who dares to mock a sick man journeying to a far-off healing spring that will only make his sickness worse and the rest of his days more painful; and so should he who looks down arrogantly on a man with a sorely afflicted heart who, to rid himself of his guilty conscience and cast off the sufferings of his soul, makes a pilgrimage to the Holy Sepulcher. Every step he takes on an unbeaten track is balm to his fearful soul, and with every day of his journey endured, his heart rests lightened of many anxieties. And you dare to call it madness, you sophists on your downy cushions? Madness? O God, Thou dost see my tears. Why didst Thou, Who made man poor, have to give him brothers who would rob him even of the little he has, of the little faith he has in Thee, Thou all-loving God? For what is faith in a healing root or in the tears of the grapevine but faith in Thee, in that Thou hast imbued all that surrounds us with the powers of salvation and the forces that ease pain, of which we stand in hourly need. Father Whom I know not, Father Who once filled my whole soul but has turned His face from me now—call me unto Thee. Be silent no longer. Thy silence will not deter this thirsting soul. Could any man—could any father—be angry with a son who comes back unexpectedly and throws his arms around his neck, crying, "Here I am, returned to thee, my father. Be not angry that I interrupted my wanderings, which according to Thy will, I should have endured longer. The world is the same everywhere—in effort and work, in reward and joy—but what concern is it of mine? Only where Thou art can I be content. There I will suffer and rejoice." Wouldst Thou, dear heavenly Father, cast out such a man?

December 1st
William! The fellow I wrote to you about, that fortunate unfortunate man, was once secretary to Lotte's father, and his passionate love for her—which he nurtured, concealed, but finally disclosed, and because of which he was dismissed—drove him mad. Try to feel, as you read these dry words, with what derangement they filled me when Albert mentioned it to me just as casually as you read about it now.

December 4th
I beg of you . . . look . . . I am done for. I cannot endure it a moment longer. Today I was with her . . . she was sitting . . . she was playing the piano . . . different pieces, and with so much expression . . . with so much . . . with so much . . . What do you want me to do? Her little sister was sitting on my knee, dressing her doll. Tears rushed to my eyes. I leaned forward and suddenly could see nothing but Lotte's wedding ring, and my tears flowed. And all of a sudden, as if by chance, she began to play that old, heavenly sweet melody, and I was consoled. And my soul was filled with the recollection of things past, of other times when I had listened to the song, and the dark intervals, the grief, the hopes dashed, and then . . . I started to pace the room, up and down, my heart stifled with the pressure of these memories. "For God's sake," I said, turning on her with a vehemence I could not control, "for God's sake, stop!"

She did and stared at me wide-eyed. "Werther," she said, with a little smile that cut me to the quick, "Werther, you are ill. Your favorite things are repugnant to you. Go. I beg of you, go and try to calm down." I tore myself away and . . . dear God, Thou seest my misery. Put an end to it, I beseech Thee!

December 6th

How the sight of her haunts me! Awake and dreaming, she fills my whole being. Here, when I close my eyes, here, behind my forehead, where we assemble our insight, I see her dark eyes. Here! I cannot express it adequately. I close my eyes and there they are . . . hers—like an abyss in front of me, inside me. They fill my whole mind.

What is man, this exalted demigod? Doesn't he lack power just when he needs it most? Whether he is uplifted by joy or engulfed by suffering, is he not stopped in both conditions and brought back to dull, cold consciousness just when he is ready to lose himself in the abundance of the infinite?

EDITOR TO READER

How I wish there was enough material left, covering our friend's last strange days, so that it would not be necessary to interrupt with narrative the flow of the letters he left behind.

I made a point of collecting precise reports from those who of necessity had a thorough knowledge of his story. It is simple, and except for a few details, all the accounts tally. Opinions differ only in accordance with the personalities and opinions of the characters involved.

There is nothing left to do but relate conscientiously what we were able to find out as a result of our meticulous efforts and include, in their proper place, letters that the departed left behind, not overlooking the smallest evidence we may have come across, since it is very difficult to uncover the true motive of even a single action when it takes place among people who are not cut of conventional cloth.

Ill humor and listlessness became more and more deeply rooted in Werther's soul until finally they took possession of his entire personality. The harmony of his spirit was utterly destroyed, and an inner passion and vehemence that confused all the forces of his nature resulted in the most objectionable effects, leaving him in the end with nothing but a feeling of exhaustion out of which he tried to rise with an even greater fear than he had felt when previously seeking to combat his misery. His anxiety destroyed all the remaining forces of his intellect, his liveliness, his wit; he became sorry company, waxing ever more unfortunate and unjust as he became increasingly unhappy. At any rate, that is what Albert's friends say. They declare that Werther could no longer evaluate that decent, quiet man who had at last taken possession of a happiness long desired with the attitude that had to accompany it—the wish to preserve this happiness in the future—not Werther, who expended his all daily only to suffer starvation at nightfall. Albert, they say, underwent no such change. He was the same man Werther had known from the beginning and learned to appreciate and respect. He loved Lotte above all else; he was proud of her and liked to see everyone else recognize her as a paragon among women. Who can blame him if he did his best to avoid any traces of suspicion and had no desire to share his treasure with anyone, not even in the most innocent fashion? They admit that Albert often left his wife's room when Werther was there—not, however, in hatred or antipathy toward his friend but because he could sense that his presence oppressed Werther.

Lotte's father was suffering from a complaint that confined him to his room. He sent his carriage for her, and she drove out to see him. It was a beautiful winter day; the first heavy snow had fallen and covered the whole countryside.

Werther walked over on the following morning to accompany Lotte home in case Albert did not come for her. The clear weather had little effect on his dour mood. His heart was heavy, his unhappy view of things was deeply rooted in him, and his spirit could only pass from one painful thought to the next. Since he lived in a state of continual dissatisfaction with himself, the condition of others appeared to him as dubious and confused, too. He felt that he had disturbed the good relationship between Albert and Lotte and reproached himself on this score, and a secret resentment against Albert crept into his confusion.

On his way to fetch Lotte, his mind reverted to this subject. Yes, yes, he told himself, his jaw set hard . . . there you have it—the ultimate, friendly, tender relationship that participates in everything, a quiet, lasting faithfulness! Satiation—that's what it is! And indifference. Doesn't every miserable bit of business he has to do attract him more than his precious wife? Does he appreciate his good fortune? Does he respect her as she deserves to be respected? He has her . . . all very well and good . . . he has her. I know he has her just as I know all sorts of things. I think I have become accustomed to the knowledge, but in the end, it will drive me mad and be the death of me. And has his friendship for me remained constant? Doesn't he see an interference in his rights in my devotion to Lotte, and a silent reproach in my attentions? I know it, I can feel it—he doesn't like to see me. He would like to see me go. My presence oppresses him.

Werther walked fast, stopped often, stood still and seemed to want to turn back, but then he persevered and went steadily forward and with thoughts such as these and mumbling to himself, finally reached the lodge almost against his will.

He walked up to the door, asked after the old man and Lotte, and found the house in quite a stir. The oldest boy told him that there had been a disaster in Wahlheim. A peasant had been murdered. The news had no particular effect on Werther. He went into the living room and found Lotte trying to talk her father out of going over to look into the matter in spite of his weak condition. The murderer was still unknown. The dead man had been found in front of his door early that morning. Suspicions centered on someone. The murdered man was the servant of a widow who had had another man in her service before him. This man had been dismissed under disagreeable circumstances.

When Werther heard this, he became very agitated. "It couldn't be!" he cried, and then, "I must go there at once!"

He rushed over to Wahlheim, every memory alive in him, and there was no doubt in his mind that the young man with whom he had spoken several times and whom he had come to like so much had committed the crime.

He had to pass under the linden trees to get to the inn where the body had been laid out and was horrified when he saw the beloved spot. Where the neighbor's children had played once it was befouled with blood. Love and faithfulness—the most beautiful human emotions—had been transformed into violence and murder. The sturdy trees stood barren and thick with hoarfrost; the pretty hedges, arched over the low wall of the churchyard, were leafless, the snow-capped gravestones were visible through the gaps.

As Werther approached the inn in front of which the whole village had assembled there was a sudden hubbub of voices. A group of armed men was approaching from a distance, shouting that they had the murderer. Werther saw him and at once his doubts were dispelled. It was the boy who had loved the widow so much, whom Werther had met some time ago in his tacit fury and despair.

"What have you done, unhappy man?" Werther cried, walking up to the prisoner. The man looked at Werther quietly and was silent for a moment; then he said, "No one shall have her, and she shall have no one." The men took the prisoner to the inn and Werther hurried away.

The impact of this horrifying experience created a state of chaos in his mind. For a moment he was torn out of his grief, his despondency and indifference to things, and sympathy for the young man overwhelmed him. He was seized by an indescribable urge to save him. He could feel the man's misery; even as a criminal—he felt the man was innocent; and he could put himself so wholeheartedly into the poor wretch's position that he was sure he could make others feel the same way. He wanted to speak for the man; he liveliest defense rushed to his lips. He tore over to the lodge, and all the way there could not keep from muttering to himself what he was going to say to the judge.

When he entered the room again, he found Albert present. For a moment this irritated him, but he soon regained control of himself and expounded to the judge how he felt about the crime. The old man shook his head several times and although Werther set forth in the liveliest fashion and most passionately and truthfully anything and everything that one man could possibly say to excuse his neighbor, still, as is quite understandable, the judge remained unmoved. He didn't even let Werther finish what he had to say, but disagreed heatedly and reproved him for defending a murderer. He explained that all law would be voided and the security of the state destroyed if Werther's viewpoint were accepted, adding that he was in no position to do anything about it without taking grave responsibility upon himself. Everything would have to take its prescribed and orderly course.

But Werther did not give up so easily. He begged the judge at least to look the other way if anyone should help the man to escape! The judge, of course, rejected him on this count too. Albert, who at last joined in the conversation, sided with the judge. Werther was outnumbered, and in a state of abject misery, took himself off, after the judge had told him several times, "The man is doomed."

How deeply these words impressed Werther can be seen from a note found among his papers, words that must certainly have been written on that day, "You are doomed, my unfortunate friend. I can see it quite clearly—we are doomed."

Werther especially resented Albert's final word in the matter, spoken in the presence of the judge, and thought he could detect resentment against himself in it, and even though, after giving the matter more thought, the fact could not have escaped him that both men were right, he still felt that he would be denying his innermost self if he admitted it.

A note referring to this, which perhaps expresses Werther's entire relationship to Albert, was found among his papers. "What good does it do me to tell myself again and again he is good, his behavior is impeccable . . . it tears me apart! I cannot be just!"

Since it was a mild evening and a thaw had set in, Lotte and Albert walked home. On the way, she looked about her every now and then as if she missed Werther's company. Albert began to talk about Werther reprovingly, accusing him of being unjust. He touched upon the young man's passionate nature and said he wished Werther would go away. "I wish it for our sakes as well," he said, "and I beg you, try to guide his attitude toward you into other channels. See to it that he visits us less often. People are beginning to notice, and I know that there has been talk about it."

Lotte was silent, and Albert seemed to feel her silence. At any rate, from then on, he never spoke of Werther in her presence, and if she mentioned him, he stopped talking or directed the conversation onto other topics.

Werther's vain effort to save the unfortunate man was the last flickering flame of a light that was dying. After it, he sank even deeper into pain and lassitude. He became especially overwrought when he heard that he might be asked to testify against the man, who now denied his guilt.

Everything disagreeable that had ever happened to him in his active life—his grievance against the embassy, every failure that had hurt him—now ran rampant through his tormented mind. He let it justify his idleness, he felt cut off from all hope of ever again being able to regain a firm grip on life. Thus he finally drew closer to his sad end, lost in a fantastic sensitivity and infinite passion, in the eternal monotony of a sad intercourse with the gracious and beloved creature whose inner repose he disturbed, stormy in the powers that were left him, working them off with no goal, no prospects.

A few letters he left behind bear witness to the confusion and tempestuousness of his restless activities and struggle, and of his weariness of life. We include them here.

December 12th

Dear William, I am in the condition in which those unfortunates who were believed to be possessed of evil spirits must have found themselves. Sometimes it takes hold of me—not fear, not desire, but an inner, unfathomable turmoil that threatens to burst the confines of my breast and choke me. Then I wander about in the dread nocturnal setting of this unfriendly season.

Last night I had to go out. We had a sudden thaw. I had heard that the river had overflowed its banks, all streams were swollen, and my beloved valley was inundated from Wahlheim down. It was after eleven. I ran outside. What a terrible spectacle, to see the turbulent flood in the moonlight, pouring down from the rocks to cover field, meadow, and hedgerow! Whichever way you looked, the broad valley was one stormy sea in a howling gale. And when the moon came out again above a black cloud, and the flood rushed by me with a dull roar in its gloriously frightening reflection,

I was overcome by a great trembling and, once more, a yearning. With my arms open wide, I stood facing the abyss, breathing down, down, and was lost in the bliss of hurling my torment and suffering into it to be carried off foaming, like the waves . . . and couldn't lift my feet from the ground to put an end to my misery! My time is not yet run out. I feel it. William, I would have given my life to be able to tear the clouds apart with the gale that was howling, and to grasp the floodwater itself! Ha! And will not this prisoner perhaps be granted such bliss one day? As I looked down in my melancholy, at a spot where I had rested once with Lotte under a willow tree during a hot walk, it too had been inundated. And I had scarcely recognized the willow, William, when I had to think, what about her meadows? Her neighborhood? The lodge? Has our summerhouse been destroyed by the torrent? And the sunshine of the past fell upon me as a dream of herds, meadows, and honors falls upon a prisoner. I stood still. I don't have to reproach myself, for I have the courage to die . . . I could have . . . and now I sit here like an old woman who gathers her firewood from broken-down hedges and begs her bread from door to door to prolong her fading, joyless existence one moment more. . . .

December 14th

What would you call it, dearest friend . . . I am afraid of myself! Is not my love for her the most sacred, chaste, and brotherly love? Has my soul ever known a culpable desire? I have no wish to protest . . . and now, my dreams! Oh, how truly those men felt who ascribed our dreams to the contrary influences of strange powers! When I think of last night . . . I tremble to tell it . . . I held her in my arms, I pressed her to my heart, her adorable lips murmured love, and I covered them with endless kisses. My eyes were lost in the intoxication that lay in hers. Dear God, am I culpable because I can still feel the bliss I experienced then and recall it with a full heart? Lotte! Lotte! It is all over with me. My mind is in a state of confusion. For days now I can't seem to come to my senses, and my eyes are constantly filled with tears. I am well nowhere and well everywhere. I wish for nothing, demand nothing. It would be best if I were to depart.

*   *   *

Under these conditions, the decision to leave this world took an even greater hold on Werther's soul. Since his return to Lotte, it had always been his last hope, yet he told himself that he dare not act hastily. He wanted to take the step with the quietest determination possible.

His doubts, his battle with himself shine forth clearly in a note that is probably the beginning of a letter to William. It was found among his papers with no date.

"Her presence, her fate, her participation in my destiny force the last tears from my parched brain.

"Oh, to be able to lift the curtain and step behind it! That is all there is to it—so why do I hesitate? Because no one knows what it looks like back there? Because no one ever returns? And because it is characteristic of our spirit to anticipate confusion and darkness in what we do not know?"

In the end, he became more and more attuned to the melancholy idea, his decision became fixed and irrevocable. The following ambiguous letter, written to his friend, attests to this.

December 20th

I can thank your love for me, William, for the fact that you understand me as you did. You are right, it would be best for me to leave. Your suggestion that I return to you does not wholly suit me; at any rate, I would like to go out of my way a little, especially since we can count on a long period of frost and good roads. But it suits me very well that you want to come and fetch me, only please let a fortnight pass and wait for one more letter from me. Nothing should be plucked until it is ripe, and a fortnight more or less can make quite a difference. Please ask my mother to pray for me and tell her that I beg her to forgive me for all the trouble I have caused her. It happened to be my fate to distress those to whom I should have brought joy. Farewell, best of friends! May all the blessings of heaven be yours! Farewell!

We scarcely dare to express in words what was going on in Lotte's soul during this time, and what her feelings were toward her husband and her unfortunate friend, although we can come to a tacit conclusion from our knowledge of her character, and any sensitive feminine soul will be able to think as she did and feel with her.

This much is certain: she was determined to do her best to keep Werther at a distance, and any hesitancy on her part must be attributed to a sincere desire to spare him, since she knew what it would mean to him to stay away and realized that it was as good as impossible for him to do so. Yet she was more inclined, during this time, to go through with her intention. Her husband meanwhile said nothing at all about it, nor did she, all of which made her more determined than ever to express her agreement with his viewpoint, at least in her behavior.

On the same day on which Werther wrote the letter, just inserted, to his friend—it was the Sunday before Christmas—he visited Lotte in the evening and found her alone. She was busy arranging a few toys she had assembled for her brothers and sisters for Christmas. He spoke about the joy the children would experience and of the days when the unexpected opening of a door and the vision of a decorated Christmas tree with its wax candles, sugar candy, and apples could transport one into paradise. Lotte tried to hide her embarrassment behind a sweet smile. "There will be a present for you, too," she said, "if you promise to be good. A pretty candle and something else."

"And what do you call good?" he cried. "How can I be good, dearest Lotte?"

"Thursday evening," she said, "is Christmas Eve. The children are coming, and my father, and all of them will receive their presents then. I want you to come, too, but not before."

Werther was stunned.

"Please," she went on, "that is how it is. I beg you, for the sake of my peace of mind, things can't go on like this. They can't."

He turned away from her and began to pace up and down the room, muttering to himself under his breath, "Things can't go on like this." Lotte, who could feel the dread condition into which her words had thrown him, tried with questions about all sorts of things, to distract him, but to no avail. "No, Lotte," he said, "I shall not see you again."

"But why?" she cried. "Werther . . . you may—you must come to see us again, only be more moderate. Oh, why did you have to be born with so much vehemence, with this fixed, uncontrollable passion for everything you touch? I implore you," she went on, taking him by the hand, "practice moderation! Your mind—all your knowledge and talents . . . think of the happiness they can give you! Be more manly! Divert this tragic devotion from a human creature who can only pity you."

His jaw set hard, he looked at her somberly. She held fast to his hand. "Think calmly, Werther," she said, "for just one moment. Don't you see that you are deceiving and ruining yourself on purpose? Why me, Werther? Why me of all people, who belongs to another? Why? I fear . . . I fear that it is just the impossibility of possessing me that makes your desire for me so fascinating."

He drew his hand out of hers, and stared at her with a benumbed, resentful expression.

"Very clever!" he said. "Very clever. Are these perhaps Albert's words? Very politic, very politic, indeed."

"Anybody could say them," she interrupted him. "Isn't it possible that in this whole wide world there might be a girl who could fulfill the desires of your heart? Master yourself and seek her. I swear that you will find her. Oh, I have been anxious for a long time now, for you and for us, because of the limitation you have imposed on yourself. Try to win control over yourself. A journey might distract you. Surely it would. Seek and find a worthy object of your affections and come back and let us enjoy the bliss of true friendship."

With a cold smile he replied, "That would look well in print and should be recommended to all tutors. Dear Lotte, give me a small respite, and all will be well."

"But just this one thing more, Werther—please do not come again before Christmas Eve."

He was about to reply when Albert entered the room. The men exchanged frosty greetings and walked up and down beside each other in some embarrassment. Werther started a desultory conversation that soon petered out; Albert did the same, then he asked his wife about a few things she was supposed to have attended to, and when he heard that they had not been done, he said something that, to Werther, sounded cold, even harsh. He wanted to leave, but couldn't seem to do so. He hesitated until eight o'clock, his discouragement and resentment increasing constantly. When he at last took up his hat and cane, the table was already set for supper. Albert asked him to stay, but Werther, who felt that the man's heart wasn't in the invitation, thanked him coldly and left.

He reached his house, took the candle from his servant, who wanted to light his way, and went to his room alone. There he wept, talked wildly to himself, paced savagely up and down, and at last threw himself fully dressed on his bed, where he was found at about eleven by his servant, who at last had dared to enter the room to ask his master whether he should not remove his boots. Werther let the man do it, then forbade the boy to enter his room the next morning until he was called.

Early on Monday morning, the twenty-first of December, Werther wrote the following letter to Lotte. It was found after his death, lying on his desk, sealed, and was brought to her. I have decided to insert it here, since it throws light on the conditions under which it was written.

Lotte, I have come to a decision. I want to die, and I am writing this without any romantic exaggeration on the morning of the day on which I shall see you for the last time. When you read these lines, my dearest one, the cool earth will already cover the rigid remains of your restless, unfortunate friend, who to his last hour knew no greater bliss than to converse with you. I have passed a terrible night, for it was the night that hardened my determination and settled it once and for all: I want to die. When I tore myself away from you yesterday, I was in a frightful state of rebellion against all that was oppressing me, and my hopeless, joyless existence beside you took me in its cold grip. I could scarcely reach my room. I threw myself on my knees, beside myself, and Thou, dear God, didst finally grant me the refreshment of the most bitter tears. A thousand blows, a thousand perspectives stormed through my soul, and in the end, there it stood—firm, whole, the last and only thought: I want to die. I went to bed, and now, in the morning, in the quietude of awakening, it still stands firm and strong in my heart: I want to die. I have come to a conclusion not of despair but of certainty. I sacrifice myself for you. Yes, Lotte, why should I remain silent? One of us three must go and I wish to be the one. Oh, my dearest one, the thought of murdering your husband . . . you . . . me, has often raged through my torn heart. So be it then. When you climb the hilltop on a beautiful summer's evening, think of me. Think of how often I used to come walking up the valley, then glance at the churchyard and look at my grave, see how the wind causes the tall grass to wave in the light of the setting sun. I was so calm when I began to write this, and now—now I am crying like a child because I can see it all so vividly.

At about ten, Werther called his servant and, as he dressed, told him that in a few days he intended to go on a journey. The man should therefore lay out his clothes and get ready to pack them. He also gave orders to collect all outstanding accounts, pick up several books he had loaned to various people, and pay two months in advance to a few poor souls to whom he customarily gave a little something every week.

He had his meal served in his room. After he had eaten, he rode to the magistrate's house, but found him not at home. Lost in thought, he walked up and down in the garden for a while, apparently wishing to burden himself with all the melancholy of remembrance.

The children didn't leave him in peace for long. They followed him, jumped around him, chattering about how, after tomorrow and one more tomorrow and one more day after that, it would be time for them to fetch their Christmas presents from Lotte. They talked about all the marvelous things that came to their childlike minds.

"Tomorrow!" he cried. "And another tomorrow, and one more day!" Then he kissed all of them tenderly and was about to leave when the littlest one had to whisper something in his ear. He betrayed the fact that his older brother had already written their New Year greetings, so big! One

for Papa, one for Albert and Lotte, and one for Herr
Werther. Early on New Year's Day they intended to distrib-
ute them. The news was too much for Werther. He gave
each of the children something, mounted his horse, left
greetings for the old gentleman, and rode off, his eyes
blinded by tears.

He reached home again at about five and told the maid
to stoke the fire and keep it going through the night. He
ordered his servant to pack his books and linen in a trunk
and fold his clothing. Then he must have written the following paragraph of his last letter to Lotte:

"You are not expecting me. You think I am going to
obey and not come to see you until Christmas Eve. Ah
Lotte, it has to be today or never! On Christmas Eve you
will hold this note in your trembling hand and it will be
bathed by your beloved tears. I shall do it. I have to do it.
Oh, I feel so content in my determination."

Lotte, meanwhile, had fallen into a strange state of mind.
After her last talk with Werther, she had begun to realize
how hard it would be for her to part with him and how
much he would suffer if forced to leave her. She had mentioned casually, in Albert's presence, that Werther was not
going to put in an appearance again until Christmas Eve,
and Albert had ridden off to see a neighbor on a business
trip that necessitated his staying away overnight.

Lotte was alone, and she was thinking quietly about their
dilemma. She saw herself tied forever to a man with whose
love and loyalty she was by now thoroughly familiar. She
was devoted to him; his serenity and reliability—attributes
on which any good woman could build her life's happiness—
seemed heaven-sent. She realized only too well what part
he would always play in her life, and that of her children.
But Werther had come to mean a great deal to her. From
the first moment of their acquaintance, the harmony of their
spirits had been very evident, and her long association with
him and several experiences they had shared had made in-
delible impressions on her heart. She was accustomed to
sharing everything that interested her with him, and his loss
threatened to tear a gap into her life that she feared could
never again be closed. If only she could have turned him
into a brother at this point, how happy it would have made

her! Or if she could have married him off to one of her friends. . . . If only she could have hoped that there might be a chance of his former good relationship with Albert being restored!

She thought of every one of her friends, one after the other, and found something wrong with all of them. She begrudged him to each in turn.

As a result of these reflections she began to realize, without admitting it to herself too clearly, that it was her secret but sincere desire to keep him for herself. At the same time she told herself, more in an aside, that she couldn't keep him, she had no right to. Her lovely spirit, usually so light and so easily able to help itself, suddenly felt the pressure of a melancholy to which all prospects of happiness were closed. She was depressed, a dark cloud obscured her vision.

It was half past six when she heard someone coming up the stairs and recognized Werther's step, and his voice asking for her. Her heart began to beat wildly, and I think we are safe in assuming that she received him in such condition for the first time. She would have liked to tell the maid to say she was not in, and as he came into the room, she cried out, in something akin to passionate confusion, "You didn't keep your promise!"

"I promised nothing," was his reply.

"Well, then at least you should have granted my request," she said. "It was made to serve the peace of mind of both of us."

Without knowing what she was saying or doing, she proceeded to send messages to two of her friends to come at once—anything so as not to be alone with Werther. He put down several books he had brought with him and spoke about a few others, while she was wishing at one moment that her friends would come and in the next that they would stay away. The maid came back with word that both girls regretted, they were unable to come.

Lotte would have liked the maid to sit in the next room with whatever she might have to do, then decided against it. Werther was pacing up and down. Lotte went over to the piano and began to play a minuet, but she could not play fluently. She pulled herself together and tried to be casual as she sat down beside Werther, who had taken his usual seat on the sofa.

"Haven't you brought anything to read?" she asked. He had not. "In my drawer over there is your translation of Ossian's songs. I haven't read them yet. I was always hoping to hear them from you, but there never seemed to be any time . . . we couldn't seem to . . ."

He smiled, got up and fetched the songs. As he took them in his hands, he shivered, and as he looked at them, his eyes filled with tears. He sat down and read:[8]

"O star of night descendent! How fair is thy light in the west, how radiantly thy head rises above thy cloud, moving toward thy hill regally! What dost thou seek on the heath? The storm winds have subsided; from far off comes the murmur of the tumbling brook; surf plays on distant rock, and hum of evening insects swarms across the lea. O beautiful light, what dost thou seek? But thou dost only smile and leave, gaily encircled by riplets that lave thy lovely hair. Farewell, calm beam of light! Arise, O magnificent effulgence of Ossian's soul!

"And it arises in all its glory. I see my departed friends assembled in Lora as in days of yore—Fingal, a moist column of mist, his heroes around him—here, there . . . see the bards! Gray Ullin, stately Ryno, Alpin—beloved singer—and thou, gentle-voiced Minona. How changed you are, my friends, since the festive days of Selma when, like spring zephyrs, we contended for our singing laurels, striving in turn to bend the weak, whispering reed!

"Minona, in all her beauty, stepped forward, eyes downcast and filled with tears, hair flowing heavy in the inconstant wind blowing from the hill. She raised her beloved voice, and the souls of the heroes were bleak, for they had oft seen Salgar's grave and the dark abode of white Colma—Colma, abandoned on the hill, Colma with her melodious voice. Salgar promised to come, but all around her night was falling. Hear Colma's voice, as she sits on the hill alone!

"COLMA: 'Night has fallen. I am alone and lost on the storm-swept hill. The wind howls down the canyon; no hut protects me from the rain. I have been abandoned on this stormy hill.

" 'Emerge, O moon, from thy cloud, stars of the night appear! Grant me a ray of light to guide me to the place where my beloved rests from the ardors of the hunt, his bow unstrung, his dogs snuffling around him. But I must needs sit here on the rocky banks of the stream, alone. Stream and storm roar, and I cannot hear the voice of my beloved.

" 'Why does he hesitate, Salgar, my beloved? Has he forgot his promise? There is the rock, and there is the tree, and here is the rushing stream. Oh, where has my Salgar lost his way?

" 'Thou didst promise to be here at nightfall. With thee I would flee, forsake father and brother—those two proud men! Our tribes have been enemies for so long, but thou and I, Salgar, we are not enemies.

" 'Be silent a while, O wind, be silent for one small while, O stream, so that my voice may resound in the valley and my wanderer hear me. Salgar, it is I calling. Here is the tree and the rock, and I am here, Salgar, my beloved. Why dost thou tarry?

" 'See . . . the moon appears, the river gleams in the valley, the rocks stand gray on the hillside—but I do not see him nor do his dogs herald this coming. Here must I sit alone.

" 'But who lies down there on the heath? My beloved? My brother? Speak to me, O my friends! They do not reply, and my soul is fearful. Ah me—they are slain, their swords are red with blood. O my brother, my brother, why hast thou slain my beloved? O Salgar, my beloved, why hast thou slain my brother? I loved you both. Among a thousand on the hill, you were beautiful, and in combat, you were terrible. Answer me! Hear me, my beloveds! Alas . . . they are mute, forever silenced, their breasts cold as the earth.

" 'Oh, speak, ye dead, from the rocks on the hill, from the top of the storm-swept mountain. Speak! I shall not shudder. Where did you go to your final rest? In which cave of the hill shall I find you? I hear no weak voice in the wind, no answer is wafted to me by the storm on the hill.

" 'I sit in my misery, bathed in my tears, and wait doggedly for the morn. Dig the grave of the dead, my friends, but do not cover it until I am come. Like a dream, my life leaves me—how can I remain behind? Here, beside the stream in the echoing rocks, I shall dwell with my friends. When night falls on the hill, and the wind sweeps o'er the heath, let my spirit stand in the wind and mourn the death of my friend. The hunter in his covert hears me, fears my voice and loves it, for the voice that mourns my friends shall be sweet. I loved them both.'

"That was thy song, O Minona, Torman's gently blushing daughter. Our tears flowed for Colma, and our souls were darkened.

"Ullin stepped forward with his harp and gave us Alpin's song. Alpin's voice was friendly, and Ryno's soul was a fiery fount; but they have both been laid to rest already in the narrow confines of their house, and their voices have echoed away in Selma. Once, before the heroes had fallen, Ullin came back from the hunt and could hear their contest on the hill. Their song was gentle but sad. They were mourning the downfall of Morar, the first of the heroes. His soul was like Fingal's, his sword like the sword of Oscar. But he fell, and his father mourned his death, and the eyes of his sister Minona were filled with tears—Minona, sister of Morar, the magnificent. She stepped back from Ullin's song like the moon in the west that foresees the rain and hides its lovely head in a cloud. With Ullin I accompanied Ryno's lament on my harp.

"RYNO: 'Wind and rain have passed, the hour of noon is clear, and the clouds are parting. An inconstant sun shines fleetingly on the hill, and the mountain stream flows red in the valley. Sweet is thy murmuring, O stream, yet the voice that I hear is sweeter—Alpin's voice. lamenting his dead. His head is bowed with age, red are his eyes from weeping. Alpin, glorious bard, where art thou, alone on the silenced hill? Why dost thou wail like the wind in the forest, like a wave on the far-off shores of the sea?'

"ALPIN: 'My tears, Ryno, are for the dead, and my voice is for the grave-dwellers. Thou art lithe on the mount, and among the sons of the heath, thou art beautiful. But thou wilt be slain like Morar, and the mourner shall sit on thy tomb. The hills will forget thee, thy bow will lie unstrung in the great hall.

" 'Thou wert swift as the deer on the hill, Morar, and

terrible as night fires in the sky. Thy anger was like a storm, like sheet lightning across the heath. Thy voice was a forest stream after rainfall, was thunder in far-off hills. Many fell beneath thy right arm, and the flame of thy fury consumed them, but when thou didst return from battle, how peaceful was thy brow! Thy countenance was like the moon on a silent night; thy breast was as calm as the waters of a lake after the blustering wind dies down.

" 'Narrow are the confines of thy house now, dark is thy abode. Three paces carry me across thy grave, thou who wert once so great—thy sole memorial now . . . for mossy, stone markers. A leafless tree, tall grass that rustles in the wind, point out the grave of mighty Morar, the hunter—but no mother to mourn thee, no maiden with tears of love. Dead is she who gave thee birth, slain is the daughter of Morglan.

" 'Who stands yonder, leaning on his staff? Who is he? His hair is hoary with age, his eyes are reddened from crying. It is thy father, Morar. Thou wert his only son. He knows all about thy fame in battle, about the enemy thou didst scatter; he has heard of Morar's fame—alas, not of his wound! Weep, father of Morar, weep! But thy son cannot hear thee. The sleep of the dead is deep, and lowly is their pillow of dust. He pays no heed to thy voice, he will ne'er awaken to thy call. Oh, when will it be morning in his grave, when will it be time to bid the slumberer awaken?

" 'Farewell, noblest of men, conqueror on the field of battle. Never again shall the field of battle see thee, nor the gloomy forest be brightened by the gleam of thy sword. Thou hast left no progeny. But our song shall keep thy name alive, and future times shall hear of Morar who was slain in battle.'

"Loud was the grief of the heroes, loudest of all though was Armin's heartbreaking sigh. For he was reminded of the death of his son who fell in the days of his youth. Carmor, chieftain of the echoing halls of Galmal, was sitting nearby. 'Why does Armin's sigh choke him?' he asked. 'What causes him so much grief? Song and voice should melt the heart and delight it. They are the gentle mist that rises from the lake and spreads into the valleys, and the blossoming trees are dampened by it. The sun, though, rises again in all its glory, and the mists are dispelled. Why art thou so wretched, Armin, chieftain of the sea-girt isle of Gorma?'

" 'Wretched? That I am. And the cause of my grief is not negligible. Carmor, thou hast not lost a son, thou hast not been deprived of a daughter. Colgar, the brave, lives, and Annira, fairest of maidens. The branches of thy house blossom, Carmor, but Armin is the last of his race. Dark is thy bier, O Daura, stifling thy sleep in the grave. When shalt thou awaken with thy songs, with thy melodious voice? Rise, winds of autumn, rise and storm across the bleak heath! Forest streams roar! Wail, thou tempests in the crowns of the pines! Move through the broken clouds, O moon, show and hide thy pale face alternately! Remind me of the dread night when my children perished, when mighty Arindal was slain, and beloved Daura died.

" 'Daura, my daughter, thou wert fair as the moon on the hills of Fura, thou wert white as the driven snow and sweet as a zephyr. Arindal, thy bow was strong, and thy spear was fleet on the field. Thy gaze was as the fog on the waves, thy shield was a cloud of fire in the tempest.

" 'Armar, famed warrior, came to woo Daura. She did not resist him long, and their friends wished them well.

" 'Erath, son of Ogdal, was angry, for his brother lay slain by Armar. He came disguised as a mariner, his locks white with age, his stern features calm. His bark crossing the waters was a beautiful sight. "Loveliest of maidens," he cried, "fair daughter of Armin—on yonder rock in the sea, not far off, where thou canst see the red fruit sparkling on the tree, Armar is waiting for thee. I come to guide his beloved across the turgid sea."

" 'Daura followed him and cried out to Armar. "Armar, my beloved, my beloved! Why dost thou frighten me? Hear me, O son of Armath! It is Daura crying out to thee!" Naught answered save the voice of the rocks.

" 'Erath, the betrayer, fled laughing back to landward. Daura lifted her voice and cried out to father and brother, "Arindal! Armin! Is there no one to save Daura?"

" 'Her voice came to them across the sea. Arindal, my son, descended the hillside, rough with the spoils of the hunt, his arrows rustling at his side. He carried his bow in his hand, and five gray-black dogs went with him. He saw bold Earth on the shore and took him and tied him to an oak, bound him firmly round his loins, and the captured man filled the air with his groaning.

" 'Then Arindal walked into the waves with his boat to bring Daura back. Armar came and in his anger let fly his gray, feathered arrow. It hummed, but it sank into thy heart, Arindal, my son! Instead of Erath, the betrayer, thou didst fall. Arindal's boat reached the rock; he sank down beside it and died. Her brother's blood ran out at Daura's feet. Oh, Daura, Daura, how terrible was thy grief!

" 'The waves shattered the boat. Armar flung himself into the sea to save his Daura or die. A gust of wind from the hill struck hard at the waves and he sank, never to rise again.

" 'Alone on the sea-washed rocks, I could hear the lament of my daughter. She cried loud and long, yet I could not save her. Throughout the night I stood on the shore. By the weak rays of the moon I could see her. Throughout the night I could hear her cry. Loud was the wind, and the rain hit sharply against the side of the mountain. By dawn her voice was weak; soon it died away like the air of evening between grasses that grow on stone. Bowed low with grief, she died, leaving Armin alone. Gone is my strength in battle, gone my prowess among women.

" 'When the mountain storms come, and the north wind rears up the wave, I sit on the echoing shore and gaze across the sea at the terrible rock. Oft, by the light of a waning moon, I see the ghosts of my children. Twilit they wander side by side in a sad unity.' "

A flood of tears streamed from Lotte's eyes, relieving her oppressed heart and preventing Werther from continuing. He threw the papers aside, took her hand, and wept bitterly. Lotte rested her head on her other hand and covered her eyes with her handkerchief. What both felt at that moment was agonizing. They experienced their own misery in the fate of these noble people, they felt it together, and their tears flowed as one. Werther's lips and eyes burned on Lotte's arm. She was seized by a shivering. She wanted to leave the room, but pain and compassion left her numb. She breathed deeply in an effort to recover her composure and begged him, sobbing, to continue, implored him to do so with the whole force of heaven in her voice. Werther was trembling; he thought his heart would break. He took up the papers again and began to read in a broken voice, "Why dost thou awaken me, O zephyr of spring? Thou dost speak of love, saying, 'I spread the dew with drops from heaven.' But the time of my fading away is high, nigh is the storm that will defoliate me. And in the morn the wanderer will come, the wanderer will come who saw me in my glory. His eyes will seek me in the field but he will not find me. . . ."

The full force of the words rained down upon the unfortunate man. In his despair he threw himself on his knees before Lotte, took her hand, pressed it to his eyes, his forehead, and a hint of the terrible thing he was planning seemed to brush Lotte's soul. She became confused and pressed his hand tightly against her breast and, with a plaintive motion, moved closer to him. Their burning cheeks touched, and the world ended for them. Werther wound his arms around Lotte, pressed her to him, and covered her trembling, stammering lips with passionate kisses. "Werther!" she cried, in a voice that was choked, turning from him, "Werther!" and with her weak hand, she pushed him away. "Werther!" she said, in a voice controlled by the noblest sentiments.

He did nothing to resist her. He let her go and threw himself down insensibly at her feet. She managed to tear herself away and, in fearful confusion, trembling between love and anger, said, "This is the last time, Werther! You shall not see me again," and with a look full of love at the miserable man, she rushed into the next room and locked the door. Werther stretched out his arms to her, but did not dare to stop her. He lay on the floor, his head resting against the side of the sofa, and remained like this for over half an hour, until a noise roused him. It was the maid, coming to set the table. He paced up and down the room and when he was alone again, walked over to the door of the room into which Lotte had fled and called softly, "Lotte . . . Lotte . . . only a word of farewell!" She was silent. He waited and begged and waited. Finally he tore himself away, crying, "Farewell, Lotte! Farewell forever!"

At the city gates, the watchmen, who were accustomed to the sight of him, let him out silently. It was drizzling, a mixture of rain and snow, and it was nearly eleven when he rapped on the gates again. His servant noted that his master came home without his hat. He didn't dare to mention the fact but undressed him silently. All his clothes were wet. The hat was found later on a rock that overlooks the valley from the precipitous side of a hill, and it is incredible that Werther could have climbed up it on a dark, wet night without falling out.

He went to bed and slept for a long time. Next morning, when his servant answered his call for coffee, he found his master writing. He was adding the following to his letter to Lotte:

"So, for the last time—yes, for the last time, I open these eyes. They shall not see the sun again. A dim, foggy day keeps them veiled. Very well then, mourn, O Nature—thy son, thy friend, thy beloved's life is drawing to a close. Lotte, it is a feeling without parallel, yet to tell oneself, 'This is the last morning,' comes very close to one's twilit dreams. The last. Lotte, I have no understanding of the word 'last.' Am I not sitting here with my whole strength, and tomorrow I am to lie stretched out limp on the floor? To die. What does it mean? Look—when we talk about death we are dreaming. I have seen many a man die, but man is so limited that he has no understanding for the beginning and end of his existence. Mine—still mine as yet— and yours! Yours, O my beloved! Then, one moment more, and separated . . . divorced from one another, perhaps forever? No, Lotte, no. How could I possibly perish? How could you pass away? You and I . . . we *are*! Perish? What does it mean? Again, nothing but a word. An empty sound with no feeling for my heart. Dead, Lotte—buried in the cold earth, so narrow, so dark. I had a sweetheart once who was my all in the days of my helpless youth. She died. I followed her bier and stood beside her grave as they let down the coffin—the ropes grating beneath it and snapping back up, the sound of the first spadeful of dirt tumbling down, and the dread casket giving off a dull tone, then a more muffled thud that became more and more muffled, until at last the coffin was covered. I sank down beside the grave, deeply moved, shattered, fearful, torn to the depths of my being, but I did not know what was the matter with me nor what was to befall me. Death. Grave. I have no understanding for the words.

"Oh, forgive me, forgive me . . . yesterday. It should have been the last moment of my life. Oh, you angel! For the first time—for the first time, a feeling of bliss burned without any doubt in the depths of me. She loves me! She loves me! The sacred fire that streamed to me from you still burns on my lips. A new, warm rapture is in my heart. Forgive me, forgive me!

"Oh, I knew that you loved me, knew it when I met your first soulful glance, with the first pressure of your hand, and yet, when I was away from you, when I saw Albert at your side, I despaired again, in a fever of doubt.

"Do you recall the flowers that you sent me when, in his irritating company, you could not say a word nor give me your hand? I knelt half the night before them, they put a seal upon your love for me. But alas, such impressions pass, just as the feeling of God's mercy—a feeling that is bestowed on a man of faith in all its divine abundance in holy, visible portent—can cede gradually from his soul.

"All such things are transient. But no eternity shall erase the glowing life that I experienced at your lips yesterday and that I feel within me now. She loves me. These arms have held her; these lips have trembled on hers; this mouth has stammered a few broken words against hers. She is mine. You are mine, Lotte, forever.

"And what difference does it make that Albert is your husband? Husband—that's a word for this world, and for this world it's a sin that I love you and would wrench you out of his arms into mine. A sin? Very well then, and I punish myself for it. I have tasted this sin in all its divine rapture, I have sucked its balm and strength into my heart. From now on you are mine—mine, Lotte! I go on ahead to my Father. To Him I will complain, and He will comfort me until you come, and I fly to meet you and enfold you and remain at your side in the sight of Infinite God in one eternal embrace.

"I do not dream, I do not think any more. Close to the grave, all grows lighter. We shall be. We shall see each other again. Your mother . . . I shall see her, find her, and oh, I shall unburden my whole heart to her. Your mother. Your image."

At about eleven, Werther asked his servant if Albert had returned. The man said yes, he had seen him riding by on his horse. Werther then gave the man an open note containing the words, "Would you be so good as to lend me your pistols for a trip I am about to undertake? My very best regards."

Lotte had slept little during the preceding night. What she had dreaded had been decided for her in a way she could neither have dreamed nor feared. Her blood, which usually coursed so chastely and steadily through her veins, was in a feverish turmoil. A thousand confused sensations disturbed her. Was it the passion of Werther's embrace that she felt in her breast? Was it resentment of his boldness? Or was it the result of an unpleasant comparison of her present condition with former days of completely unabashed innocence and carefree confidence in herself? How was she to meet her husband? There was nothing to hide, yet how was she to explain the scene to him? She didn't dare to. They had been silent for such a long time on this subject—should she break the silence and make such an unexpected disclosure, perhaps at the wrong time? She feared that even the mention of Werther's visit would make a disagreeable impression, and on top of that—this unexpected catastrophe! Could she hope that her husband would see things in their true light and accept what she had to say entirely without bias? And did she want him to look into her soul and read what was there? But then, again, could she dissemble before a man to whom she had always been frank and clear as crystal, from whom she had never been able to keep any of her feelings secret? All these things troubled and embarrassed her. Again and again her thoughts reverted to Werther, who was lost to her, whom she could not abandon, yet, alas, had to abandon, to whom—once he had lost her—nothing was left.

The estrangement which had closed in upon all three of them weighed heavily upon her now, but it was something she could not see clearly at the moment. Good, sensible people often withdraw from one another because of secret differences, each becoming absorbed by what he feels is right and by the error of the other. Conditions then grow more and more complicated and exasperating, until it becomes impossible to undo the knot at the crucial moment on which everything depends. If only a fortunate intimacy had brought them closer again before this, if only they could have felt love and consideration for one another mutually, and confided in one another, Werther might have been saved.

Another strange circumstance must be mentioned here. As we know from his letters, Werther had never made any secret of his longing to leave this world. Albert had argued the point with him often and had even discussed it with Lotte. Since such behavior was so distasteful to him, he had declared several times, with an irritability that was quite foreign to his character, that he doubted the seriousness of Werther's inclination. One day he had even gone so far as to joke about it and had mentioned his skepticism to Lotte. On the one hand, this helped to calm her whenever she dwelled on the unhappy prospect, on the other hand, she was reluctant for the same reason to share with her husband the anxieties that were tormenting her now.

Albert came home, and Lotte went to meet him in a state of self-conscious haste. He was not in good spirits. He had had to leave his business incompleted; the neighboring magistrate had turned out to be an inflexible, narrow-minded man. The bad roads had added to his irritation.

He asked if there was any news. She replied, a little too hastily, that Werther had been there the evening before. He asked if there was any mail and received the reply that some letters and packets had been placed in his room. He went there, and Lotte was left alone. The presence of the man she loved and respected had made a fresh impression on her heart. The thought of his generosity, his love and kindness, had calmed her. She felt the urge to follow him, took her work and went into his room, something she did quite often. She found him unwrapping the packets and reading the contents. Several seemed to contain unpleasant news. She asked a few questions, he replied curtly and sat down at his desk to write.

They were together like this for an hour, and Lotte's

spirits sank increasingly lower. She realized how difficult it was going to be to disclose to her husband what was oppressing her, even if he were in the best of moods, and she lapsed into a melancholy that became more and more frightening as she tried to hide it and fight down her tears.

The appearance of Werther's groom put her in a very embarrassing position. He handed the note to Albert, who turned to his wife and said casually, "Give him the pistols." To the boy he said, "Tell your master that I wish him a pleasant journey."

The words fell like a thunderclap on Lotte's ears. She swayed as she rose to her feet; she didn't know what to do. Slowly she walked over to the wall and, with hands that trembled, took the pistols from the rack, dusted them, hesitated, and would have hesitated longer if Albert had not forced her with his questioning eyes to go on with what he had asked her to do. Incapable of uttering a word, she gave the unfortunate weapons to the boy, and when he had left the house, she picked up her work and went to her room in a state of the most indescribable anxiety. Her heart foretold all terror. At one moment, she was on the point of throwing herself at her husband's feet and confessing everything—what had happened last night, her culpability, and her awful premonitions—then again she realized how futile that would be. The last thing she could hope for was that her husband would go over to see Werther.

The table was set. A good friend, who had only come to enquire about something, stayed and made the conversation at table at least tolerable. Lotte forced herself to some semblance of self-control, conversed, and forgot herself.

The servant brought Werther the weapons. He was delighted when he heard that Lotte had given him to the boy. He had bread and wine brought to him, told the boy to have his dinner; and sat down to write.

"They have passed through your hands. You brushed the dust from them. You touched them. I kiss them a thousand times. The spirit of heaven favors my decision, and you, Lotte, hand me the weapon—you, from whom I wished to receive death and now receive it. Oh, how I questioned my boy! You trembled, he said, as you handed them to him. You said no farewell. Alas—no farewell! Have you closed your heart to me, because of that moment that bound me to you forever? Lotte, not a thousand years can erase that impression. And—I feel it—you cannot hate him who glows with his whole heart for you."

After dinner he ordered the boy to pack, tore up some papers, and went out and settled a few minor debts. He returned home; then, disregarding the rain, he went out again as far as the gate, from there into the Count's garden, after which he wandered about the countryside. When night was falling he came home and wrote, "William, I have seen fields, wood, and sky for the last time. Farewell to you, too. Dear Mother, forgive me. Console her, William. God bless you both. All my affairs are in order. Farewell. We shall meet again under happier circumstances.

"Albert, I have rewarded you poorly, but you will forgive me. I disturbed the peace of your household; I sowed distrust between you and Lotte. Farewell. It is my wish to terminate things. Ah, if only you could be made happy through my death! Albert, make my angel happy! And may God's blessing be on you both."

He spent the rest of the evening going through his papers again, tore up many and threw them into the stove, sealed several packets and addressed them to William. The latter contained a few short articles and random observations, several of which I have seen. After having had the stove stoked once more at ten o' clock and ordering a bottle of wine for himself, he sent his servant to bed. The boy's room, like the bedrooms of the other domestics, was far off in the back of the house. He lay down with his clothes on in order to be ready to leave early the next morning, for his master had told him that the post chaise would be at the house before six.

After eleven.

Everything is so still around me and so calm within my soul. I thank you, God, who gave this last moment of mine such warmth, such strength.

I walk over to the window, my dearest one, and look out. Through the storm clouds flying by, I can still see a few stars in the eternal sky. No, you will not fall. The Eternal One carries you in his heart, as he carries me. I can see the handle of the Big Dipper, my favorite of all the constellations. When I left you that night, as I walked out the gate, it stood in the sky facing me. In what a state of intoxication I have been often when I looked at it. Then I would lift my hand and make a sign of it, a sacred marker for my present bliss. And I still do! Oh, Lotte, what does not remind me of you? Are you not all around me, and haven't I snatched all sorts of little things and held onto them like an insatiable child—things, my angel, that you touched?

Beloved silhouette. I leave it to you, Lotte, and beg you to respect it. I have pressed thousands of impassioned kisses on it and waved it a thousand greetings when I left the house or returned.

In another note I have asked your father to take care of my remains. There are two linden trees in the cemetery, back in a corner, near the field. That is where I wish to rest. He can—he will do it for his friend. Please ask him, too, to do so. It would be too much to expect a faithful Christian to lie beside a poor unfortunate like me. Oh, how I wish you could bury me by the wayside or in a lonely valley, so that priest and Levite might bless themselves as they pass the stone marker and the Samaritan could shed a tear there.

Here, Lotte . . . see, it does not make me shudder to grasp the cold and terrible cup from which I shall drink the transport of death. You hand it to me, and I do not hesitate. All! All of it! Thus all the wishes and hopes I had of life are fulfilled . . . to knock so coldly, so rigidly, on the brazen gates of death.

That I was granted the good fortune to die for you, Lotte, to sacrifice myself for you . . . I would die courageously, joyously, if only I could re-establish the repose and bliss of your existence. But oh, it has been granted to only a few noble men to shed their life's blood for those they love and, by their death, kindle a new life for their friends.

I want to be buried, Lotte, in the clothes I have on. You have touched them and made them sacred. I have asked your father, too, to do this for me. My soul floats over the coffin. Please let no one go through my pockets. The pale pink bow that you wore at your breast when I saw you for the first time with your children . . . kiss them a thousand times and tell them the fate of their unfortunate friend. The darlings . . . they are tumbling all around me. Ah, how I attached myself to you from the first moment and could not let go. This bow is to be buried with me. You gave it to me on my birthday. Oh, how greedily I absorbed it all, never thinking that the way would lead here. Be calm, I beseech you, be calm.

It is loaded. The clock strikes midnight. So be it then, Lotte. Farewell. Farewell.

A neighbor saw the flash of gunpowder and heard the shot, but since all remained silent, he paid no further heed to the occurrence.

Next morning at six, the servant came into the room with a light. He found his master lying on the floor, the pistol, and the blood. He cried out, touched him—no response. Werther's last breath was rattling in his throat. The boy ran for the doctor and for Albert. Lotte heard the bell, and a shiver ran through every member of her body. She woke her husband. They got up. The servant, sobbing and stammering, delivered his message. Lotte sank fainting to the ground at Albert's feet.

When the doctor arrived, he found the unfortunate man on the floor. There was no hope of saving him. His pulse could still be felt but all his limbs were paralyzed. He had shot himself in the head above the right eye, driving his brains out. Quite superfluously, the doctor undertook a bloodletting of one vein. The blood ran out, Werther was still breathing.

The blood on the armchair was evidence of the fact that he had shot himself while sitting in front of his desk, then had slumped down and twisted himself convulsively out of the chair. He was lying on his back, against the window, fully clad in his blue coat and yellow vest, with his boots on.

The house, the neighborhood, the whole town were filled with commotion. Albert came in. They laid Werther on the bed and bandaged his forehead. His face was already like that of the dead; he did not move a muscle. His breathing was terrible—weak at one moment, then a little stronger. They were waiting for the end to come.

He had drunk only one glass of the wine. *Emilia Galotti*[9] lay open on his lectern.

There are no words to express Albert's consternation or Lotte's misery.

The old judge came bursting in as soon as he heard the news. With the hot tears streaming down his cheeks, he kissed the dying man. His oldest sons soon followed him on foot. They fell on their knees beside the bed in attitudes of the wildest grief, kissing the dying man's hand, his mouth. The oldest one, whom Werther had always loved best, clung to his lips as he expired and had to be forcefully removed. At twelve noon, Werther died. The presence of the judge and the arrangements he made silenced the crowd. That night, at about eleven, he had the body buried in the spot Werther had chosen. The old man and his sons walked behind the bier; Albert found himself incapable of doing so. They feared for Lotte's life. Workmen carried the body. There was no priest in attendance.

REFLECTIONS ON WERTHER

> The word *Dichtung* should not be understood in
> the sense of fabrication or as a collection of fac-
> tual details, but as the revelation of higher
> truths. . . . [It was my] endeavor to present and
> express to the best of my ability the actual basic
> truths that controlled my life as I understood
> them. . . . We are of course prone to set forth
> and stress results and the past as we see it now,
> rather than the detailed events as they took
> place at the time . . . all this—belonging as it
> does to the narrator and to history—I have in-
> cluded here under the word *Dichtung*, so that I
> might employ the truths of which I am conscious
> to suit my ends.
>
> —GOETHE on the meaning
> of the word *Dichtung*

Wetzlar, May to September 1772

All my reflections and endeavors left my old resolve unchanged: to explore the inner and outer manifestations of
nature and, in loving emulation, let them hold sway over
me. As part of this reaction—which would not let me rest
by day or night—I was confronted by two grand, indeed, I
should say, gigantic conceptions. All I had to do was estimate their wealth to some extent and I would have already
produced something significant. The life of *Götz von Berlichingen* falls into the older epoch, and the unfortunate
flowering of the new is described in *Werther*. . . .

The decision to let my inner self rule me at will and
permit all outside events to penetrate in a way characteristic

of them drove me into the wonderful element in which *Werther* was conceived and written. I tried to release myself from all alien emotions, to look kindly upon what was going on around me and let all living things, beginning with man himself, affect me as deeply as possible, each in its own way. The result was a marvelous affinity with nature and a warm and heartfelt response—a harmony with all things— that made me capable of being deeply touched by every change, whether of place or region, of day or season, or by anything else. The eye of the painter was added to that of the poet. A beautiful landscape, enlivened by a friendly stream, heightened my inclination for solitude and favored my quiet but extensive observations. My departure from the family circle in Sesenheim[10] and now, again, from my friends in Frankfurt and Darmstadt, had left an emptiness in my heart that I was unable to fill. I found myself there- fore in the position where any attraction, as long as it ap- pears in a semblance of disguise, succeeds in creeping up upon one unawares and can thwart all one's best intentions.

Having reached this stage of my undertaking, I can feel lighthearted about it for the first time, because it looks as if this book were going to be what it should be. It did not announce itself as anything independent but was intended rather to fill in gaps in the author's life—to complete a few fragments and preserve the memory lost, the forgotten adventure. But what has already been done cannot and should not be repeated, and the poet too would call upon the darkened powers of his soul in vain and demand to no avail that they re-establish those former pleasant circum- stances that made his stay in the Lahn valley so beautiful. Fortunately the genius of inspiration saw to it for him at the right time and gave him, in the precious days of his youth, the impetus to hold fast and describe events just passed, and the boldness to publish what he had written at a propitious hour. I presume I need say no more. It must be clear to everyone that I am referring to that slim volume

Excerpts dealing with the conception and writing of *Werther*, from Goethe's memoirs, *Aus Meinem Laben: Dichtung und Wahrheit* (*My Life: Poetry and Truth*), Books XII and XIII, published in 1814.

entitled *Werther*. From time to time I shall have something
to say about the characters in it, as well as about the sentiments ascribed to them.

Among the younger men assigned to the embassy who
were preparing themselves for their future duties, there was
one whom we referred to simply as "the betrothed." He
was notable for his calm, steadfast behavior and the clarity
of his opinions, and his diligence made such a good impression on his superiors that he was promised a post in the
very near future. This justified his engagement to a girl who
suited his inclinations perfectly. After her mother's death
she had become the head of a numerous younger family
and had been the sole comfort of her widowed father in his
grief. Any future husband could hope to find the same comfort in her for himself and his children, and could expect
the happiest conditions to prevail in his household. But
everyone had to admit that, even without these selfish con-
siderations, she was a highly desirable young lady. She was
the type who, even though they cannot arouse violent passion, are so constituted as to excite general admiration. A
slight, pretty figure; a wholesome nature and the joyous
vitality that springs from it; and a way of doing, without
self-consciousness, what had to be done daily—all were contained in her. I have always enjoyed such attributes and
liked to join forces with those who were blessed with them;
and even if I did not always find an opportunity to be of
service to such persons, I much preferred to share with them
the enjoyment of those innocent pleasures that are always
easily accessible to young people and can be found without
much effort or expense. Since it is, moreover, an established
fact that women adorn themselves only for one another and
never tire of growing fancier and fancier, I liked those fe-
males best who, with a simple neatness, gave their friend
or fiancé the tacit assurance that they adorned themselves
only for him and that a whole lifetime could be spent like
this, without great fuss and expense.

Persons like that are not overly absorbed with themselves. They have time to observe what is going on around
them and are sufficiently easygoing to adjust to the outside
world and enjoy a sense of equality with it. They become
clever and understanding without undue exertion and re-

quire few books for their education. The girl's nature was like that. Her fiancé, with his thoroughly honest and trusting attitude toward life, soon introduced her to everyone he thought well of, and liked it—because he was busy during the greater part of the day—when, after having completed her household duties, she amused herself in other ways and enjoyed sociability in the form of walks or excursions into the countryside with friends. Lotte—I suppose we might as well call her that—was undemanding in two ways: first, according to her nature, which was intent on creating general good will rather than on attracting any specific attention, and secondly, she had already chosen someone who was worthy of her, who had declared himself willing to join his fate with hers for life. Wherever she was, it was always gay. It is indeed a pleasant sight to see parents devoting themselves to their children, but it is even more beautiful to see brother and sister doing the same thing for each other. In the former we see a more natural drive and more traditional origins; in the latter, greater freedom of choice and spirit.

The new arrival was completely free of all ties and blithe in the presence of this girl who, already betrothed to another, did not interpret his favors as a wooing and could thus enjoy them all the more. He could therefore afford to let himself go and was soon so deeply infatuated, and at the same time receiving such trustful and kind treatment from the pair, that he didn't know his own mind! Idle and dreamy—since the present could not satisfy him—he found what he missed in this girl who, because she lived for time as a whole, seemed to live only for the moment. She enjoyed the young man as a companion. Soon he did not know how to get along without her, for she opened up the outside world to him, and they became inseparable companions in field, on meadow, and in garden. When her fiancé's work permitted, he accompanied them. They became accustomed to being three quite unintentionally, without knowing how or when they had reached this point of mutual need. Thus a glorious summer passed by, a true German idyl. The fruitful earth provided the prose and their pure attraction the poetry. They refreshed themselves on dewy mornings by wandering through the ripe cornfields; the lark's song and the quail's cry delighted them. Hot days followed, there were terrible thunderstorms—all of which succeeded only in bringing them closer—and numerous little family spats were quickly forgotten thanks to their steadfast love. One ordinary day followed another, and every day seemed to be a feast day. The whole calendar might have been printed in red! He will understand me who recalls what was prophesied about the unhappy friend of the new Héloïse, "Sitting at the feet of his beloved he shall break flax, and he shall want to break flax, today, tomorrow, and the day after tomorrow, yea, for his entire life."[11]

And now I can tell a little, but as much as is necessary, about a young man whose name will be mentioned often in the pages to come—Jerusalem, the son of a liberal-minded and highly sensitive theologian. He also held a post at one of the embassies. He was pleasant-looking, of medium height, and well built. His face was round rather than long, his features were soft and tranquil, and he possessed everything else that a nice-looking, blond young man should have—even blue eyes that were appealing rather than expressive. He dressed in a style which the North Germans had copied from the English—a blue coat, a leather-yellow vest and breeches, and boots with brown cuffs. I never visited him, nor was he ever a guest at my house. We met sometimes at the houses of friends. The young man expressed himself with moderation, but amiably. He took part in our various artistic endeavors and seemed especially attracted to those drawings and sketches that succeeded in conveying the silent aspects of a lonely region. Sometimes he would show us etchings by Gessner and would encourage us amateurs to study them. But he took little or no part in our efforts to re-create the chivalric aspects of an earlier life,[12] or our masquerades. He lived according to his convictions. There was some talk about his passion for the wife of a friend, but they were never seen together in public. Altogether very little was known about him except that he was interested in English literature. He was the son of a wealthy man and therefore had neither to worry about business nor seek a lucrative post anywhere.

The Gessner etchings just mentioned heightened our longing for pastoral scenes, and a short poem that was ecstatically received in our small circle also affected us so that we seemed to have eyes for nothing else. "The Deserted Village," by Goldsmith, was enjoyed by people on every level of education. In it all those things were described, not as living or still effective but as part of a past, lost existence, which we wanted to see with our own eyes, which we loved and valued and sought avidly in the present, in order to play our youthful, lively part in it. Feast and holiday in the country, church fair, and market, to say nothing of the serious assembly of town elders under the village linden tree being jostled by the robust dancing of the young people or perhaps even by the gentler folk—these pleasures seemed to be so fitting, tempered as they were by the village priest who knew just how to take care of any situation that got out of hand or might give cause for bickering and strife. Here we found our honest Wakefield again in his well-known surroundings, no longer vividly portrayed, but a shadow recalled by the elegiac poet's soft lament. The very idea of such a description is felicitous as soon as one has decided to recall the innocent past in a mood of sweet sadness. And how the English succeed in this amiable pursuit! I shared Gotter's enthusiasm for this charming poem. He was more successful in translating it than I was, for I approached the task of reproducing the delicate meanings of the original in our language too timidly and succeeded in some passages, but not with the thing as a whole.

If, as they say, our greatest happiness rests in our longings, and if true longing may have only what is unattainable as its goal, then all things certainly had come together to make our young man, whom we are accompanying on his erratic journey, the happiest of mortals. His attraction to a girl already affianced, his urge to assimilate the masterpieces of a foreign language, thereby making them his, his efforts to re-create all things natural not only in words but with stylus and brush as well, and this without any actual technique—all these things could have sufficed to oppress him and bring his heart to the breaking point. . . .

I could hardly wait to introduce Merck to Lotte, but alas, his presence in our little circle didn't do me any good, for just as Mephistopheles may go where he pleases but can hardly be expected to act as a blessing, Merck's indifference to my dear girl did not exactly cause me to waver in my affections but it certainly did not add to my pleasure. I might have known this would happen; I should have remembered that it was just such slight, dainty persons, who know how to spread a vital gaiety around them without making any demands, that Merck did not care for. He soon showed his preference for a more Junoesque friend of Lotte's, and since he lacked the time to start an affair with her, he scolded me quite acridly because *I* was not wooing this magnificent female, especially since she was free and unattached. I didn't know what was good for me, he declared, and he didn't like to see, even here, my special penchant for wasting my time.

It is dangerous to introduce a friend to the merits of one's beloved because he may find her attractive too, but his rejection is no less a danger, for he may confuse us with it. This was not the case now—I was far too deeply touched by the magic of her sweetness for the picture ever to be erased—but his presence and his powers of persuasion hastened my decision to leave the place. He made a trip along the Rhine that he was about to undertake with his wife and son sound fascinating, and aroused in me the longing at last to see with my own eyes a region that I had always heard about with envy. After he had left, I took leave of Charlotte with a clearer conscience than I had said farewell to Friederike, but still not without pain. Through habit and indulgence, our relationship had become more ardent on my side than had been my intention. She, on the other hand, and her fiancé, had always been so carefree and behaved toward me in a fashion that could not have been more sweet and friendly, and the feeling of security resulting from this had made me forget any idea of danger. But there was no hiding the fact that this little episode was about to end, for their marriage now depended only on his imminent promotion, and since a man, if he is resolute, does what is necessary of his own free will, I decided to remove myself before what was unbearable might drive me away.

Frankfurt, September 1772

He who dares go out into the world is like a man who has decided to become a soldier and go to war. Courageously he takes upon himself the idea of enduring perils and hardship, wounds and pain, even death, but he never takes the trouble to imagine the specific circumstances under which these universally anticipated misfortunes may choose to surprise him disagreeably. An author especially finds himself in such a position, and that is what happened to me. Since most readers are inspired more by the material than by the way it is treated, the sympathy of young men to my plays was, for the most part, for their content. They thought they saw in the events a standard behind which everything that was wild and boorish in youth could rally. And it was just the keenest minds—those who were trying to cope with something similar—that were most enchanted with them. . . . More sober men, on the other hand, accused me of portraying the policy of the mailed fist too sympathetically and went so far as to accuse me of wanting to bring back such uncertain times. Some took me for an erudite man and demanded that I publish a new edition of the original story of Götz, with footnotes, which I did not feel at all like doing, although I permitted them to put my name on the title page of a new printing. Because I had known how to pick the fruits of a great life, they took me for a scrupulous gardener, but this supposedly tremendous erudition of mine was the subject of doubts in others.

An esteemed merchant paid me an unexpected visit. I felt greatly honored, especially since he started the conversation by praising *Götz von Berlichingen* and my fine insight into German history, but I soon began to feel hurt when I noticed that he had really come only to inform me that Götz von Berlichingen had not been a brother-in-law of Franz von Sickingen, and that I was offending history with such poetic license. I tried to excuse myself by pointing out that Götz himself had called the man that, but I was told that this was a manner of speech meant only to express a more intimate relationship, similar to the current fad of calling the stagecoach driver "brother" without enjoying any family ties with him. I thanked the man for his information as best I could and expressed my regret that there wasn't much we could do about it now. He expressed the same regret and proceeded to exhort me, in a quite friendly way, to make a further study of Germany's history and constitution, and offered me the facilities of his library toward that end, an offer which I promptly made good use of.

But the most amusing incident of this kind was the visit of a bookdealer who blithely asked me for a dozen such plays and promised to pay well for them. Of course, this amused all of us highly, yet the man was not so far wrong, for I was quietly toying with the idea of moving backward and forward from this turning point in German history and of treating the main events in a similar way, a praiseworthy intention that was thwarted by the swift passage of time, like so many other things. But Götz was not the only theme on my mind, for while I was reflecting on it, writing and rewriting it, and it was being printed and distributed, many other ideas and suggestions occupied my thoughts. Those that would have to be treated as dramas took first place. I thought them through most often and brought them closer to realization. At the same time, however, there was developing in me the transition to another representational form that is not usually categorized with the drama, yet has strong kinship with it. This transition took place because of a peculiarity of mine that enabled me to transform a conversation with myself into a dialogue.

Accustomed by preference to spending my time sociably, I succeeded in transforming solitary thinking into friendly conversation in the following manner: When I saw that I was alone, I would summon some person or other from my circle of friends, in spirit. I would ask this person to sit down and would pace up and down or stand still before him and discuss any problems with him that were on my mind. Every now and then my companion would reply and agree or disagree with the usual gestures—every person has his own way of doing so. I would then elaborate on whatever seemed to have pleased my guest or would qualify what had not; perhaps I would be more precise about it and probably, in the end, let the subject drop. Strangely enough I never chose to summon my more intimate friends, but only those I saw seldom—even some who lived far away, with whom I enjoyed only a fleeting relationship. But the ones I called in were, for the most part, of a receptive rather than effusive nature, capable of participating quietly and clear-headedly, even when I chose to summon contradictory spirits to join in these dialectical exercises. Toward this end, persons of either sex and every age and rank were good enough to appear and all of them were amiable, since nothing was mentioned except subjects that were clear and agreeable to them. And it would have been a marvelous revelation to some of them, if they had found out how often they were called in to such an idealized conversation, since quite a few of them would have been heard to come by for a real one!

It is clear that a conversation in spirit, such as this, is closely related to correspondence, the only differences being that in the latter one sees one's confidence reciprocated and in the former one creates one's own fresh and constantly changing unrequited confidences. When it came to the point, therefore, of my wishing to describe the weariness with which people often experience life without having been forced to such a dismal outlook by want, I hit upon the idea, as author, of expressing my feelings in letters. For this weariness, this disgust with life, is born of loneliness, it is the foster child of solitude. He who gives himself up to it, flees from all opposition; and what could oppose him more than all blithe company? The joy of life in others is an embarrassingly painful reproach to him. Thus he is thrust back upon himself by the very things that should serve to take him out of himself. If he ever does want to discuss it, then surely only in letters, for a written effusion, whether it be joyous or morose, does not antagonize anyone directly, and an answer filled with counterarguments gives the lonely man an opportunity to harden in his peculiarities and offers the inducement to become more obdurate. Werther's letters, which were written with this in mind, probably enjoyed such a diversified popularity because the various events were first discussed in idealized dialogues with several individuals but then, in the composition itself, they are directed at one friend and participant only. I don't think it would be advisable to say more about the treatment of this much-discussed little volume, but quite a bit remains to be told about the content.

A repugnance toward life has its physical and moral origins. We shall leave the explanation of the former to the doctor, of the latter to the moralist, and, in material that has been worked over again and again, let us pay attention to the salient point where this phenomenon expresses itself most clearly. All one's gratifications in life are based on the regular reappearance of external things. The change from day to night, of the seasons, of flower and fruit, and all the other things that confront us at regular intervals so that we may and should enjoy them—these are the actual wellsprings of our daily life. The more openly we avow these pleasures, the happier we are. But if these divers spectacles revolve in front of us and we take no part in them, then we are unreceptive to these precious gifts, then the greatest evil, the most dire sickness breaks out in us—we look upon life as a repulsive burden. There is the story of an Englishman who hanged himself because he didn't want to dress and undress himself any more. I knew a gardener, a stalwart fellow in charge of a big park, who in his bleakness cried out one day, "Am I to spend my whole life watching the rain clouds move from eve to morn?" And then I have heard tell of one of our best men that he hates to see the greening of springtime and wishes that, for a change, everything would come up red! All these are symptoms of a weariness of life that quite often culminates in suicide and is more prevalent among thoughtful introverts than one would care to believe.

Nothing, however, can further such a weariness of life as much as the repetition of love. First love is truly described as the only love, for in the second, and through the second, the emotion in its highest sense is already lost. The idea of forever and eternal—which is really what uplifts and sustains love—is destroyed, and it becomes a transient thing like all events that are repeated. The separation of its sensual and moral aspects, which in our confused civilization has split our loving and desiring sensations, also produces harmful exaggerations.

Furthermore, a young man soon becomes aware—if not in himself, then in others—of the fact that moral epochs change just as the seasons do. The graciousness of the great, the favor of the powerful, the promotion of those who are diligent, the adulation of the crowd, the love of an individual—all fluctuate without our being able to hold fast to any of them, any more than we can grasp the sun, moon, or stars. And these things are not all natural phenomena. They elude us through our own fault or the fault of others, by chance or by fate, but they change, and we can never be sure of them.

But what makes a sensitive youth most fearful is the irresistible repetition of his errors. Only too late does he recognize that in the cultivation of his virtues he at the same time raises his mistakes. The former rest on the roots of the latter as well as on their own, and the latter branch out in all directions, secretly but just as powerfully, and as varied as those that flourish in the open. Since we practice our virtues, for the most part, willfully and consciously, whereas our faults take us unconsciously by surprise, the former occasionally give us a little pleasure, but the latter worry and torment us constantly. And here lies the most intricate aspect of self-recognition, an aspect that makes it virtually impossible. Add to all this the turgid blood of youth, the powers of an imagination that is easily paralyzed, the imbalance of the day's motion—and the impatient urge to free oneself of the dilemma does not seem so unnatural.

Such dire reflections, however, that must lead him who gives himself up to them to endless speculation, would not have developed so decisively in the hearts of German youth if an external inducement had not incited and encouraged him. And this was offered by English literature, especially English poetry, the excellencies of which are accompanied by a profound melancholy that it seems to pass on to anyone studying it. The intellectual Briton sees himself surrounded from his youth by a world of eminence that stimulates all his energies. Sooner or later he becomes aware of the fact that he is going to need all his thinking capacities to put up with it. How many English poets there are who led profligate lives in their youth and felt justified early in life in accusing all earthly things of being naught but vanity! How many tried to make their way in business, in parliament, at court, in the ministry, how many played prominent or secondary roles at embassies, participated in internal unrest, state and governmental changes, and had more sad than good experiences, if not with themselves, then with their friends and benefactors!

But even being only a spectator of such great events

forces a man to take life seriously, and where can such earnestness lead except to the contemplation of transitory things and an awareness of the worthlessness of all earthly matters? The German can be serious too. English poetry therefore suited him very well, and because it was conceived on such lofty heights, he found it impressive. A grandiose, vigorous, and worldly sagacity can be found in it, a profound and gentle spirit, a splendid will, a passionate activity—all glorious qualities for which the intellectual, erudite man can only be lauded, yet all these things combined do not make a poet. True poetry proclaims itself as a secular gospel in its ability to liberate us from the earthly burdens that oppress us by producing in us serenity and a physical sense of well-being. It lifts us and our ballast into higher spheres like a balloon, leaving the confused and labyrinthine path of our earthly meanderings below us in bird's-eye perspective. The liveliest and most serious works should have the same aim—to alleviate passion and pain through a felicitous and ingenious presentation. With this in mind, one should take a look at the majority of English poems, most of which are highly moral and didactic, and one will find that, for the most part, they display a dreary weariness of life. All English contemplative poems, even Young's "Night Thoughts," in which this dreariness has been gloriously realized, straggle on before you know it into such sad regions, where the mind is given a problem it cannot solve, where even religion, if the poet has any, does not help him. Volumes could be printed as a commentary to the dread verse:

> Then old Age and Experience, hand in hand
>   Lead him to death, and make him understand,
> After a search so painful and so long,
>   That all his life he has been in the wrong.[13]

What furthermore makes a complete misanthrope of the English poet and spreads an unpleasant aura of repugnance against all things over his writing is that, because of the numerous schisms in his communal existence, he must dedicate if not his whole life than the better part of it to one political party or other. Such a writer is not permitted to glorify his loved ones, to whom he is devoted, or the cause he favors, because he might otherwise arouse ill will. He therefore uses his talents to speak as harshly as possible of his opponent, and satiric weapons, however adeptly used, always serve to sharpen and poison the atmosphere. When this takes place on both sides, the world that lies between is destroyed, with the result that, in a great and intellectually active nation, one finds at best nothing but folly or madness in their verse. Even the most tender poem is concerned with sad subject matter. Here an abandoned young girl is dying, there a faithful lover drowns or, swimming as fast as he can, is eaten by a shark before he can reach his beloved. And when a poet like Gray settles down in a village churchyard and starts to sing the same old melody, he can be sure of attracting a following among the friends of melancholy. Milton, in "Allegro," must first dispel all gloom with some violent verse before he can arrive at a very moderate measure of joyful expression, and even our blithe friend Goldsmith loses himself in elegiac sentiments in his "Deserted Village" when he lets his "Traveler" cross the face of the earth to find a lost Eden, which the author describes very beautifully, but sadly.

I do not doubt that it would be possible to confront me with lively and gay English poems as well, but most of the best of them belong to an older epoch, and the latest ones that might be included tend toward satire, are bitter, and especially lack a respect for women.

Suffice it to say that the more general, serious poems mentioned above, which tended to undermine human nature, were our favorites. We picked them out from among all others. One person, according to his personality, chose the lighter lament, another sought a more oppressive despair that was ready to sacrifice all. Strangely enough, our father and teacher, Shakespeare, who knew so well how to spread brightness, also helped to increase our gloom. Hamlet and his monologues remained ghosts that haunted us. We knew the main parts by heart and loved to recite them, and every one of us felt he had to be just as melancholy as the Prince of Denmark, even if he hadn't seen a ghost and didn't have a royal father to avenge.

But in order that all this melancholy might not lack a suitable setting, it was left to Ossian to lure us to a final

Thule, where we wandered across gray, unending moors, amid prominent, moss-covered gravestones, surrounded by grass that was being eerily swept by the wind, and looked up into a sky that was leaden with clouds. This Caledonian night became day only in the moonlight. Defunct heroes and wan maidens hovered around us until, in the end, we really thought we could see the terrible shape of the spirit of Loda.[14] In such an atmosphere, with fancies and studies of this nature, tortured by unsatisfied passion, with no external inspiration to do anything really important, our only prospect to succumb, in the end, to a dreary, uncultured, bourgeois existence—we began to think kindly of departing this life should it no longer seem worth living, or at any rate of doing so whenever it suited us. Thus we helped ourselves meagerly over the wrongs and boredom of the day. Sentiments such as these were so universal that *Werther* had to have the powerful effect it did, because it touched every heart and depicted the innermost workings of a sick youthful madness openly and comprehensibly. The following lines attracted little attention and were written before the publication of *Werther,* but they prove how well acquainted the English were with this type of misery.

> To griefs congenial prone
>   More wounds than nature gave he knew
> While misery's form his fancy drew
>   In dark ideal hues and horrors not its own.[15]

Suicide—however much may already have been said or done about it—is an event of human nature that demands everyone's sympathy, and it should be dealt with anew in every era. Montesquieu gives his heroes and great men the right to surrender themselves to death in that he says it should be left to every man to end the fifth act of his tragedy as he sees fit. Here, however, we are not dealing with people who have lived active and eminent lives, who have spent their days in the service of some great kingdom or in the cause of freedom and cannot be blamed if they wish to follow the ideal that inspired them, once it has disappeared from this earth. We are dealing here with people who are weary of life from a lack of activity under the most peaceful conditions imaginable, through the exaggerated demands they make upon themselves. Since I found myself in such a condition once and know how I suffered and what efforts I had to make to escape it, I do not wish to hide the conclusions I reached after giving much consideration to the various forms of death one might choose.

It is so unnatural for a man to tear himself away from himself—not only to harm but to destroy himself—that he invariably turns to mechanical devices to put his design into action. When Ajax falls on his sword, it is the weight of his body that does him this last service; when a warrior orders his shield bearer not to let him fall into the hands of the enemy, he also assures himself on an external power, in this case a moral, not a physical one. Women seek to cool their despair in the water, and the most mechanical device of all, the pistol, assures quick action with no exertion at all. No one likes to mention hanging, because it is a dishonorable death. You find it in England more frequently than anywhere else, because there, even in one's youth, one may have seen someone hang without the punishment's being considered a disgrace. Poison or the slashing of a vein is for the man who is considering taking leave of this life slowly; and the most subtle, quick, and painless death, by the bite of an asp, was worthy of a queen who had lived a life of splendor and passion. But all these things are external aids, are enemies with whom man forms an alliance against himself.

When I contemplated these means and at the same time went on searching in history, I found that of all those who had taken their lives not one had done the deed with the grandeur and freedom of Emperor Otho.[16] Although he was at a disadvantage in battle, yet by no means driven to extremity, he decided to leave this world for the salvation of thousands and the welfare of a kingdom that, in a way, was as good as his. He celebrated a festive supper with his friends; next morning they found that he had thrust a dagger into his heart. This death alone seemed to me worthy of emulation, and I was convinced that he who could not behave like Otho had no right to take his life. And with this conviction, I saved myself not only from the dire intention itself, but from the whole caprice of suicide that had crept in upon a bored youth in those magnificent times of peace.

As a part of a rather impressive collection of weapons, I owned a costly, well-sharpened dagger. I used to put it beside my bed before I snuffed out the light and would try to see if it was possible for me to sink the sharp point a few inches into my breast. But I never could and I finally laughed at myself, threw off all hypochondriac specters, and decided to live. But in order to do so happily, I had first to complete a poetic work in which I could express everything I had felt and considered about this important subject. Toward this end, I proceeded to collect all the elements that had been fermenting inside me during the past few years. I tried to reconstruct the events that had oppressed and frightened me most, but nothing wanted to take shape. I lacked an incident, a legend, in which I could incorporate them.

Suddenly I heard of Jerusalem's death, and hot upon the general rumors, an exact and involved description of the entire incident. In that moment, the plan of *Werther* was found, the whole thing crystallized, like water in a glass that is on the point of freezing and can be turned to ice immediately with the slightest motion. To hold this strange prize fast and realize a work of such major importance and diverse content was all the dearer to me since I again found myself in an embarrassing situation that left me even less hope than the one that had preceded it and seemed to presage nothing but discontent and unpleasantness. . . .

Jerusalem's death—the result of his unfortunate attraction to the wife of a friend—shook me out of my dream, and since I did not look upon what had happened to him and me dispassionately, but was startled by the similarity with what was going on in my heart at the same time, I naturally breathed into the work I now undertook all the passion that results when there is no difference between fact and fiction. I isolated myself completely, forbade even my friends to visit me and laid aside inwardly as well everything that was not concerned with my enterprise. On the other hand, I assembled all I possibly could that was in any way connected with it and recapitulated my immediate past, of which I had made no poetic use until now. Under those conditions, and after long and much secret preparation, I wrote *Werther* in four weeks without ever making a plan of the whole or previously putting any of it down on paper.

And now the finished manuscript lay before me—the entire conception, with very few corrections or changes. I had it bound immediately, for covers are to a book what a frame is to a picture—they make it so much easier to see if the thing can really stand on its own. Since I had written this little volume more or less unconsciously, rather like a sleepwalker, it astonished me when I read it through with the idea of changing a few things and improving it. However, with the feeling that I might want to improve it after more time had elapsed and I could see it in better perspective, I now gave it to my young friends to read. Since, contrary to my usual habitude, I had told no one about it beforehand, nor had anyone been able to find out what I was up to, it made a tremendous impression. Of course, here again, the material was more effective than anything else, proving that their frame of mind was the exact opposite of mine—for I had saved myself from a tempestuous element with this composition, from a situation into which I had been driven through my own fault and the fault of others, through a chance and a chosen way of life, through intent and haste, through stubbornness and compliancy. I felt like a man after absolute confession—happy and free again, with the right to a new life. This time an old household remedy had done me a lot of good. But just as I felt relieved and lighthearted because I had succeeded in transforming reality into poetry, my friends were confusing themselves by believing that they had to turn poetry into reality, enact the novel and shoot themselves! What actually took place now among a few, happened later en masse, and this little book that had done me so much good acquired the reputation of being extremely harmful!

But all the evil that it is said to have done and the misfortune that is supposed to have brought in its wake were almost avoided by chance, for very soon after its completion, it was nearly destroyed. This came about in the following fashion:

Merck had just returned from Petersburg. He was always busy, so I didn't see much of him and was only able to tell him more or less generally about this book, *Werther*, that was so dear to my heart. One day he visited me, and since he didn't seem to have much to say, I begged him to listen to me. He sat down on the sofa and I began to read the work aloud, letter by letter. After I had been reading for a while without having been able to wring a word of praise from him, I began to hold forth with even more emotion. You can imagine how I felt when, during a pause, he dashed me completely by saying, "Well, that's quite nice," and, without another word, withdrew. I was beside myself. Although the things I wrote usually pleased me without my being able to pass any judgment on them at first, I now firmly believed that as far as subject matter, mood, and style were concerned—after all, every one of them was dubious—it was all wrong, and I had produced something impossible. If there had been a stove handy I would have thrown the whole thing into it, but I pulled myself together and lived through some painful days, until at last Merck confessed to me that he had been in the most dreadful predicament humanly possible when I had read the story to him. He had therefore not heard a word I had said and didn't have the slightest idea what the manuscript was about. In the meantime things had righted themselves, insofar as this was possible, and since Merck, in his energetic days, was the type who could bear even the most terrible fate, he regained his good humor, although he was more bitter now than ever before. He disapproved vehemently of my intention to revise *Werther* and demanded to see it in print just as it was. I had a clean copy made, but it did not remain in my hands long. Quite by chance, on the day my sister married George Schlosser, a letter came from Weygand in Leipzig, asking for the manuscript. The whole house was filled and glittering with the gay festivities, and I took the coincidence to be a good omen, sent *Werther* off, and was pleased when my fee was not swallowed up entirely by the debts I had incurred for *Götz von Berlichingen*.

The effect of *Werther* was great—indeed, one might say immense—and excellent because it came at exactly the right time. For just as only a small firing charge is needed to detonate a powerful mine, the explosion *Werther* caused was so far-reaching because the young people of that era had already undermined themselves; and the shock was so great because everyone could now burst forth with his own exaggerated demands, unsatisfied passions, and imaginary sufferings. The reader should not be asked to receive an intellectual work intellectually; the only thing he really pays any attention to is the content, the material, just as I had experienced with my friends, and this is usually accompanied by the old prejudice which the dignity of the printed word arouses—it should have a didactic purpose. But true representation has none. It neither approves nor disapproves but develops character and action chronologically and in that way illuminates and instructs.

I paid little attention to criticism. For me the book was finished, and all good people could digest it as they pleased. But of course my friends collected the reviews, and since they knew a little more about my opinions, they could have great fun with them. "The Joys of Young Werther," which was Nicolai's idea, provided us with plenty of laughs. This good, worthy, and knowledgeable man had already begun to suppress everything that did not suit his viewpoint, which, narrow-minded as he was, he felt was the only true one. He had to pit his strength against me, too, and his little brochure fell into our hands. Chodowiecki's very fine vignette gave me great pleasure. He was an artist whom I admired profoundly. But Nicolai's work was really cut of rough cloth. Oblivious of the fact that there was actually nothing much to be done about it, that the flowering of Werther's youth appears from the start as fatally blighted, the author let my version stand until page 214, and just when the deranged fellow is taking his last fatal step, this judicious psychic doctor lets his patient use a pistol that is loaded with chicken blood, which makes for quite a filthy mess but unfortunately does no further harm. Lotte marries Werther and the whole thing has a happy ending!

That's as much as I remember of it, for I never came across it again, but I cut out the vignette and put it away with my favorite engravings. Then, in a secret, harmless mood of revenge, I wrote a little satirical poem, "Nicolai at Werther's Grave," that I couldn't very well publish. The urge to dramatize everything was alive in me this time, too. I composed a dialogue in prose between Lotte and Werther that turned out to be quite funny. Werther complained bit-

terly that his salvation through chicken blood had ended so
badly. He had remained alive, true, but he had shot out his
eyes and was in despair because he was Lotte's husband but
could not see her, for the sight of her as a whole meant
more to him than the sweet details he could now assure
himself of only by feeling. Lotte, as can be imagined, wasn't
too happy either, with her blind husband, all of which offered an opportunity to give Nicolai a dressing down for
meddling, without being asked to, in affairs that were none
of his business. The whole thing was written drolly and was
in a way an early reaction to Nicolai's unfortunate and be-
nighted urge to concern himself with things to which he
wasn't equal, with the result that he soon made a lot of
difficulties for himself and others and in the end completely
lost his literary reputation. The original draft of this little
joke was never printed and has been lost for years. The
piece was a special favorite of mine. The pure and passionate feelings of the two characters were intensified rather
than weakened by the comic-tragic situation in which they
found themselves. The whole thing was handled tenderly;
I even treated the antagonist humorously, not bitterly. But
I wasn't so considerate when, paraphrasing an old rhyme, I
wrote:

> Presumptuous man! We'll let him
>   As dangerous me defame—
> A clumsy fellow who can't swim
>   The water likes to blame.
>
> What care I for the Berlin ban?
>   A bigoted lot, indeed!
> Let him who cannot understand
>   First of all learn to read!

Prepared as I was for any objections that might be raised
against *Werther,* such controversy didn't bother me in the
slightest, but I had not taken into consideration that sympathizing, well-wishing souls were going to become such an
unbearable nuisance. Instead of saying something nice
about the book just as it was, all of them wanted to know
how much of it was true! This made me very angry, and

my reply was invariably extremely rude. For, in order to answer this question, I would have had to tear apart and destroy the form of this little book over which I had brooded for such a long time to give it some elements of poetic unity; and the actual parts—even if they were not ruined—would have been scattered and dissipated. On second thought, I couldn't really blame these people. Jerusalem's fate had created a sensation. A cultured, likable, blameless young man, the son of a leading theologian and writer, healthy and well-to-do, suddenly decides to leave this world without any apparent reason. Everyone was asking how it could possibly have happened? When there was talk of an unhappy love affair, the young people became excited; when there was talk of the minor vexations he had encountered in high society, the middle class was in an uproar, and everyone wanted to know the facts. Now, in *Werther,* they had a comprehensive description in which they thought they could find the life and character of the young man. Locale and personalities were right, and the naturalness of the representation made them feel that now they knew all, and satisfied them. On the other hand, anyone who cared to take a closer look could find that many things did not fit; and those who were seeking the truth found it an unprofitable business, because the critics who like to sift things had to come up with quite a few doubtful factors. It turned out to be impossible to get to the bottom of the matter, because it was impossible to clarify what I had contributed to the composition from my own life and sufferings, since, as an unnoticed young man, I had lived my life, if not secretly, then certainly inconspicuously.

It had become evident to me as I worked, how advantageous it had been for the artist who was given the opportunity to compose a Venus out of many beauties.[17] Similarly, I took the liberty of composing Lotte according to the shape and characteristics of several pretty young girls, although I took her main features from the one I loved best. My investigative readers could therefore discover in her a similarity to several women, and it was not a matter of indifference to the ladies to believe that they were the one. This profusion of Lottes was a terrible nuisance because everyone who

even looked at me wanted to know where the real one was.
I tried to extricate myself like Nathan with the three rings,[18]
and took a way out that might have been very well suited
for loftier purposes but satisfied neither my credulous nor
my reading public. I hoped I would soon be rid of these
embarrassing inquiries, but unfortunately they pursued me
throughout my entire life. I tried to protect myself from
them by traveling incognito, but was thwarted in this respect as well. So, if I did something wrong or harmful in
writing *Werther,* I was certainly punished for it sufficiently—
I would say more than sufficiently—by all these inescapable
importunities.

Oppressed in this fashion, I became only too aware of
the fact that the author and his public are separated by an
immense abyss, both of them fortunately having no idea of
its dimensions. And I had recognized long ago how useless
all forewords were, for the more one tries to explain one's
intentions, the more confusion one causes. The author may
write as many prefaces as he likes, the reader will always
go right on demanding that which the author is trying to
avoid. I also came in contact early with a related and hu-
morous attribute of the reader who likes to see his opinions
in print. He lives in the delusion that, because the author
has accomplished something, he has become the critic's
debtor, and of course the author always falls short of the
mark, even if the man—before he saw the work—hadn't
the slightest idea that any such thing existed or was even
possible.

But putting all this aside, the greatest good fortune—or
disaster—was the fact that everyone wanted to know more
about the strange young author who had suddenly put in
such a bold appearance. They demanded to see me and talk
to me; those far away wanted to hear something about me.
I therefore experienced a high degree of popularity that was
sometimes pleasant, sometimes disagreeable, and always
distracting. For plenty of unfinished work lay before me—
in fact I had things planned that would take years to complete, even if I applied myself to them ardently. But I had
been dragged out of my stillness, out of the twilight and
darkness that alone favor the purity of creation, into the
noise of daytime, where one loses oneself in others and

becomes confused by sympathy as well as by coldness, by praise as well as by reproof, for these external encounters never coincide with the present stage of one's inner life. Therefore, since they cannot benefit us, they must do us harm.

GOETHE
IN SESENHEIM

Very few biographies succeed in portraying the straightforward, serene, and regular progress of an individual. Our life is like the Allness in which we are contained, and it is put together in an unfathomable fashion out of freedom and necessity. Our intention is a foretelling of what we are going to do under any circumstances, but these "circumstances" affect us in their own way. The "what" of things lies in us, the "how" rarely depends on us, and we are not allowed to ask "why." We are therefore justly advised to say "because."

—GOETHE,
Dichtung und Wahrheit, Book XI

How far behind I was in all things concerning modern literature is demonstrated quite clearly by the kind of life I led in Frankfurt and what I chose to study there, and my sojourn in Strassburg did very little for me in this respect. Then Herder came, bringing with him—apart from his profound knowledge—so many other resources, and the latest writings. Among these, he assured us that *The Vicar of Wakefield* was an excellent work and he intended to intro-

Excerpts from *Aus Meinem Leben: Dichtung und Wahrheit*, Book X, published in 1812, and Books XI and XII, published in 1814.

duce it to us by reading the German translation aloud to us himself.

His way of reading aloud was unique. Whoever has heard him preach will have some idea of it. He propounded everything, including this piece of fiction, earnestly and simply. Far from seeking any dramatic effects, he even avoided the diversity of expression that is not only permissible but actually prerequisite for epic delivery—a slight change of expression when more than one character is speaking so that what each man says stands out and the actor is separated from whoever is telling the story. Without being monotonous, Herder read aloud in *one* tone, as if nothing were happening in the present but everything were historical, as if the shades of these poetic creatures were not behaving in a lively fashion but were only passing gently by. Even so, coming from him, this way of reading had infinite charm because he felt deeply everything that was happening and knew how to appreciate the diversity of such fiction. The result was that its merits stood out all the more clearly and purely, since one was not disturbed or jolted out of one's impressions by any sharply expressed detail, all of which served to make a lasting impression.

A Protestant country clergyman is perhaps the most beautiful subject for a modern idyl; he appears like Melchizedek, as priest and king in one, and he can be associated with the most innocent of all conditions—that of a tiller of the soil—because his occupation is very often similar, and his family relationships may well be the same. He is father, master of his house, a man of the earth, and thus completely a member of the community. His lofty profession rests on this clear and beautiful terrestrial foundation. It has been entrusted to him to lead his flock through this life, to attend to their spiritual education, to bless them at all the major milestones of their existence, to give them strength and console them, and, when the comfort he can give is inadequate for their present misery, it is he who invokes and guarantees the hope for a happier future. If one can conjure up such a man, with pure human convictions and strong-minded enough not to deviate from them under any circumstances—which already elevates him above the multitude from whom purity and resoluteness cannot be expected—if one gives this man the knowledge that goes with his office, and a blithe, even-tempered way of officiating that may even be called passionate, since he never misses an opportunity to do good, then one can say that he has been well equipped. At the same time, one should endow him with the modesty necessary to endure life, not only in his own small circle—he should be capable of passing over into even narrower confines. He should be given good humor, a forgiving heart, steadfastness, and every other laudable attribute that stands out in any resolute character and, above all, a gay tractability and smiling tolerance of his own mistakes and those of others, and we have more or less assembled our admirable Wakefield.

The description of this character as he experiences joy and suffering and the growing interest of the story itself through a combination of the completely natural with the extraordinary, make this novel one of the best ever written. In addition, it has the great advantage of being utterly moral and, in the purest sense, Christian. It demonstrates the rewarding of good and the perseverance of justice; it reaffirms an unquestioning faith in God and confirms the final triumph of good over evil—and all this without a trace of bigotry or pedantry. The author was preserved from both pitfalls by a fine intuition that makes itself felt throughout as irony, enabling this little work of art to make an impression that is not only pleasant but wise. The author, Dr. Goldsmith, unquestionably has great insight into the world of morality, its values and frailties; at the same time, he should acknowledge gratefully the fact that he is an Englishman and should rate highly the advantages his country has to offer. The family he describes lives on the very lowest level of social comfort yet comes in contact with the highest; their narrow circle, which in the course of the story becomes even more constricted, intervenes in the events of a larger world via quite natural and bourgeois course of events; their little bark moves on the rich, agitated waves of English life and can expect harm or aid in good or ill fortune from the immense fleet sailing all around it.

I am taking for granted that my reader knows this work and remembers it, but whoever hears about it here for the first time as well as he who may be stimulated to read it again, both will thank me for it. For them I would like to say, just in passing, that the vicar's wife is a good, active

soul who doesn't let herself or her dear ones lack anything
and consequently thinks quite well of herself and them. And
I do not want to leave out two daughters—Olivia, beautiful
and inclined to be superficial, and Sophie, charming and
more serious—and a diligent, rather austere son who tries
to emulate his father.

If Herder could be reproached for one thing when he
read aloud, then it was his impatience. He couldn't wait
until his hearers had heard and grasped a certain aspect of
the events and felt them properly, as was their due; he was
always in a hurry to see the effect they made, yet wasn't
pleased with what he saw when it was produced! He reprimanded me for an excess of emotion, which overflowed step
by step as we moved along. I experienced everything he
read as a human being, and as a young man. All of it came
to life for me, was true and present. But he, who paid
attention only to content and form, of course noticed at
once that I was letting myself be overwhelmed only by the
events, and he didn't approve of that. Pegelow's reflections,
which were not the most refined, made an even worse impression on him. But he was especially furious over our lack
of discernment—that we didn't foresee the contracts of
which the author made so much use, but let ourselves be
touched and carried away by them without noticing the literary devices that turned up again and again. He couldn't
forgive us for not recognizing or at least suspecting, right
at the beginning, that Burchell, when he switches from the
third person to the first in the course of something he is
telling, is actually the lord of whom he is speaking, and
when we were childishly delighted over the discovery and
transformation of a poor, miserable wanderer into a rich
and eminent gentleman, he referred us back to the place
we had overlooked, just as the author intended; and gave
us a lecture berating our stupidity. It is clear, therefore,
that he looked upon the novel only as a work of art and
expected the same of us, who were still meandering along
in the condition in which it is permissible to let a work of
art affect one like a product of nature.

I did not let Herder's invectives confuse me in the slightest, for young people have the good or bad fortune that
they must assimilate anything that has affected them by

themselves. Sometimes this has good, sometimes disastrous results. *The Vicar of Wakefield* made a very strong impression on me, which I could not rightly account for. All in all, though, I was in agreement with the irony that raises itself above circumstances, above happiness and misfortune, good and evil, life and death, and can thus embrace a truly poetic world. I became conscious of this, naturally, only much later; just the same, even at the time, it gave me plenty of food for thought. But I had never expected to be removed from this fictitious world into a similar real one.

Weyland, my companion at table, who from time to time brightened his tranquil, industrious life by visiting friends and relatives in Alsace—he was born there—was most helpful to me on my short excursions in that he introduced me to various places and families, sometimes personally, sometimes by recommending them to me. He had spoken to me often of a country parson who had a good parish six hours from Strassburg, near Drusenheim, where he lived with an intelligent wife and two attractive daughters. Whenever Weyland spoke of the family, he praised their hospitality and charm. More was scarcely necessary to inspire a young horseman who had already formed the habit of spending all his leisurely days and hours riding in the fresh air. So we decided to take this little trip, and I made my friend promise to say nothing good or bad about me when he introduced me. He was to treat me with indifference and permit me to appear, not exactly badly dressed, but looking rather poor and neglected. He agreed and seemed to think he would get some fun out of it, too.

To lay aside his material advantages on occasion and let his own innermost, human aspects shine forth more clearly, is an excusable caprice in the eminent man. That is why princes traveling incognito and the adventures resulting from it somehow always have a pleasant effect. Gods appear disguised and can count every kindness they receive double, and are in a position to take every unpleasantness lightly or go out of its way. That Jupiter with Philemon and Baucis, or Henry IV among his peasants after the hunt, enjoyed being incognito is as natural as it is pleasing. But that a young man of no importance or fame should hit upon the idea to get some fun out of traveling disguised, might seem unpardonable arrogance to some people. However, our interest here is not in applauding or criticizing this viewpoint and these actions but rather in determining how much they reveal and what the results are, so let us, this time at least and for our entertainment, forgive the young man his presumption, all the more since I must add that the urge to disguise myself had been alive in me ever since I could remember and was even stimulated by my very serious father.

With some of my own old things and a few borrowed items, and by the way I combed my hair, I did not exactly disfigure myself—still, I was so marvelously put together that my friend couldn't restrain his laughter as we rode along, especially since I could imitate perfectly the position and behavior of persons who, when they are on horseback, are referred to as "bookworm" riders. The beautiful highway, the glorious weather, and the proximity of the Rhine put us in the best of moods. We stopped for a few moments in Drusenheim—Weyland to spruce up, I to find my way back into my characterization, which I was very much afraid of losing. The region there has all the characteristics of Alsace—it is wide open and flat. We rode across fields on a pretty little footpath and soon reached Sesenheim, where we left our horses at the inn and walked in a leisurely fashion to the parsonage.

"Don't let yourself be misled because it looks like a poor old peasant house," Weyland said, pointing out the house from a distance. "For that it's all the younger inside."

We walked into the courtyard. The whole place appealed to me because it was what is called picturesque, a quality that enchants me in all Dutch works of art. The effect time produces on human handiwork was very evident. House, barn, and stables were in just that condition of deterioration in which, undecided between preservation and reconstruction, one fails to do the former without being able to make up one's mind to attend to the latter.

It was quiet, there was no one about, not in the village nor in the courtyard. We found the vicar alone—a slight, reserved, yet friendly man. His family was out in the fields. He bade us welcome and offered us refreshment, which we declined. My friend hurried off to find the girls and I remained alone with our host.

"You are perhaps astonished," he said, "to find me so poorly housed in a prosperous village, and in a quite lucrative office, but that is the result of a lack of decision. For a long time now the community, or I should say, those in high positions, have been promising to rebuild my house. Several plans have been made, studied, and altered, but none has been completely rejected or carried out. All this has taken so many years that I don't know how to contain my impatience."

I said what I considered the correct thing to strengthen his hopes and encourage him in following the matter up. He went on, confidentially, to describe the persons on whom such matters depended, and although he was not a very good outliner of character, still I was able to get quite a good impression of how the whole business had come to a standstill. There was something unique about the man's truthfulness. He spoke to me as if he had known me for ten years, yet there was nothing in his expression to let me think that he was paying any attention to me. At last, Weyland came in with the vicar's wife, who seemed to see me with different eyes. His features were regular, her expression highly intelligent. In her youth she must have been beautiful. She was tall and rather gaunt, but not more than went suitably with her age. From the back, she still looked quite young and attractive. Then her oldest daughter came storming gaily into the room. She asked after Friederike, as did the other two. The father declared he hadn't seen her since all three of them had left. The daughter rushed out of the room again to look for her sister, the mother brought some refreshment, and Weyland continued his conversation with the couple, all of it about persons and situations that were known to all concerned, as is customary when acquaintances meet after a long separation and want to find out what has been going on among members of a quite large circle and take turns in exchanging information. I listened and soon found out what I could expect from this little group.

The older daughter burst into the room again, agitated because she had not found her sister. She and her mother seemed worried about her and spoke reprovingly of this and that bad habit of hers, but her father said quietly, "Let her go. She'll come back." And just then she actually did appear and truly a most adorable star rose into this pastoral sky with her coming. Both girls were still dressed "German," as it was called, and this folk costume, which has almost disappeared, suited Friederike exceptionally well. A short, wide, circular skirt with a flounce, not so long but that it left her pretty little feet visible to the ankle; a tight, white bodice and black taffeta apron—there she stood on the borderline between peasant and town girl. Slender and light, she came into the room as if she had no weight to carry, and the heavy blonde braids that hung down from her charming little head seemed almost too heavy for her delicate neck. She glanced brightly about with her blue eyes and stuck her little turned-up nose courageously into the air, as if there couldn't possibly be a care in the world. Her straw hat hung on her arm. That was how I had the pleasure of seeing her first and recognizing her in all her charm and sweetness.

I now began to play my part more moderately. I was a little ashamed to be deceiving such good people, whom I could go right on observing, for the girls picked up the conversation with *élan*. Every neighbor and relative was introduced all over again, and a swarm of uncles and aunts, cousins, people coming and going, godfathers and guests was presented to my imagination and made me feel at home in the liveliest of worlds. Every member of the family addressed a few words to me. The mother gave me a look every time she came in or went out, but Friederike was the first to start a conversation with me. When I picked up some music that was lying around and began to leaf through it, she asked me if I played. When I said yes, she begged me to play something for them. Her father, however, wouldn't hear of it; he declared that the proper thing was to entertain one's guests first with a piece or a song.

Friederike played several pieces quite fluently, as people play who live in the country, and this on a piano that the schoolmaster was supposed to have tuned long ago, if he had had the time. Then she went on to sing a certain tender, sad song, but this she could not do at all. She stood up and, with a smile—or rather, with the serene, radiant expression she seemed to wear constantly—said, "If I sing badly, I cannot blame the piano and the schoolmaster. But let us go outside—then you can hear my Alsatian and Swiss songs. They sound much better."

During supper, I was absorbed with a revelation that had already struck me a while before and I became thoughtful and silent, although the liveliness of the older sister and charm of the younger girl served often enough to shake me out of my reflections. I was astonished beyond words to find myself actually in the Wakefield family! The father, of course, could not be compared with that admirable man, but then, where could one find his equal? On the other hand, all the dignity inherent in that good husband could be found in this man's wife. You could not look at her without respecting yet fearing her at the same time. She displayed all the marks of a good upbringing—she was calm, poised, gay, and hospitable.

The older daughter did not, perhaps, possess Olivia's famed beauty, but she had a good figure and was lively, almost too lively. She busied herself with everything and helped her mother with whatever she was doing. To put Friederike in the place of Primrose's Sophie was not difficult, for Sophie gets so little mention. All that is said of her is that she is amiable, and the girl certainly was that. Since a similarity of office and circumstances, wherever they turn up, have similar if not the same effect, quite a few things came up for discussion here that had occurred in the Primrose family. But when, in the end, a young son, whose arrival had been announced some time before and whose father was awaiting him impatiently, came bounding into the room and brashly sat down with us, paying practically no attention to his father's guests, I could scarcely keep myself from crying, "Moses, *you* are here, too?"

The conversation at table broadened my vision of the county and family circle as the talk centered upon all sorts of amusing things that had happened in one place or another. Friederike, who sat next to me, took this opportunity to describe to me the various places that apparently were worth visiting. Since one story invariably produces another,

I was now better able to take part in the conversation and tell of similar events, and since no one was being sparing with the wine while all this was going on, I was in great danger of falling out of character. However, my cautious friend, Weyland, used the beautiful moonlight as an excuse to suggest a walk, an idea that was immediately popular. He gave the older girl his arm, I gave mine to the younger, and so we wandered across the wide pastures, the heavens above us more real than the earth below, which was lost in space all around us. But there was no moonlight in Friederike's chatter. The clarity with which she spoke made day of night, and though she said nothing that might have indicated any sentiment, what she said was directed more than ever at me, as she introduced herself, the region, and her friends, from the viewpoint of how *I* would get to know them, because, she explained, she hoped that I would not be an exception but would visit them again, as every stranger had done who had ever come to see them.

I found it very pleasant to listen silently to her describe the small world in which she moved and to hear her speak of the people whom she especially esteemed. In this way she gave me a very clear and, at the same time, charming idea of her condition, and it had a quite miraculous effect on me. Suddenly I felt deeply chagrined that I had had no part in her life before and was embarrassingly envious of everything that had had the good fortune to surround her until now. I at once began to pay close attention—as if I had the right to do so—to any description of men, whether they turned up in the shape of neighbor, cousin, or godfather, and let my conjectures run wild. But how could I hope to uncover anything with no knowledge whatsoever of the situation? In the end, she became more and more talkative and I more and more silent. Listening to her was just too enjoyable, and since all I could do was hear her voice while her features, like the rest of the world, floated in the twilight, it was as if I were looking into her heart, and I found it very chaste as she laid it bare before me in her uninhibited chatter.

When my traveling companion and I retired to the guest room that had been prepared for us, he at once began to joke complacently, very pleased with himself for having

managed to surprise me so completely with this replica of
the Primrose family. I agreed with him and expressed my
gratitude. "Truly," he said, "the fantasy is completely
cast. The family is exactly like that one, and you can pass
for Mr. Burchell. Furthermore, since we don't need villains so badly in real life as we do in novels, I am perfectly
willing to play the nephew and behave better than he!"

I immediately changed the subject—pleasant as it was—
and asked him before anything else, could he swear that he
truly hadn't given me away? He assured me he had not,
and I could see that he was telling the truth. They had
peppered him with questions, he said, about his jolly companion who ate with him in the same pension in Strassburg,
of whom they had heard all sorts of conflicting reports. I
then went on to another question: Had she ever been in
love? Was she in love with anyone now? Was she engaged?
He replied to all my questions in the negative. "I must say,"
I declared, "such a blithe spirit by nature is unbelievable.
If she had loved and lost and found herself again, or if she
were betrothed, that I could grasp."

So we chatted far into the night, and I was wide awake
with the dawn. The desire to see her again was uncontrollable, but as I was getting dressed, my accursed wardrobe,
which I had so wantonly chosen to put on, shocked me. The
further I progressed with my dressing, the more despicable I
felt—after all, everything was based on this effect. I could
have resigned myself to my hair, but after I had finally
managed to ram myself into my borrowed gray, threadbare
jacket, with its sleeves that were much too short, I saw
how really impossible I looked; and I became even more
desperate when I couldn't get a full view of myself in the
little mirror and each part of me that I could see looked
more ridiculous than the rest.

During this procedure of getting dressed, my friend had
awakened and, with the satisfaction of a clear conscience,
was looking about him from the protection of the pink silk
comforter, filled with joyful hope for the day. I had already
envied him his fine clothes draped over a chair, and if he
had been my size, I would have decamped with them before
his very eyes, changed outside and hurried into the garden,
leaving him my accursed shell. He would have been good-

natured enough to put on my apparel and the deception
would have come to a jolly end in the early morning. But
there could be no thought of that nor of any other suitable
intervention. However, I was determined not to appear
again in the shape that had made it possible for him to pass
me off as an industrious and clever but poor student of
theology to Friederike, who had chatted in such a friendly
fashion with my disguised self the night before. There I
stood, vexed and brooding, mustering all my inventive
powers—alas, they had forsaken me. But then, when my
comfortably outstretched friend, after having stared
fixedly at me for a few moments, suddenly burst into up-
roarious laughter and cried, "No! But truly, you look
ghastly!" I replied violently, "And I know what I am
going to do about it. Farewell. You are going to have to
excuse me."

"Are you mad?" he cried, jumping out of bed with the
idea of stopping me, but I was already out the door and
down the stairs. Leaving house and yard behind me, I
headed for the inn. In no time, my horse was saddled and
I galloped off to Drusenheim in a tearing bad temper,
through that town, and onward.

When I felt safe, I began to ride more slowly and realized
only then how reluctant I was to withdraw. But I bowed to
my fate, calmly recalled last night's walk, and quietly nourished the hope that I would see Friederike again soon. But
this calm was soon transformed into impatience again, and
I decided to ride quickly into the city, change, take a fresh
horse, and then—according to the reflections of my passion—I could be back in Sesenheim before lunch, or what
was more probable, after lunch, at any rate, toward evening, and could beg to be forgiven.

I was about to give my horse the spurs when another
thought occurred to me, a splendid idea. The day before,
in Drusenheim, I had noticed the innkeeper's very neatly
dressed son. Early this morning, busy with his rustic chores,
he had greeted me from the farmyard. He was built like me
and had fleetingly reminded me of myself. No sooner said
than done! I had scarcely turned my horse around and I
was in Drusenheim again. I rode to the stable and without
much further ado made my suggestion to the boy—he was

to lend me his clothes because I had a little joke planned
in Sesenheim. I didn't have to finish my story; he accepted
my proposition gleefully and praised me for wanting to provide the "mamsells" with some fun. They were such good,
kind girls, especially "Mamsell Riekchen," and their parents
liked things cheerful and gay too. He looked me over carefully, and since he could only take me for a poor fellow,
judging by the way I was clad, he said, "If you want to get
on the good side of them, you're doing the right thing."
We had meanwhile come quite far along in my transformation, and he really shouldn't have entrusted his best suit
to me in exchange for what I had on, but he was a trusting
fellow and, after all, he had my horse. Soon I was standing there, looking quite smart. I thrust out my chest, and
my friend seemed pleased as he looked at his counterpart.
"Very fine, brother," he said, stretching out his hand,
which I grasped firmly. "But I would advise you not to
get too close to my girl. She might try to make up to
you!"

My hair had grown long again, and I was able to part it
to resemble his, and looking at him again and again, I
found it amusing to imitate his thicker eyebrows with a
burnt cork and draw them closer together in the middle—
in short, I made myself look as questionable as my project. As he handed me his beribboned hat, I asked him,
"Isn't there any errand you have to do at the parsonage
that would allow me to announce myself in a natural fashion?" "There is," he said, "but then you must wait two
hours. We have a woman in labor here. I'll offer to de-
liver the christening cake to the parson's wife and you can
take it over. Vanity must learn to endure hardships, and
so must a prank!"

I decided to wait, but the two hours that followed seemed
interminable, and I was dying of impatience as the third
dragged by before the cake came out of the oven. At last
I had it, still warm, and hurried off with my credential in
the most glorious sunshine, accompanied for a short while
by my counterpart, who offered to come after me toward
evening and bring my clothes. But I rejected his offer hastily
and reserved the right to return his to him.

I hadn't gone far with my offering, which I was carrying

wrapped in a clean napkin, when I saw my friend and the two girls in the distance, coming toward me. I felt uneasy, which somehow didn't go well with the jacket I was wearing. Stopping to catch my breath, I tried to think what I should do; then I noticed that the terrain was to my advantage, for they were walking on the other side of the stream that, with the strip of meadow through which it flowed, kept the two footpaths quite wide apart. When they were abreast of me, Friederike, who had caught sight of me earlier, cried out, "George, what have you got there?" I was smart enough to raise my hat and let it cover my face as I held the napkin with its contents high up in the air. "The christening cake!" she cried, when she saw it. "How is your sister?" "Very well," I replied. I couldn't speak their Alsatian dialect, but I did my best to speak in a foreign fashion. "Take it to the house," said the oldest girl, "and if you can't find Mother, give it to the maid. But wait for us, we won't be long, do you hear?"

I hurried on my way with a happy feeling, my hopes high that all would go well since the thing had started off so propitiously, and I soon reached the parsonage. I found no one there, not in house nor kitchen; I didn't want to disturb the parson, who I felt must be busy in his study, so I sat down on a bench outside, next to the door, the cake at my side, and rammed my hat down on my face.

I cannot remember ever having felt more pleased with myself. To be sitting on this threshold again, over which I had stumbled in such despair a short while before, to have seen her again and heard her sweet voice once more, so shortly after my despair had envisioned a long separation, to be expecting her at any moment, and my unmasking—a thought that made my heart beat fast, although in this ambiguous case, it was a disclosure of which I did not have to be ashamed and such a good joke, right away on entering, better than any laughed over the day before! Truly, love and need are the best matters! Here they were working hand in hand, and their apprentice had proved himself equal to them!

But the maid came out of the barn, "Well," she said, "how did the cake turn out? And how is your sister?" "All are well," I said, pointing to the cake without looking up.

She took it and grumbled, "What's the matter with you today? Has Barbara looked at somebody else again? That's going to be a nice marriage, is all I can say, if you two go on like that." Since she spoke in quite a loud voice, it brought the vicar to his window, and he wanted to know what was going on. She told him. I got up and turned toward him, again holding my hat before my face. He said a few friendly words and told me to stay, whereupon I walked over toward the garden. I was about to enter it when the vicar's wife came into the yard and called out to me. The sun happened to be shining in my face. So I again made use of the advantage offered by my hat and greeted her with a bow. She went into the house after calling out to me not to leave without having partaken of some refreshment.

I proceeded to walk up and down in the garden. Until now, everything had been a complete success; still, I drew a deep breath as I reflected that very soon the young people would be returning. But the mother came back quite unexpectedly and was about to ask me a question when she looked into my face, which I could no longer hide, and her words remained stuck in her throat. "I was expecting to find George," she said after a little pause, "and whom do I find? Is it really you, young man? How many shapes do you have?"

"Seriously speaking," I replied, "only one; but in fun, as many as you like."

"I don't want to spoil your fun," she said, smiling. "Why don't you go beyond the gardens toward the fields and stay there until noon? Then you can come back; meanwhile, I shall have paved the way for your little joke."

I did as she suggested, but when I had passed the hedges of the village gardens and was about to enter a field, I could see, to my embarrassment, some countryfolk coming toward me on the footpath. I therefore turned off in the direction of a small glade that crowned a nearby hill to hide there until the time agreed upon. Imagine my surprise when, on entering, I found myself in a clearing with benches, from each of which one had a very pretty view of the region. There was the village and the steeple, yonder lay Drusenheim, behind it the wooded Rhine islands, the Vosges

Mountains opposite, and finally, the Strassburg Cathedral. All these varied, heavenly-light vistas were enclosed in bushy green frames. The result was the most delightful sight imaginable. I sat down on one of the benches and noticed, on one of the stoutest trees, a small board with the inscription, "Friederike's Rest." It never occurred to me that I might have come to disturb that rest, for the beauty of a burgeoning passion is that it is not conscious of its source nor can it have any idea of how it is going to end; and when it is happy and carefree, there can be no suspicion that one day it may do harm.

I had scarcely time to look around me and was just losing myself in a sweet dreaminess when I heard someone coming. It was Friederike herself. "George," she cried from afar, "what are you doing here?" "Not George," I called out as I ran to meet her, "but one who begs to be forgiven." She looked at me, astounded, but at once pulled herself together and, after drawing a deep breath, said, "You horrid man! How you startled me!"

"My first masquerade drove me to the second," I explained, "and the first would have been unpardonable if I had known to whom I was going. You will forgive me the second, I am sure, because it portrays a person to whom you are friendly."

Now her pale cheeks were suffused with the loveliest pink. "Well, I am certainly not going to treat you worse than George," she said. "But let us sit down. I must confess that the shock has made me feel shaky."

I sat down beside her, deeply moved. "We know what happened up to this morning," she said. "Your friend told us everything. Now you tell the rest."

I didn't have to be urged twice, but described my repugnance for the figure I had cut the day before and my stormy departure from the house in such a droll fashion that she laughed heartily and enchantingly. Then I told her the rest, modestly yet passionately enough to pass for a declaration of love in narrative form. At the end, I celebrated the joy of finding her again by kissing her hand, and she let it rest in mine. The night before, on our moonlit walk, she had taken the burden of the conversation upon herself; now I did my share extravagantly. The joy of seeing her again, of

being able to tell her everything I had had to hold back
yesterday, was so great that in my talkativeness I did not
notice that this time she was thoughtful and silent. Once or
twice she drew a deep breath, and I begged her over and
over again to forgive me for startling her. I don't know how
long we sat there, but suddenly we heard a voice crying,
"Riekchen! Riekchen!" It was her sister.

"This is going to make a wonderful story," the dear girl
said, suddenly blithe again. "She is coming up on my side,"
she went on, leaning forward a little to hide me. "Turn
away a bit so that she doesn't recognize you at once." Her
sister walked into the clearing, but she was not alone. Weyland was with her, and both of them stood still as if petrified
when they saw us.

If we were to see a flame suddenly shoot forth from a
peaceful rooftop or meet a monster with an outrageous de-
formity, we could not be more horrified than when we saw
with our own eyes, something that we believe is morally
impossible. "What is the meaning of this?" the older girl
cried, with the haste of someone startled. "What does it
mean . . . you and George . . . hand in hand . . . what am
I supposed . . ."

"My dear sister," Friederike said very seriously, "the
poor fellow . . . he has asked me to forgive him. He wants
your forgiveness, too, but you must promise in advance that
you will forgive him."

"I don't understand, I don't understand," said her sister,
shaking her head and looking at Weyland, who in his calm
way stood there quietly watching the scene. Friederike got
up, pulling me up after her.

"Don't hesitate!" she cried. "Forgiveness asked for and
granted!"

"And in truth, I need it," I said, as I approached the girl.

She stepped back, let out a loud scream, and blushed
furiously, then she threw herself on the grass, laughing up-
roariously, and simply couldn't get over it. Weyland smiled
amiably and said, "You're an excellent fellow!" Then he
shook hands with me. Ordinarily he was not affectionate,
so there was something hearty and refreshing about his
handshake, yet he was chary with it, too.

After a short pause to permit the two to recover their

composure, we started back to the village. On our way I heard how this miraculous meeting had come about. Toward the end of their walk, Friederike had left the other two in order to rest in her favorite spot for a while before lunch, and when they had reached home, the girl's mother had sent them to fetch her, because lunch was ready.

Friederike's sister was wild with glee, and when she heard that her mother already knew the secret, she cried, "Then all that is left is for Papa, my brother, the groom, and the maid to be tricked!" When we reached the garden hedge, she made Friederike walk on ahead to the house with Weyland. The maid was busy in the garden, and Olivia (we might just as well call the older sister that) cried out to her, "Listen! I have something to tell you!" Leaving me by the hedge, she went over to the girl. I saw them talking earnestly. Olivia was telling her that George had quarreled with Barbara; and wanted to marry her. The maid didn't seem averse to the idea, and now they called me over to confirm what had been said. The pretty girl—she was a trifle coarse—lowered her eyes and remained standing like that until I was quite close to her. But then, when she suddenly saw my strange face, she too let out a loud scream and ran off. Olivia told me to go after her and catch her, so that she should not run into the house and noise everything abroad; while she would go and see where her father was. On the way, she met the stableboy who was courting the maid. I meanwhile had caught the girl and was holding her fast. "Just think!" Olivia cried. "It's all over between George and Barbara. He's going to marry Lisa."

"That's what I've been thinking for a long time," the boy said and remained standing there, looking morose.

I told the maid that all we wanted was to play the joke on the vicar. We walked over to the boy, who turned his back on us and tried to get away, but Lisa ran and fetched him back, and he too—when he realized that he had been duped—carried on in a wonderful fashion. Then all of us went up to the house together. The table was set, the vicar was already in the room. Olivia, who was holding onto me behind her, walked in the doorway and asked, "Papa, is it all right if George eats with us today? But you must let him keep his hat on."

"It makes no difference to me," the old man said, "but why something so unusual? Has he hurt himself?"

She dragged me forward, just as I was, with my hat on. "No," she said, "but he has a brood of birds under it. They'd fly out and create a devilish uproar because they're very wild birds."

The vicar didn't resent the joke, although he couldn't make out what it was all about. But then she took my hat off for me, bowed low and demanded that I do the same. The old man gave me a look, recognized me, but never lost his clerical dignity for a moment. "Well, well!" he said, raising a warning finger. "If it isn't my bright young theologian! You certainly managed to change horses quickly, and overnight I've lost an assistant who only yesterday promised me faithfully that he would go up into the pulpit for me sometimes." He laughed heartily, bade me welcome, and we sat down at table. Moses came in only much later. Being the youngest and rather spoiled, he had formed the habit of not hearing the stroke of twelve. Moreover, he paid little attention to those present, even when he spoke. In order to make sure he would be fooled, I was not seated between the sisters but at the end of the table, where George sometimes actually did sit. When Moses came in, my back was turned to him. He slapped me on the shoulder roughly and said, "Good appetite, George!" "Thank you, sir," I replied. My strange voice, and then my face, startled him. "Isn't it amazing?" cried Olivia.

"Yes, indeed," he replied, recovering quickly. "From the back you could take him for anybody."

He didn't give me another glance but busied himself exclusively with swallowing the courses he had missed as fast as he could. Every now and then, he took it upon himself to get up from table and attend to something in yard or garden. During the dessert, the real George came in and enlivened the proceedings even more. Everyone teased him about his jealousy and declared that they didn't approve at all of his having dressed me up to be his rival. But he was a modest fellow and quite adroit, and knew how to get his betrothed, me—his counterpart—and the young ladies, all mixed up in such a tipsy fashion that, in the end, nobody knew who was being talked about, and everyone was glad to let him enjoy his christening cake and glass of wine in peace.

When the meal was over, there was talk of going for a walk, which wasn't very well possible with me in my peasant garb. But already that morning, when they had discovered who had left the house in such a hurry, the girls had remembered that a perfectly good jacket, belonging to a cousin, was hanging in the clothes press, a coat in which he hunted when he was there. But I declined the offer, ostensibly making a joke of it, but inwardly with the vain emotion of not wanting to spoil, as the cousin, the good impression I had made as a peasant. The vicar had left the room to take his nap; his wife was busy with her household duties, as usual. My friend Weyland suggested that I tell a story, to which I at once agreed. We retired to a roomy summerhouse, and I told them a tale I have since written down called "The New Melusina."[19] It compares with "The New Paris"[20] like a young man to a boy, and I would insert it here were I not afraid of interrupting the pleasant pastoral realism and simplicity that surround us now. Anyway, I succeeded in achieving the desired reward of a creator and raconteur of such tales—I aroused the curiosity of my listeners; held their attention and inspired them to seek an earlier solution to the impenetrable puzzle; dashed their expectations by putting something even more extraordinary in place of what was already strange; confused them; aroused pity and fear; worried them; touched them and in the end satisfied them emotionally by twisting what had looked serious into an ingenious and amusing joke, leaving their imaginations with the material to crate new pictures, and their minds with food for thought.

If anyone should one day find the tale in print and read it and doubt that it could have such an effect, he should reflect that man is really only qualified to make an impression in the present. Writing is a misuse of language; reading alone quietly is a sad substitute for talk. A man makes every impression he possibly can on others through his personality—the young most powerfully on the young—and that is where the purest effects are achieved. It is the young who enliven the world and don't let it die, either morally or physically. From my father I inherited a certain pedagogic loquacity; from my mother the ability to represent clearly and gaily everything my imagination could evoke and grasp, to revive familiar fairy tales and invent new ones, invent them even as I talked. My father's heritage often made me rather a trial to be with, for who likes to hear the opinions and convictions of others, especially of a young man whose judgment must seem inadequate because of the gaps in his experience? My mother, on the other hand, had equipped me rather well for sociability and conversation, and I soon discovered that the most insubstantial fairy tale holds a certain charm for the imagination, and the slightest content is often gratefully received.

Through entertainment such as this, which cost me nothing, I made myself popular with children, excited and delighted young people and attracted the attention of older ones. But in the common run of society, I soon had to put a stop to such habits, and so deprived myself of a lively enjoyment and found the powers of my imagination curtailed. But both these parental gifts accompanied me throughout my entire life, with a third—the urge to express myself metaphorically and in parables. The brilliant and judicious Dr. Gall[21] recognized these traits in me and declared that, according to his teaching, I was born to be a public speaker. This startled me somewhat, for if there was any truth in it, anything else I might undertake—since in my nation there simply was no forum for such a career—would unfortunately be a wrong profession![22]

When I had finished my tale in the summerhouse in Sesenheim—a story in which ordinary events and the improbable were pleasantly interwoven—I could see that the two young ladies, who had listened with unusual attentiveness, were enchanted by my strange invention. They begged me to write it down so that they might read it aloud among themselves and to others. I promised to do so, all the more happily because this gave me an excuse to visit them again, and the chance of a closer association. We parted company for a short while, and anyone could have feared that, after such a lively day, the evening might be dull. But my friend relieved me of this anxiety by suggesting that we leave right away. He was a very studious fellow, most conscientious about his work, and wanted to spend the night in Drusen-heim in order to be in Strassburg early the next morning.

We reached our quarters in silence, I, because my heart was dragging me back to Sesenheim, he, because something else was on his mind. When we had arrived at our destination, he told me about it. "It is really extraordinary," he said, "that you should have hit upon just this tale. Didn't you notice that it made a quite unusual impression?" "Of course I did," I replied. "How could I help noticing that in some places the older girl laughed more than was called for and the younger one sat there shaking her head? And I also saw you looking at each other knowingly every now and then, and even you seemed disconcerted. I must say, it almost confused me, because the thought passed through my mind that perhaps it was improper to tell the good children such a grotesque tale and give them such a poor idea of men as they had to get from my adventurous hero."

"Not at all!" cried Weyland. "You haven't guessed what I am talking about—and why should you? The dear children are not so unfamiliar with such things as you think. The society that surrounds them gives them food for all sorts of speculation, and there happens to be a married couple on the other side of the Rhine very like the one you described, only yours is exaggerated, of course, and more fey. He is just as big, coarse, and clumsy, and she is pretty and dainty enough for him to carry her on his hand—well, almost. And their situation, their story, fits your tale too, so exactly that the girls asked me quite seriously if you knew the people and were portraying them mischievously. I assured them that you were not, but I think it would be wise if you never transcribed the tale. We can find good enough excuses in delay and subterfuge."

I was very surprised, for I had not had any specific couple in mind, not on this side of the Rhine nor on the other! In fact, I wouldn't have known how to explain whence I got the idea. I liked to pass my time inventing such amusing little stories. They had no connection with reality, and I felt that my listeners should accept them as such.[23]

When I got back to my affairs in town, I could feel how everything irked me more than usual, for a person who is born active is prone to exaggerate his planning and overburden himself with work. And that can turn out well enough, until some physical or moral obstacle enters the picture and clarifies the discrepancy between strength and project.

I was studying law as diligently as was necessary to pass my examinations with honors of sorts; the study of medicine attracted me because, although it did not completely reveal nature, it at least made me aware of it, and I was attached to it by association and habit; I had to spend some time and attention on sociabilities because quite a few families had shown me kindness, and everything could have gone on like this had it not been for the burden Herder had imposed on me. He had torn away the curtain that had hidden the poverty of German literature from me and had brutally destroyed quite a few of my prejudices. Only a few stars remained shining in my native sky because he had brushed away all the others as falling fragments shooting by. He had even spoiled my hopes and expectations of myself to such an extent that I began to doubt my own capabilities. At the same time he had swept me away with him onto the broad and glorious paths he liked to follow. He had brought his favorite writers to my attention—Swift and Hamann at the top of the list—and had roused me even more than he had depressed me. Add to all this the confusion of an incipient passion that, by threatening to consume me, was quite capable of distracting me from these preoccupations, not, however, of helping me to rise above them; and on top of that, a feeling of physical ill-being that threatened to choke me after every meal. I was able to rid myself of it only later when I stopped drinking a red wine which was served regularly at the pension where we ate, and which we enjoyed. This horrible feeling of discomfort had not plagued me in Sesenheim, with the result that I had been doubly gay there; however, as soon as I returned to my city diet, there it was again, to my profound irritation. All these things combined to make me thoughtful and morose, and my outer appearance probably reflected what was going on inside me.

More out of sorts than ever, because my ailment had made itself felt quite violently after my last meal, I accompanied the doctor on his rounds. The carefree way in which our venerable teacher led us from bed to bed; his precise comment on important symptoms; altogether, his ideas on the course of an illness, the beautiful Hippocratic method with which he expounded the science, without theorizing, just from his own experience, and the final remarks with which he usually brought his lecture to a magnificent conclusion—all this drew me to him and made a strange subject at which I was merely peering as through a slit, more attractive to me. My revulsion to sick people lessened constantly the more I learned to transform a condition of illness into a conception through which healing and the restoration of the human body was made possible. The doctor probably looked upon me as a peculiar young man and forgave me the anomaly that attracted me to his classes. On this particular day, he did not end his lecture as usual with a theory that concerned the illness under observation, but said blithely, "Gentlemen, we have a few days of vacation ahead of us. Use them to refresh yourselves. Your studies should be treated not only with earnestness and diligence—they require gaiety and freedom of spirit as well. Give your bodies some exercise, too. Wander through the beautiful countryside on foot or on horseback. If you are a native, you will enjoy the accustomed beauties, and whoever is a stranger will gain new impressions and have happy memories."

There really were only two of us at whom this advice could have been aimed; all I can hope is that the prescription was as clear to the others! I thought I was listening to a voice direct from heaven and went off as fast as I could to order a horse and spruce myself up. I sent for Weyland, but he was nowhere to be found. This didn't deter me, but unfortunately I was held up by final arrangements and didn't get away as early as I had hoped. I rode my horse hard; still, night had fallen before I reached my destination. However, the way was clear and the moon lighted up my passionate exploit for me. The night was windy and eerie, and I spurred my horse on so that I would not have to wait until morning to see her.

It was late when I stabled my horse in Sesenheim. The innkeeper, in reply to my question as to whether there was still light in the parsonage, assured me that the girls had only just gone home. He thought he had heard them say that they were expecting someone. This didn't suit me at all; I had hoped to be the only one. I hurried over so as at

least to be the first to arrive, however late. I found the two
sisters sitting outside. They didn't seem at all surprised to
see me, but I was when I heard Friederike whisper to
Olivia, but loud enough for me to hear, "What did I tell
you? There he is!" They led me indoors and I found some
refreshment waiting for me. Their mother greeted me like
an old friend, but the older girl burst out laughing when
she saw me in the light—she had very little control over
herself.

After this first, rather amazing, reception, the conversation was at once free and gay, and whatever remained hidden that evening was disclosed to me next day. Friederike
had predicted that I would come, and who does not feel
satisfaction when his prophecy is fulfilled, even when it is a
sad one? All presentiments, when confirmed by events, give
a man a higher conception of himself. They make him feel
that either he is so perceptive he can sense things that are
still far off or so discerning that he is aware of a logical yet
still-obscured chain of events.

Friederike called me to go for a walk very early in the
morning. Mother and sister were busy preparing for a number of guests. I enjoyed a glorious Sunday morning in the
country at the side of my dear girl, just as Hebel, that
priceless poet, has immortalized for us. She described the
company they were expecting and begged me to stand by
and help her see to it that all festivities were enjoyed com-
munally and with a certain sense for order. Usually, she
explained, people tended to scatter, and fun and games
were enjoyed only superficially, so that in the end some
people found nothing better to do than play cards, and others sought a wilder outlet in dancing.

We therefore concocted a plan for what should take place
before and after lunch, and initiated each other into all sorts
of new party games. We got along famously, and were of
good cheer when the church bells called us to service. At
her side I didn't find the vicar's dry sermon at all long.

The nearness of a beloved serves always to shorten time,
yet this hour passed quickly for me also because of my own
specific reflections. I went over all the girl's fine qualities
in my mind as they unfolded before my eyes—her sunny
nature, her quite conscious naïveté, which was gaiety com-

bined with circumspection. They were qualities that didn't seem to go together, yet in her they did, and they also made her physically beautiful. But then I had to apply the same serious reflections to myself, and this tended to mar any carefree gaiety on my part.

Since the passionate girl had cursed and blessed my lips,[24] I had been careful not to kiss another girl out of superstition, because I feared I might harm her in some incomprehensible and uncanny fashion. I therefore fought down every desire that impels a young man to wrest this mixed blessing from some charming girl or other. But apparently even in this very respectable company, such burdensome temptation awaited me. Even those so-called harmless games that serve to assemble and unite a lively group of young people are for the most part based on forfeits, and a kiss is considered one of the most important media of exchange. I had made up my mind once and for all not to kiss, and since any lack or handicap can incite us to activities for which we would otherwise feel no inclination, I now summoned every talent I had and all my wit to get by without kissing, yet at the same time gain rather than lose in the eyes of the company. When the forfeit was to be redeemed by a verse, I was usually called upon. On such occasions I was always prepared and could come up with something in praise of the hostess or one of the girls who had been nice to me. If I happened to be saddled with a kiss, I tried to wriggle out of it with a witty remark that usually satisfied everyone just as well. Since I had time to think about it beforehand, I was not short of a variety of compliments, although they really come off best when they are spontaneous.

When we reached home, the guests, who had arrived from various directions, were already milling around merrily. Friederike assembled them, suggested a walk to her beautiful spot, and led the way. Here they found refreshments and were happy to play games until it was time for lunch. With Friederike's consent—although she knew nothing of my secret—I was able to set up and lead off in games that did not include forfeits.

My ingeniousness was all the more necessary since this group of people, all of whom were strangers to me, might very soon have suspected a more intimate relationship between me and the dear girl, and tried playfully to force upon me just what I was secretly trying to avoid. For if any incipient inclination between young people is noticed by a group like this, they will always try to embarrass them or bring the two closer, just as efforts are usually bent toward separating people who have disclosed a passion for each other. In any case, it is a matter of complete indifference to the sociable man whether he is being helpful or harmful, as long as he is being entertained.

On this particular morning, I paid a great deal of attention to Friederike and gained an insight into the essence of her nature that was never to change. The especially friendly greetings of the peasants revealed the fact that they liked her and that she made them feel at ease. In the house, Olivia was helping her mother. Nothing that required physical strength was demanded of Friederike. She was treated with consideration, I was told, because she had a weak chest.

There are women who are at their best in a room, others who shine outdoors. Friederike was one of the latter. Her personality and appearance were never more attractive than when she moved across an elevated footpath. The charm of her behavior seemed to vie with the fruitful earth, the indestructible gaiety of her expression with the blue sky. She brought the refreshing air home with her, and I soon discovered that she could also allay confusion and erase any poor impression made by petty little incidents.

The lover's purest joy is to see his beloved charm others. Friederike's behavior at the party pleased everyone. On our walks she seemed to tread on air like an enlivening spirit, back and forth, knowing just how to fill in gaps every now and then. I have already mentioned how liltingly she walked, but she was most graceful when she ran. Just as the deer seems to be fulfilling its destiny completely when it flies lightly across the sprouting seed, she seemed to demonstrate her nature most clearly when she ran lightly over hill and dale to fetch something forgotten, to search for something lost, to call back a couple who had strayed away or order something that was necessary, in the course of which she was never out of breath and never got excited. I therefore felt that her parents' anxiety about her chest may have been a little exaggerated.

Her father, who occasionally accompanied us across the meadows and fields, didn't always find the right company. I therefore joined him and of course we got involved in his favorite topic, the proposed rebuilding of the parsonage. He was especially annoyed about the fact that he couldn't get the carefully drawn plans back. He wanted to give them some more thought and come up with this or that improvement. I replied that it would be easy to replace them and offered to draw a ground plan myself, which would after all have to be the starting point for everything else. This seemed to please him. The schoolmaster was to help with the measurements, and the vicar hurried off then and there to suggest this to him, so that he would have his yardstick ready early the next morning.

When he had left, Friederike said, "It is very good of you to cater to Papa's weakness, not like the others, who are sick and tired of the topic and either try to avoid him or break away. But I must confess that we don't really want a new building. It would cost the community too much, and us too. A new house means new furnishings. Our guests would not feel happier in a new house; they are used to the old one. Here we can entertain them lavishly; in the big rooms of a new house we would feel constrained. That's how it is—but don't stop being kind to him. I thank you for it with all my heart."

Another young girl, who had joined us, asked Friederike about several novels. Had she read them? Friederike said she had not; altogether she had not done much reading. She had been reared in a gay, moral enjoyment of life and was educated in accordance with it. It was on the tip of my tongue to mention *The Vicar of Wakefield,* but I didn't dare to offer her the book. The similarities of the situation were too conspicuous and far-reaching. "But I like to read novels," she said. "One meets such nice people in them. It would be pleasant if one could be like them."

Next morning we figured out the measurements of the house. It took quite some time, since neither the schoolmaster nor I was very experienced in this art, but in the end we produced a passable sketch. The good old man told me what he had in mind, and was pleased when I departed to finish the plan more conveniently in town. Friederike bade me farewell happily. Now she was sure of my attachment to her, as I was of hers to me, and the six hours that separated us no longer seemed like any distance at all. It was easy to drive to Drusenheim by stagecoach and to keep in touch through it or use the ordinary and the special messenger services, in which latter case George was to be the messenger.

Once I got back to the city, I spent the early morning hours—for there could be no thought any more of long nights spent in sleep—redrawing the plan as neatly as I could. Meanwhile, I sent Friederike some books and accompanied them with a few friendly words. She replied right away, and her light, pretty, generous handwriting delighted me. Content and style were just as natural, good, and affectionate, and what she wrote came from the heart. Thus the pleasant impression she had made on me remained intact and was constantly renewed. I loved to reflect on her sweet personality and nourished the hope of seeing her again soon, and then for a longer time.

Now I no longer needed my good professor's exhortation. He had cured me with those last words at just the right time and so thoroughly that I was in no hurry to see him and his patients again. My correspondence with Friederike became more and more animated. She invited me to a festival, to which people from the other side of the Rhine had also been invited. I should leave myself time for it. I did so, and sent a sizable bag by stagecoach. In a few hours, I was at her side, where I found a large, jolly crowd. Taking her father aside, I handed him the plan, and he was delighted with it. I discussed with him what had occurred to me while I had been working on it. He was beside himself with pleasure and especially praised the neatness of my drawing. This was something I had practiced since youth, and this time I had taken special pains on the very best paper. Unfortunately, my host's delight was soon spoiled when, against my advice, but in his sincere pleasure, he showed the plan to those present. Far from expressing the desired enthusiasm, some paid no attention to the precious thing while others, who thought they knew something about draftsmanship, were worse. They criticized the plan as unprofessional, and when the old man wasn't looking, took my neat drawing and—using it as a rough draft—one of them drew his suggestions for improvement all over the fragile paper with a hard pencil, so crudely that there could be no thought of restoring it to its pristine condition.

I could scarcely console the disgusted old man whose pleasure had been so rudely spoiled, although I tried to assure him that I too had considered the plan something which should be open to discussion and upon which we could construct a new design. Paying no attention to me, he took himself off with his ill humor, and Friederike thanked me for being so attentive to her father and so patient with the rudeness of the guests.

But I didn't know the meaning of pain or grievance when I was near her. The company consisted of young, rather noisy friends, whom an older gentleman was trying to outdo by holding forth in an even more astonishing fashion. Already at breakfast they had not been sparing with the wine and they lacked for nothing on the laden luncheon table, either. Everyone enjoyed the food, especially after having indulged in physical exercise in rather warm weather. The old magistrate had a little too much to drink, but the young folk didn't lag far behind him.

I was blissfully happy at Friederike's side. I was talkative, gay, witty, bold, yet tempered by my feelings for her, and by my respect and devotion. She, who felt the same way for me, was frank, blithe, interested, and communicative. We seemed to have nothing on our minds but the party, yet actually had nothing on our minds but each other.

After lunch, everyone sought the shade, games were played, and the time came for games with forfeits. With the redeeming of the forfeits, all behavior became exaggerated—the pantomime demanded, the tasks that had to be fulfilled—everything that took place reflected a bold joy that seemed to know no bounds. I augmented the wild proceedings with some pranks of my own, and Friederike shone with her droll ideas. To me she seemed more adorable than ever. All my hypochondriac, superstitious foibles had disappeared, and when the opportunity came to kiss my dearly beloved warmly, I did not avoid it, even less did I avoid a repetition of the pleasure.

Everyone was hoping that there would be music; at last we could hear it, and all of us hurried off to dance. The *allemande*—waltzing and turning—was the beginning, middle, and end of our dancing. Everyone had grown up with this folk dance, and I did ample honor to the two girls who had taught me. Friederike, who danced as she walked, jumped, and ran, was delighted to find such a good partner in me. She danced with me most of the time, but soon had to stop because she was being advised from all sides to calm down. We compensated ourselves by taking a walk alone, hand in hand, and by a warm embrace at her tranquil resting place, where we exchanged assurances that we loved each other deeply.

Some old people who had left the games brought us back. During the evening refreshments, we found just as little time to ourselves. The dancing continued until late in the night, and there were as many toasts and temptations to drink more as there had been at noon.

I had slept only a few hours when my hot, tumultuous blood roused me. It is at such times and under such circumstances that anxiety and remorse tend to overwhelm the defenseless man as he lies stretched out in his bed. My imagination conjured up the liveliest visions. I saw Lucinda, how she had drawn back from me after kissing me passionately, her cheeks glowing, her eyes sparkling, pronouncing the curse that was intended to threaten only her sister, yet with it unwittingly menacing strangers and innocents. I could see Friederike facing her, pale, petrified at the sight of her, feeling the effects of a curse of which she knew nothing. And I saw myself in the middle, incapable of rejecting the spiritual effects of that adventure or of averting that accursed kiss. Friederike's frailty seemed to hasten the threatened disaster, and my love for her now appeared to me as most unfortunate. I wished myself a thousand miles away.

But I won't conceal what lay even more painfully in the back of my mind. I was, to a degree, made conceited by the superstition. My lips, blessed or accursed, seemed more significant than before, and I was conscious with no less self-satisfaction of the attitude of self-denial with which I had rejected many innocent joys, partly to preserve that magical advantage, partly to avoid hurting a harmless creature if I renounced it.

But now all was irrevocably lost. I had returned to an ordinary condition and I was sure that I had hurt Friederike and done her irreparable harm. Instead of being rid of Lucinda's curse, it had struck back from my lips to my heart.

All this raced wildly through my blood—which was already excited by love, passion, wine, and dancing—and tormented me, confusing my thoughts so that, especially when compared with yesterday's agreeable joys, I felt a profound despair. Fortunately the dawn was peeping through a slit in the shutters, and the rising sun, overcoming the powers of the night, put me back on my feet. Soon I was out of doors and quickly refreshed, if not completely restored.

Superstition, like a lot of other beliefs, loses much of its strength when, instead of flattering our vanity, it gets in its way and decides to give this frailty of ours a bad time. Then we can suddenly see quite clearly that our superstitions can be banished at will, and we let them go all the more readily when it is to our advantage. Just to see Friederike and to experience her love and the gaiety of her surroundings reproached me for harboring such sad night shades on such a happy day, and I thought I had dispelled them forever. Friederike was more close and confiding than ever, which made me deeply happy, and I was overjoyed when she offered to kiss me good-by openly, as she did her friends and relatives.

In the city, a great deal of business and distraction awaited me, out of which I often joined my beloved in a correspondence that now became quite regular. In her letters too, she was always the same. She could tell something new or refer to facts I already knew a little about; she could describe things lightly or be fleetingly reflective—it was always as if she were coming, going, running, jumping, surefooted and light, with her pen too. I also enjoyed writing to her, and to imagine her good qualities present increased my attachment to her in her absence, making this type of conversation just as effective as a personal one—in fact, in time it meant more to me. I found it pleasanter and more precious.

For my superstition had been completely banished. It had been based on impressions made in earlier years, but the spirit of the day, the fleetness of youth, the intercourse with cold, rational men, all tended to discourage it, and it would not have been easy to find anyone in my surroundings who would not have dismissed my foible as ridiculous. But the sad part of it was that, as this madness fled, it left behind a true reflection of the condition in which young people always find themselves who, in their early attachments, cannot hope for a lasting union. It didn't help me much to be rid of my error, because my common sense and reflective powers gave me an even worse time. My passion for the good girl grew the more I learned to value her, and the time was approaching when I would perhaps have to lose so much love and goodness forever.

We had been living thus as one for some time, quietly and very pleasantly, when friend Weyland played a joke on us by bringing *The Vicar of Wakefield* to Sesenheim. When someone mentioned reading aloud, he handed me the book as if there were nothing to it. I managed to control myself and read as freely and spiritedly as I could. The faces of my listeners soon brightened too, and they didn't seem to mind at all having to make comparisons again. If they had found amusing counterparts for Raymond and Melusina, they now saw themselves in the mirror—and it was by no means an ugly picture. Nobody mentioned it specifically but no one could deny either that they were being presented with people who thought and felt as they did.

All people of quality, as they increase their knowledge, feel that they have to play dual roles on earth—a realistic and an ideal one—and the basis of everything noble can be found in this feeling. What is bestowed upon us as reality, we experience only too vividly, but we seldom learn to see our ideal role clearly. A man may seek his higher destiny on earth or in heaven, in the present or in the future, still—and because of it—he remains inwardly prone to eternal hesitation, outwardly to ever disturbing impressions, until he finally decides to declare that what is right is what suits him.

Among the more pardonable efforts to achieve something noble or to compare oneself with a superior is the youthful urge to draw comparisons between oneself and the characters in a novel. This urge is quite innocent and—however much may be said against it—utterly harmless. It amuses us at times when we are in danger of perishing of boredom or would have to resort to a more passionate pastime.

How often one hears a litany of the harm done by the novel, and why it should be considered a misfortune when a good little girl or a handsome young man put themselves in the place of a character who is better or worse off than they! Is our middle-class life worth so much, or do man's daily needs occupy him to such an extent that he must reject all higher demands?

The use of historic-poetic Christian names in place of the names of saints, which has found its way into the German church, very often to the vexation of the priest who is baptizing the child, can doubtlessly be considered a minor side effect of romantic-poetic fiction. This trend—which may have nothing behind it but the urge to ennoble a child by giving it a melodious name—is praiseworthy, and this joining of a fictitious world with reality can even spread an enhancing glow over that person's entire life. We would be insulting a beautiful child, whom we are pleased to name "Bertha," if we had her baptized "Urselblandine!"[25] Any educated person—to say nothing of a lover—would find his tongue tripping over such a name. A cold, one-sided world is not to blame when it spurs everything from the world of fantasy as ridiculous and reprehensible, but the thoughtful connoisseur of humankind knows how to estimate such things according to his sense of values.

For the two lovers on the banks of the Rhine, this comparison, which had been forced upon them by a joke, had the most delightful consequence. One doesn't necessarily think about oneself when one looks into a mirror, but one is made aware of oneself and feels one's own importance. The same applies to moral images, in which one recognizes one's customs and inclinations, one's habits and peculiarities, as in a silhouette, and tries with brotherly fervor to grasp and embrace them.

The habitude of being together became stronger and

stronger; that I belonged to this circle was irrefutable. It had taken place without anyone's asking how it was to end. And where are the parents who do not find it necessary to leave daughter or son in such a condition of uncertainty for a while, until something turns out to be for life, and better than any long-plotted plan could have produced?

They had complete faith in Friederike's character and in my integrity, of which they had formed a favorable impression because of my peculiar abstinence from even the most innocent caress. We were left unobserved, which was customary anyway at the time, and it was left to us to wander across the countryside with much company or little, and to visit friends and neighbors as we pleased. On both banks of the Rhine—in Hagenau, Fort Louis, Philippsburg, in the Ortenau—I found those people scattered whom I had seen united in Sesenheim. In their homes, they were friendly hosts, hospitable, and so willing to open up to us kitchen, cellar, gardens, and vineyards—indeed, the entire region! The islands in the Rhine were often the goals of our boat rides. There we mercilessly tossed the cool inhabitants of that clear river into a pot or onto a grill or roasted them in spluttering fat, and we might have settled down happily there in some fisherman's homely cottage if the horrible Rhine gnats had not chased us away. Once, when we had been driven home awkwardly and inopportunely ahead of time, I held forth in quite blasphemous terms, in front of Friederike's good clerical father, on the insupportable disruption of a perfectly good picnic which had until then turned out so well in every respect, and our loving feelings for one another had seemed to grow with the success of the outing. I assured the vicar that these gnats alone could dissuade me from believing that a good and wise God had created the world. The pious old man called me to order sternly and explained that gnats and other insects had been created only after the fall of our first parents—or, if they had existed in Paradise, then certainly only to hum pleasantly, never to sting! I at once felt calmer, for an angry man is easily pacified if he can be made to laugh. Still, I assured him that there really could have been no need for an angel with a flaming sword to drive the sinful couple out of the Garden of Eden; he was pleased to let me believe that huge gnats from the Tigris and Euphrates had done it. Thus I succeeded in making him laugh, for the good man could appreciate fun or, at least, knew how to let it pass.

More serious and uplifting, though, was the enjoyment of the various hours of the day and the seasons in the glorious countryside. One had only to give oneself up to the present in order to delight in the clarity of the pure sky, the glow of the rich earth, the mild evenings, the warm night beside or near one's beloved. For months on end we were blessed with the clear air of mornings on which the sky presented itself in all its glory; the earth was drenched by a profuse dew, and, so that the drama might not be too simple, occasional clouds often towered above the far-off mountains. At times they would hover there for days, for weeks, without diminishing the clarity of the sky, and even the passing storms refreshed the land and glorified the green, glistening in the sunlight before it dried. A double rainbow in the sky—two colored seams on a dark gray, almost black strip of heaven—were more magnificent, more colorful, and stronger, but also more fleeting, than I had ever seen them.

In these surroundings the urge to write poetry awoke in me quite unexpectedly. I had not felt it for a long time. I composed several verses to melodies for Friederike. They would have made a nice little volume, but few are left. It should not be difficult to find them among the others.[26]

Since I had to return to the city often because of my strange studies and other circumstances, a new life was created for our love and it preserved us from all the unpleasantness that can ordinarily be the tiresome result of such a love affair. Separated from me, she lived for me in that she thought of something new with which to amuse me on my return. Separated from her, I busied myself on her behalf in order to appear new to her with some gift or idea when I saw her again. Painted ribbons had just come into style. I at once painted several for her and sent them to her, with a little poem, at a time when I had to stay away longer than I had anticipated.[27] In order to keep my promise to her father to produce a new plan for the house, I persuaded a young architect to do the work for me. He seemed to enjoy doing it as a favor to me and even more in the expectation of receiving a good reception in such a friendly family. He finished off the ground plan and cross section of the house, didn't forget yard and garden, and added a detailed but reasonable estimate of cost to make the execution of such an extensive project look easy and practical.

This evidence of our friendly efforts was most affectionately received, and since the vicar saw that we were pleased to serve him, he came forward with one more request— would we paint a chaise, which was all one color, with flowers and other decorative motifs? We were happy to oblige him and fetched paint, brushes, and other materials we might need from the apothecary and another shop in the next town. However, so that a Wakefield failure might not be missing, we noticed only when everything had been busily and very colorfully painted that we had used a defective varnish that would not dry. Sunshine, fresh air, clear or damp weather—nothing would make it behave as it should. Meanwhile, they had to use an old rattletrap, and there was nothing left for us to do but scrape off all the fine decoration again, which was much harder work than it had been to put it on. Our disgust with the job was heightened when the girls begged us for heaven's sake to proceed slowly and carefully so as to preserve the paint underneath, which after our efforts never did regain its original high polish.

As with Dr. Primrose and his friendly family, such unpleasant little incidents did nothing to disturb the joy of our life, for we encountered all sorts of good fortune too, as did our friends and neighbors. Weddings and baptisms, the celebration when the framework of a new house was completed, inheritances and lottery winnings, were alternately announced and enjoyed by everyone. We gathered all joy together as communal property, and head and heart knew how to enhance it. It was not the first nor the last time that I found myself in a family or sociable circle at the very height of its flowering, and if I may flatter myself, helped to add something to the glow of such a period. On the other hand, I had to face the fact that such felicitous times don't last and are quick to disappear.

But now our love was put to one more strange test. I like to call it a test, although it was not exactly that. The rustic family, whom I counted as my friends, had relatives in the city, people of good standing and repute, and comfortably off. The young city people often came to Sesenheim. The older ones, mothers and aunts who were less mobile, heard a lot about life in Sesenheim and of the increasing charm of the daughters, even of my influence. They consequently expressed a desire to meet me, and after I had visited them several times and been received well by them too, they decided that they wanted once to see all of us together, especially since they felt that they owed the Sesenheimers a friendly return invitation.

The arrangements took quite some time. The vicar's wife didn't find it easy to leave her household, Olivia had a horror of the city, into which she did not fit, and Friederike did not feel drawn there either. Thus the whole project was delayed until it was finally decided by the fact that I couldn't get out into the country for a fortnight, and we preferred to see each other in the city, even under pressure, rather than not to meet at all. And so I found my girls—whom I was accustomed to seeing only in a rustic setting, against a backdrop of swaying trees, tumbling books, nodding field flowers, and a free horizon miles wide—for the first time in the rooms of a town house, which were large enough; still, they were hemmed in against a backdrop of wallpaper, mirrors, clocks, and figurines.

One's relationship to one's beloved is so decisive that one's surroundings mean little, yet the spirit demands that they be fitting, natural, accustomed surroundings. With my animated response to all things present, I was unable to reconcile myself at once to the contradictions of the moment. The mother's respectable, serene, and dignified behavior fitted perfectly into the new circle; she could not be told apart from the other women, but Olivia was as restless as a fish tossed up on shore. She was used to calling out to me in the garden or waving at me in the fields to come over when she had something special to tell me, and she did the same thing now, dragging me off to a window niche. She did it clumsily, with embarrassment, because she could sense that it was not the right thing to do—still, she did it. She had something of absolutely no importance to tell me, nothing that I did not know already—that she was utterly miserable, that she wished she were across the Rhine, yes, even in Turkey, for all she cared! Friederike, on the other hand, behaved quite remarkably under the circumstances. She didn't fit in either, but it spoke for her character that, instead of trying to adapt herself to the situation, she unconsciously adapted the situation to herself. She behaved here just as she did in the country and knew how to enliven every moment. Without making a special effort, she set things in motion, thereby putting everyone at their ease, for it is really only boredom that makes people uneasy. And with that she fulfilled the wishes of the city aunts who had wanted, just once and from their own sofas, to witness rustic games and entertainment. And when everyone had had enough, the Sesenheimers looked at the wardrobe, jewelry, and all the other things that distinguished the French-dressed city women, and my girls admired it all without a trace of envy. With me too, Friederike made things easy for herself by treating me as she always did. She didn't seem to single me out in any way except by directing any wishes she had at me rather than anyone else, therefore acknowledging me as her humble servant.

She used my obligingness on the following day with assurance, when she confided in me that the ladies would like to hear me read. Their daughters had spoken a lot about it, because in Sesenheim I read aloud whatever was requested, whenever desired. I was ready immediately and asked only for their silence and attention for a few hours. They agreed, and in one evening, without interruption, I read *Hamlet* in its entirety, trying to penetrate the true meaning of the drama as best I could, expressing myself animatedly and passionately as only the young can. I was greatly applauded. Every now and then, Friederike drew a deep breath, and her cheeks were suffused with pink. I knew these symptoms of a sensitive and deeply moved heart that remains outwardly blithe and tranquil, and they were the only reward I wanted. She joyfully accepted the thanks for the fact that she had suggested the reading and in her gentle way, did not deny herself a little pride in having shone through me.

The visit was not intended to last long, but their departure was delayed. Friederike did what she could to be entertaining; so did I. But the rich resources that can be found in such abundance in the country are soon exhausted in the city, and the situation was made even more embarrassing because Olivia lost her composure entirely. The two sisters were the only ones in the entire company who dressed in the style we called "German." Friederike had never thought of wearing anything else and felt she could pass this way anywhere; she made no comparisons. But Olivia found it unbearable to look like a maid in a society of such refinement. When she was in the country, she scarcely noticed how differently those who came from the city were dressed, and had no desire to dress like them, but in town she detested her country clothes. This, on top of all the other accomplishments of the city ladies and the hundred little incidents of a completely contrary milieu, created such a turmoil in her excitable little self that, to pacify her—which I did because Friederike asked me to—I had to pay her the most flattering attention. I was afraid there would be a dreadful scene. I could see the moment coming when she would throw herself at my feet, imploring me for heaven's sake to save her from this situation. She was such a good girl when she could behave naturally, but pressures such as she was faced with here made her feel dreadfully ill at ease and in the end drove her to despair. So now I tried to hasten that which Olivia and her mother desired and to which Friederike was also not averse. I did not refrain from praising the latter's behavior when compared with her sister's. I told her how happy I was to see her unchanged and as free as the birds in the trees, even in these surroundings. She was sweet enough to reply that I was there, and she didn't care where she was if only I was with her. At last I saw them off, and a load fell from me, for my feelings lay just between those of the two girls—I did not feel hysterically fearful like Olivia, but neither did I feel at ease like Friederike. . . .

Such a youthful, carefree attachment can be compared with a rocket set off at night, which rises up in a gentle, glowing arc, mingles with the stars, appears to linger among them for a while, then, as it falls, describes a similar path, only this time in the opposite direction, and finally brings ruination where it ends its flight. Friederike remained always the same. She didn't seem to think or want to think that our relationship might end. Olivia also did not like to see me stay away, but she did not lose as much as her sister by my absence. She could therefore be more farseeing and candid about it. She spoke to me sometimes about a parting that she could see was probable and tried to find some consolation for her sister and herself. A girl who gives up a man to whom she has not denied her affection is not in nearly such an embarrassing position as the youth who has gone just as far in the declaration of his love. He always cuts a sorry figure, because as a maturing man a certain perspicacity is expected of him and rashness does not suit him. The reasons of a girl who withdraws always seem valid; a man's never!

But how can a flattering passion possibly grant us the foresight as to where it may lead? Even when we have very sensibly decided to give it up, we can't let it go, but continue to find delight in the beloved custom, even if in a completely altered fashion. And that is what happened to me. Although Friederike's presence caused me anxiety, still I could conceive of nothing more pleasant than to think of her and converse with her when I was not with her. My visits to Sesenheim became less frequent; our correspondence, however, grew more and more lively. She knew how to write merrily about events and described her feelings with great charm, and I passionately recalled all her good qualities. Absence set me free, and my attachment to her blossomed all the more through our conversation across the distance. At such moments, I could deceive myself thoroughly about the future. I was distracted enough anyway by the passing of time and important business. Until now I had managed to accomplish a great variety of things by a constant lively participation in everything going on around me, but in the end all things conspired to create a too powerful pressure, as happens when the time has come to withdraw from a place. . . .

In this state of pressure and confusion, I could not avoid seeing Friederike once more. They were embarrassing days, and I do not remember them. As I stretched out my hand to her—I was already seated on my horse—there were tears in her eyes, and I felt utterly miserable. Then I rode along the footpath to Drusenheim, and there I had a very strange vision. I saw myself—not with my physical but with my mind's eye—approaching myself on horseback, dressed in a suit I could not remember ever having had on, leaden gray with a little gold. I shook myself out of the dream, and the figure was gone. The strange thing is that, eight years later, I found myself on the same path, riding to visit Friederike in the suit I had seen in the vision, and I was wearing it quite by chance. One may think what one will of such things, but the miraculous vision gave me a little comfort in this hour of parting. The pain of leaving beautiful Alsace forever, and everything I had so richly experienced there was eased; and with the confusion of farewell behind me at last, I again found myself, in a fashion, on a peaceful and inspiring journey. . . .

How can young people be expected to find the highest interests in life, how can they hope to arouse interest among their own kind if they are not animated by love? If an affair of the heart, whatever kind it may be, is not alive in them? I was mourning a lost love in secret, and it made me mild and acquiescent and more pleasant company than in brighter times, when there was nothing to remind me of my errors of a deficiency in me, and I would storm along rootlessly. Friederike's reply to a final letter of mine tore my heart. The same handwriting, the same sensitivity, the same feeling that had tended toward me and been encourged by me. Now I could feel the loss she suffered, but could see no possibility of replacing it or of consoling her. Suddenly she was present again; I missed her constantly, and what was worst, I could not forgive myself for my own misfortune. Gretchen[28] had been taken from me; Annette[29] had forsaken me; but here, for the first time, I was at fault. I had deeply wounded a beautiful heart, and a period of gloomy remorse, unrelieved by an accustomed, refreshing love, became extremely painful—one might almost say unbearable.

But a man wants to live. I therefore began to take serious interest in those around me and tried to extricate some from their dilemmas and unite others who were thinking of parting, so that they might not share my fate. People began to call me "the confidant," and because it was my wont to rove all over the countryside, "the wanderer." The comfort I felt under the open sky, in valleys, on heights, in field and forest, was helped by Frankfurt's location. It lay between

Darmstadt and Homburg, two pleasant cities that were amiably disposed toward each other because of the relationship between their two courts. I made a habit of living in the open, of wandering like a messenger between mountains and flatlands. Sometimes I walked alone through my native town, sometimes with company, as if the place were no concern of mine. I ate in the public restaurants on the main thoroughfare and, after the meal, wandered on. I was more than ever attuned to the wide-open world and nature's freedom. On my way, I would sing to myself—strange hymns and wild lyrics in free verse. Of them all, one, called *"Wanderers Sturmlied,"* is still in existence. And I would sing all this half-nonsense aloud, passionately, as if a terrible storm that I had to escape were about to break over me. . . .

But during this period, when the pain caused by Friederike's situation made me fearful, I tried in the old way that was habitual to me to find consolation in the art of poetry. I turned once more to the traditional poetic confession in order to become worthy of absolution through this self-scourging atonement. Both Marias, in *Götz von Berlichingen* and *Clavigo,* and their lovers who play the part of villains, are probably the results of my remorse.

But in one's youth, one overcomes hurt and illness quickly, because a healthy system of organic life takes over and gives a young man time to recover. Fortunately quite a few opportunities for physical exercise offered themselves at the appropriate time, and I was stimulated by new enjoyments. Riding gradually replaced my slow, melancholy, fatiguing, and aimless wanderings. I got where I wanted to go more quickly, happily, and comfortably. The younger generation reintroduced fencing, and with the onset of winter, a new world was opened up for us. I soon made up my mind to try skating—something I had never done before—and in a short time, through practice, concentration, and doggedness, I reached the point necessary for the enjoyment of a gay and lively rink, even if I could not distinguish myself.

We really had Klopstock to thank for this joyous new activity. His enthusiasm is confirmed by private accounts, and his odes give undeniable proof of it. I remember so well jumping out of bed one bright, frosty morning, and recalling the verse:

> Filled with joy alone by my own soundness,
>   I have made white the spreading crystal, far, far down.
> How gently winter's dawning day doth light the snow!
>   Hoarfrost like stars has scattered a whole glittering night
>   across it. [30]

My hesitant and fluctuating decision was fixed at once. Off I flew, straight to the place where an old beginner like me could do best with his efforts. And in truth, this trial of strength deserved to be recommended by Klopstock, for it brings us in contact with the freshness of childhood, challenges the young man to enjoy his litheness, and is suited to defend us against the stagnation of old age. And we became absolutely addicted to the pleasure. It didn't suffice to spend a glorious Sunday on the ice; we went on skating far into the night. Other forms of exercise may tire the body, but skating gives it ever fresh *élan*. The full moon rising over the wide nocturnal meadows, frozen to ice fields, the night air rushing toward us as we glided forward, the somber thunder of sinking ice as the water level went down, the strange echoing of our own motions, were perfect reminders of scenes by Ossian. First one then another of our friends would recite an ode of Klopstock's in declamatory half tones, and when we met again in the twilight, the sincere praise of the instigator of our joys could be heard:

> How could He who created health and joy,
>   Such as horse trotting briskly ne'er conveys,
> Which e'en the bouncing ball doth lack,
>   Not be immortal? [31]

A man who knows how to ennoble any of our earthly activities by intellectual stimulation, and understands how to propagate them appropriately, merits all our thanks. Then we forgo our calling to higher things only too easily, like talented children whose gifts have been developed marvelously early in life and who, when given a chance, turn again to the simplest boyhood games.

THE NEW MELUSINA

Honored Gentlemen! I am fully aware of the fact that you do not like forewords or introductions; therefore I hasten to assure you that this time I intend to pass with flying colors. I know that quite a few of the true stories I have told turned out to everyone's satisfaction, but today I am going to tell you one that far surpasses all the others. Although it happened several years ago, it still disturbs me whenever I recall it and I hope that someday there may be further developments. I think it would be hard to find its equal.

First, let me confess that I have not always lived in a way that could insure my immediate future—frankly, not even the next day! In my youth, I was not a good manager and often found myself in quite embarrassing straits. Once I undertook a journey that was intended to be profitable, but I aimed too high, and after having begun the trip in a private coach, had to continue by ordinary diligence and finally found myself traveling on foot.

I was a bright young man and it was a custom of mine, whenever I arrived at an inn, to look around for the landlady or the cook and to ingratiate myself with them, a practice that usually helped to reduce my bill.

One evening, as I walked into the stagecoach inn of a small town and was about to proceed in my usual fashion, a beautiful carriage, a two-seater drawn by four horses, rattled up to the entrance behind me. Turning, I saw a woman, alone—no maid, no footman. I hurried forward to open the door for her and assure her that I was her servant. As she descended, I could see that she was beautifully built and, on looking more closely, that her lovely face betrayed a hint of sadness. Again I asked if there was anything I could do for her. "Yes," she replied, "would you take out the casket on the seat for me? But be careful, please, and carry it upstairs. I must beg you, though, to be sure to hold it level and not to move or shake it in any way." I picked up the casket carefully; she closed the door of the carriage and told the domestic that she intended to stay the night.

Soon we were alone in her room. she asked me to put the casket on a table that stood against the wall, and since I could gather from her behavior that she wished to be alone, I withdrew after kissing her hand respectfully and fervently, whereupon she said, "Order dinner for both of us." You can imagine how delighted I was to carry out her orders. In my exuberance, I scarcely gave landlady and cook a nod! I awaited the moment that would bring us together again with the greatest impatience. The dinner was served, we sat down opposite each other, I enjoyed my first good meal in a long time, and with it—what a delectable sight! I must say, she seemed to grow more and more beautiful by the minute!

She was most gracious, but she rejected any efforts on my part to be more intimate. The dishes were removed, I lingered on, racking my brains for a ruse that might bring me closer to her—in vain. A certain dignity on her part held me back. I could not overcome it and had to take my leave early, quite against my will.

After a wakeful night filled with restless dreaming, I was up early and inquired whether she had ordered fresh horses. I was told No, and walked out into the garden. From there, I could see her at the window of her room, fully dressed, and hurried up to her. When I found her to be just as beautiful—nay, more beautiful than the day before, I was overwhelmed by a wicked audacity. Rushing up to her, I took her in my arms.

"Angelic, irresistible creature!" I cried. "Forgive me, but I cannot help myself."

She extricated herself from my embrace with unbelievable dexterity. I wasn't even able to kiss her cheek. "You will have to curb such outbursts," she said, "or you will forfeit a happiness that lies within your reach. But you shall not take possession of it until you have passed several tests."

"Ask of me what you will, angelic spirit," I cried. "Only do not drive me to despair!"

Smiling, she said, "If you want to serve me, hear my conditions. I have come here to visit a friend with whom I intend to stay a few days. During that time I would like my carriage and this casket to travel on ahead. Would you undertake the assignment? All you have to do is place the casket in the carriage and lift it out again, sit beside it when it is in the carriage and take good care of it. Whenever you arrive at an inn, place it on a table in a room all by itself where you are not to live or step. You must lock this room every time with this key, which can open all locks. It has a special power that prevents anyone else from opening them in the meantime."

I stared at her and suddenly I began to feel quite strange, but I promised to do everything she said, if only I could hope to see her again soon and she would seal my hopes with a kiss. She did, and from that moment on I was hers, body and soul. Now, she said, I was please to go and order fresh horses. We discussed what route I was to take and the places where I was to stop and wait for her. Finally, she gave me a purse full of gold, and I kissed her hand. As we parted, she seemed touched, and I—I didn't know what I was doing!

When I came back after having ordered the horses, I found the door of her room locked. I tried the passkey at once, and it stood the test perfectly. The door opened, I found the room empty, only the casket was standing on the table where I had placed it.

Meanwhile the carriage had been brought to the front entrance. I carried the casket down carefully and placed it on the seat beside me. The landlady asked, "Where is the lady?" A child replied, "She went into town." I bade them farewell and left them triumphantly—I, who had arrived the night before with dusty leggings. You can readily imagine that, with nothing else to do, I began to give the whole business a lot of thought. I counted the money, made a few plans of my own, and every now and then gave the casket a sidelong glance. I drove straight on, didn't tarry at quite a few stops and didn't rest until I had arrived at one of the larger towns she had specified. I obeyed her instructions meticulously and placed the box in a room by itself with candles on either side, as she had ordered. I locked the room, moved into my own, and made myself comfortable.

For a time I was able to pass the hours thinking of her, but after a while I became bored. I was not used to living alone, and I soon found the sort of company I liked at inns and public places, in the pursuit of which my money began to dwindle away. One evening, after having carelessly indulged in a wild game of chance, I found my purse empty. When I got back to my room, I was beside myself. I looked like a rich man and could expect a stiff bill next morning; I had no idea when my beautiful lady would turn up again, if ever; in short, I could not have found myself in a more embarrassing situation. I longed for her doubly and felt I couldn't live a moment longer without her and her money.

After supper, which I couldn't enjoy because, for the first time, I had to dine alone, I paced my room, up and down, spoke loudly to myself, cursed myself, threw myself on the floor, tore my hair, altogether behaved abominably. Suddenly I heard a slight movement in the next room, which I had locked, and after that, a knocking. I pulled myself together, took my passkey, but I did not need it. The double door opened all by itself, and my lovely lady was coming toward me by the light of the candles. I threw myself at her feet, kissed the hem of her dress, her hands. She helped me to my feet. I didn't dare to embrace her. I scarcely dared to look at her, but I confessed my sins honestly and remorsefully.

"I forgive you," she said, "but unfortunately you are delaying your happiness and mine. Now you must travel another stretch out into the world before we may meet again. Here is more gold, enough if you know how to manage at all. Since wine and women brought you to this pass, avoid them in the future, and let us hope to meet again happily."

She stepped back into the room, and the doors closed. I knocked, I pleaded, but I could hear nothing more. Next morning when I asked for the bill, the waiter smiled and said, "Now we know why you lock your doors in such a puzzling fashion, so that no passkey can open them. We thought you must be the bearer of a great treasure and much money, and when we saw your treasure coming downstairs, we had to admit that you are right to secure her so carefully."

I had nothing to say to that, but paid my bill and got into the carriage with the casket. This time I drove out into the world firmly determined to heed my mysterious lady's warning, but I had scarcely reached the next big town when I found myself surrounded by attractive women from whom I simply could not tear myself away. They seemed determined to make me pay dearly for their favors, for they managed to keep me at a distance yet plunge me into one expenditure after the other, and since I had nothing on my mind but to keep them amused, I again gave no thought to what I was spending, but paid and played host whenever the opportunity arose. You can imagine my astonishment and delight when I discovered a few weeks later that my sack of gold was as round and full as ever.

I had to assure myself of this wonderful characteristic of my purse, so I sat down and counted the money, then memorized the sum total carefully, and went on living as merrily and sociably as ever. I didn't miss an excursion into the country or a boat trip, singing, dancing or any other pleasures. But it soon became quite evident that now my purse *was* growing smaller, as if with my accursed counting, I had robbed it of its virtue of being countless! By now though, my pursuit of pleasure was in full swing again, and there seemed to be no way back, although I was again almost at the end of my resources. I cursed the situation I found myself in; I ranted against the beautiful creature who had led me into this temptation and was offended because she did not put in an appearance again. Angrily I renounced all my obligations to her and decided to open the casket and see if I couldn't find some assistance in it. For, although it was not heavy enough to contain money, there could have been jewels in it, and they would have been most welcome too. I was about to carry out my intention, then decided to wait for the night in order to be able to do so undisturbed, and hurried off to a banquet that was being held. There was the usual carousing, and all of us were wildly excited by wine and trumpet blast, when something very unpleasant happened. The meal was almost over when an older friend of my favorite beauty at table entered the hall quite unexpectedly, having returned from a journey. He sat down beside her without much ado and tried to assert his old rights. The result was bad feeling, dispute, and strife. We drew swords, and I was carried home more dead than alive.

A surgeon bound my wounds and left me. It was already past midnight and my attendant was asleep, when the door to the next room opened, and my mysterious lady walked into my room and sat down at my bedside. She asked me how I felt. I didn't reply because I was too weak and miserable. She went on speaking to me with much compassion and rubbed my temples with a certain balm that made me feel stronger at once—so strong, in fact, that I could become angry and upbraid her. In a violent speech, I laid all the blame for my misfortune at her feet, railed against the passion with which she filled me, against her appearing and disappearing, and the boredom and longing that had to be the result. I became more and more vehement, as if attacked by a fever. Finally I swore that if she still refused to be mine and would not submit to me, I no longer wished to live; and I demanded an immediate reply. When she hesitated with some sort of excuse, I was beside myself and tore off my bandages with the intention of bleeding to death. Imagine my astonishment when I found my wounds healed, my body in as fine condition as ever, and her in my arms!

Now we were the happiest couple in the world. Alternately we begged each other's forgiveness without really knowing what for. She promised to travel with me from now on, and soon we were sitting side by side in the carriage, the casket opposite us like a third person. I had never spoken of it in her presence, and it didn't occur to me to do so now, although there it was before our eyes. In a tacit understanding, both of us looked after it whenever necessary, but I was the one who put it in the carriage and lifted it out again, and I was also the one who attended to the locking of the doors.

As long as there was still something in the purse, I paid, and when all the money was gone, I said so. "We can soon remedy that," she said, pointing to two small bags hanging on either side of the carriage. I had noticed them before, but we had never made any use of them. She put her hand into one and drew out a few pieces of gold, out of the other some silver, thus demonstrating to me how it would be possible for us to continue to live as we pleased. And so we traveled from city to city, from country to country, were gay whether we were alone or with others, and it never occurred to me that she might leave me again, especially since she had been pregnant for some time now, a circumstance that only served to increase our joy and love for each other. But alas, one morning I could not find her, and since I didn't like the idea of remaining without her, I proceeded on my way, with the casket. I tried both moneybags and found them full.

The trip was a pleasant one, and although I had no desire to reflect on my recent fantastic adventures—I expected them to come to a quite natural end somehow—something happened now that amazed and worried me. Yes, I would go so far as to say that it frightened me. Since, to get away from a place, I was accustomed to traveling by day and night, I quite often found myself driving in the dark. Then, if the lanterns happened to fail, it was black as night in the carriage. Once, on such a dark night, I had fallen asleep. When I awoke, I saw a ray of light above me on the hood of the carriage. I followed its course down and discovered that it came from the casket, which evidently had a crack, as if it had split a little in the hot, dry summer weather that had just set in. I thought again of jewels—a diamond might be in the casket—I had to find out if I was right. I moved so as to bring my eye down to the crack and was overwhelmed with astonishment when I found myself looking into a brilliantly lit room that was richly furnished in excellent taste. It was as if I were looking through an archway into a palatial hall. Of course, I could see only a part of the room, but I could guess what the rest must look like. A fire was burning on the hearth, an armchair was standing beside it. I held my breath and went on looking. Now a woman came from another side of the room, a book in her hand, and I immediately recognized my beautiful lady, although she was minute. She sat down in the armchair beside the fire to read, first fixing some branches that were burning with the prettiest little fire tongs, in the course of which I could see quite clearly that this darling little creature was pregnant too. But now I simply had to move—my position was so cramped—and soon after that, when I wanted to look again and convince myself that I had not been dreaming, the light was gone, and I found myself staring into the dark.

You can imagine how shocked I was. I couldn't stop thinking about what I had discovered, yet couldn't think clearly about it at all. At last I fell asleep, and when I awoke, I was sure I had dreamed the whole thing, yet I also felt a little estranged from my lovely lady; and the more carefully I carried the casket, the less I could say whether I wanted her to reappear again full size or not.

One evening, some time later, she really did appear, dressed all in white. Since the room was twilit, she looked taller than usual, and I recalled having read that all water sprites and elves grew taller when night was falling. As usual, she flew into my arms, but I could not embrace her with my customary carefree fervor.

"My beloved," she said, "I can tell by your reception what, alas, I already know. You have seen me since last we met and know what shape I must assume at certain times, and this knowledge has affected your happiness and mine. In fact, our happiness is in danger of being utterly destroyed. I must leave you, and I don't know if I shall ever see you again."

Her presence, and the graciousness with which she spoke, succeeded in almost completely eradicating from my memory that other shape of hers that had haunted me until now. I embraced her ardently and convinced her of my love; I assured her of my innocence, explaining how I had discovered everything quite by chance; in short, I did what I could to calm her, and she did the same for me.

"Think it over carefully," she said. "has this discovery hurt your love for me? Can you forget that I live with you in two shapes? Doesn't the diminution of my form also diminish your love for me?"

I looked at her—she was more lovely than ever—and I thought to myself, "Is it such a misfortune to possess a woman who, from time to time, is so tiny that one can carry her in a casket? Wouldn't it be much worse if, instead of becoming a pixie, she were to become gigantic, and put her man in a casket?" By this time my good humor had been restored, and I would not have let her go for anything in the world.

"Dear heart," I said, "let all things remain as they are. Could two people be more blessed? Do whatever is best for yourself, and I promise you that all I shall do is carry the casket more carefully than ever. How could the prettiest little thing I have ever seen in my life make a bad impression on me? How happy all lovers would be if they could possess such a miniature of their beloved! For that's what it is, a miniature, a most artful deception. You may test and tease me, but you shall see how stanch I shall be!"

"The situation is more serious than you realize," she said, "but I am glad to see you take it so lightly, for things may still turn out happily for both of us. I am going to trust you and will do the best I can, only promise me never to think with reproach of what you have discovered. And I want to add one more, most urgent request—be more cautious than ever of wine and anger."

I promised everything she asked and would have gone on protesting, but she changed the subject, and all things were as they had been before. There was no reason for us to move from where we were staying—the town was large, the sociabilities were varied, and the season was favorable for picnics and garden parties.

At all such festivities my lady was very popular; in fact, she was in demand. Her ingratiating behavior, her refinement, accompanied by a certain natural dignity, drew everyone to her. Moreover, she could play the lute beautifully and sing to her own accompaniment, and she graced all our nocturnal outings with her talents.

I have to admit that I was never one to enjoy music; in fact, it always impressed me unfavorably. My beautiful beloved had noticed this and therefore never tried to entertain me with music when we were alone. But when we were among people, she seemed to make up for it, in the course of which she attracted many admirers.

And now, why shouldn't I admit that, despite my best intentions, our last conversation had not completely satisfied me? I could not throw the thing off, my reaction to it was strange without my actually being conscious of it, until one night, at a large gathering, my suppressed resentment burst forth with dreadful results for me.

As I look back, I must confess that I did love the charming creature much less after my unfortunate discovery, and now I was jealous of her, something that would never have occurred to me before. That evening at dinner, we were seated diagonally opposite each other and quite far apart. I was feeling very happy between two ladies whom I found most attractive. With jokes and foolish love-talk we were not sparing with the wine. Meanwhile, two music-loving gentlemen had taken possession of my lady and were encouraging the others to sing—solos and in harmony—which didn't suit me at all. I found the art-loving gentlemen forward, the singing irritated me, and when even I was asked to contribute a solo, I did nothing to hide my bad temper, but drained my glass and slammed it down again on the table, hard.

My neighbors' charms soon pacified me somewhat, but anger once aroused is a pernicious thing. It continued to rage within me, although my surroundings should have kept me amused and had a conciliatory effect. But I only felt more vicious when someone brought my beautiful lady a lute, and she sang to her own accompaniment and to everyone's delight. Unfortunately someone asked for absolute silence. So I wasn't even to be allowed to talk! Her singing grated on my nerves. No wonder only a small spark was needed to set off an explosion!

She had just finished a song, the applause was tremendous, and she looked across at me with true affection in her eyes. Unfortunately, her glance failed to touch me. She could see me draining my glass and hear me demand that it be refilled. She shook a warning finger at me lovingly. "Don't forget that it is wine," she said, loudly enough for me to hear. "Water is for nixes!" I cried. She turned to the women sitting at my side and said, "Ladies, lace his goblet with your charms so that it isn't emptied so often."

"You're not going to let yourself be ruled by her, are you?" one of them hissed in my ear, and I cried aloud, "What does my dwarf want of me?" and accompanied my words with such a violent motion of my arm that I knocked over my glass.

"You have upset much," my beautiful lady said, and strummed her lute once, as if trying to attract the attention of those present from the disturbance back to herself. And she actually succeeded in doing so, especially when she stood up—which she did as if it were easier for her to play standing—and picked up the interrupted melody.

When I saw the red wine spill across the cloth, I came to my senses. Realizing what a terrible thing I had done, I was crushed. For the first time, music appealed to me. The first verse she sang was a friendly farewell to the company, who still felt united; with the next they gradually began to disassociate themselves from one another—every man for himself, apart, no one felt present any more. And what can I tell you about the last verse? It was aimed at me alone, the voice of love wounded, bidding farewell to all bad temper and bravado.

Silently I took her home, expecting the worst, but we had scarcely reached our room when she became very friendly and behaved enchantingly—she was even quite mischievous—and made me the happiest of men.

Next morning I said cheerfully and lovingly, "You have often sung when asked to do so at a gathering, as for instance last night, that touching farewell ballad. Sing just once for me now, a happy welcome to this morning hour, so that we may feel as if met for the first time."

"I cannot do that, my friend," she said seriously. "The ballad I sang last night was our farewell, and we must part at once. All I can tell you is that your offense against promise and vow has had the most dreadful consequences for both of us. You have frivolously thrown away all your chances of happiness, and I too must deny myself everything I desire."

I begged, I implored her to explain herself. "I can do so now," she said, "since I cannot remain with you any longer. So, hear what I would have liked to keep hidden from you forever! The shape and form in which you saw me in the casket is the way I was born, it is my natural shape. For I am of the race of King Eckwald, mighty prince of all pixies. Authentic history has much to tell of him. My people are still as active as they were in days of old and are therefore easily ruled. But I don't want you to think that they have remained backward in their activities. They used to be famed for making swords that pursued the enemy when hurled at him, invisible and secretly binding chains, impenetrable shields—things like that. But now they busy themselves mainly with objects that give man comfort and adorn him, and in this they surpass every race on earth. You would be amazed if you were to go through our workshops and storehouses. And all this would be well and good, if a certain condition did not prevail among us—especially in the royal family." She paused for a moment, and I begged her to go on revealing her miraculous secret.

"It is well-known fact," she continued, "that when God created the world, and the earth was dry, and the mountains stood powerful in their glory, He created the pixies first, before all living things—this is what I believe—so that there might be sensible creatures to admire His miracles in the earth's interior as well, in the caverns and crevasses. It is, moreover, common knowledge that these little people rose up and tried to grasp the dominion of the earth for themselves, and that is why God created the dragons, to subdue the pixies. But since dragons also liked to settle in great caves and fissures, and many of them spat fire and perpetrated other outrages, the pixies were sorely afflicted. They didn't know what to do. They turned to Almighty God and humbly and beseechingly implored Him to destroy this wicked race of dragons. He could not bring Himself to destroy creatures whom He had created according to His wisdom, but the despair of the pixies touched Him so deeply that He created the giants to fight the dragons—not to destroy them, but to at least decrease their number.

"But when the giants had more or less done away with the dragons, they too became haughty and presumptuous and began to persecute the pixies. Again the little people turned to God in their need, and He, in His omnipotence, created the knights to fight giants and dragons, and to live in harmony with the pixies. And with that, this aspect of God's creation was completed, and it came to pass in times to come that giant and dragon always held together, as did knight and pixie. So, you see, my friend, we are one of the oldest races in the world, which is a greater honor but results in quite a few disadvantages. For since on this earth nothing lasts forever, and all things that once were great must grow small, we too find ourselves diminishing constantly and growing smaller—especially the royal family, which is subject above all others to this fate because of its pure blood. Our sages therefore decided long ago that, from time to time, a princess from the royal house should be sent out into the land to marry an honorable knight, so that the race of pixies might be renewed and not die out completely."

My beautiful lady told me all this most sincerely, but I could not help watching her with some suspicion, for it occurred to me that she might be pulling my leg. I didn't doubt her story insofar as it concerned the fairylike quality of her origin, but that she had chosen me instead of a knight filled me with some distrust. I knew myself too well to believe that any of my ancestors might have been created directly by God. However, I hid my astonishment and doubt and asked amiably, "But tell me, dear child, how did you grow to be so tall and imposing? For I know few women who can equal your magnificent figure."

"I shall tell you," she said. "It was the policy of the pixie kings of old to beware of resorting to any extraordinary measures as long as possible, and I find this a quite natural and reasonable policy. And they might have hesitated much longer before sending a princess out into the land, if my little brother, who was born after me, had not turned out to be so tiny that his nurse lost him in his swaddling clothes, and no one ever found out what had become of him. Nothing like this unique case could be found in the whole annals of our kingdom. The wise men therefore held a conclave and . . . in short . . . it was decided to send me out into the world to find a husband."

"It was decided!" I cried. "All well and good, things can be decided, but to give a pixie the form of a goddess . . . how did your wise men manage that?"

"That, too," she said, "was ordained by our ancestors. In the royal treasure chest there was a huge gold ring. I speak of it now as it looked to me when I was shown it as a child. It is the ring I have on now, and this is how they set about it. I was carefully instructed in everything that was to take place, and told what I could and could not do.

"A magnificent palace was built after the pattern of my parents' favorite summer residence. It had a main building, two ells, everything one could wish for, and it stood in the entrance of a rocky crevasse, embellishing it marvelously. On a certain day, the whole court repaired to it, and my parents with me. The army paraded, and twenty-four priests carried the miraculous ring on a precious litter, not without a great deal of effort. It was laid down on the threshold of the palace, just inside as you step over it. A ceremony followed; then, after bidding everyone a fond farewell, I set to work. I walked up to the ring, laid my hands on it, and at once began to grow noticeably. In a few minutes, I had attained my present stature and I at once put on the ring. In no time at all, windows, doors, gate, and ells shrank into the main building, and in front of me, instead of the palace, stood a casket, which I immediately picked up and carried off, feeling quite pleased to be so big and strong even if I was still tiny compared to the trees and mountains, the rivers and vast plains. Still, beside grass and herbs, I was a giant, especially when compared to an ant. We pixies do not get along with the ants and are therefore often plagued by them.

"There would be much to tell of all the things that happened to me on my pilgrimage before I met you, but let it suffice to say that I tested many, and only you seemed to be worthy of renewing the wonderful line of Eckwald and perpetuating it."

As she spoke, I could feel my head move every now and then, but I was careful not to shake it in negation. I asked a lot of questions, but did not receive very satisfactory answers to any of them. To my dismay, however, I heard that, after what had happened between us, she would have to return to her parents. She hoped to be able to come back to me, but at this moment there was no getting around her putting in an appearance at home or all would be lost for both of us. The sacks would soon cease to pay, and there would be other disastrous consequences. When I heard that there was a possibility of our running out of money, I asked no further questions. I shrugged and was silent, and she seemed to understand.

We packed and took our seats in the carriage, the casket

opposite us. It didn't look like a palace to me. Thus we drove past several stations. The moneybags provided simply and liberally for tips and the fare until we reached mountainous terrain. We stopped, my lovely lady got out and hurried on ahead, and I followed with the casket at her request. She led me up a steep path to a narrow valley where a clear spring bubbled and wound its way through a meadow. Pointing to a rise in the ground, she told me to put the casket down and said, "Farewell. You won't have any difficulty in finding your way back. I hope we shall meet again."

But I could not leave her. It was one of her most beautiful days or, if you like, her loveliest hour. To be alone with such a ravishing creature on a green sward, between grass and flowers, hemmed in by rock and rushing water—what heart could have remained unfeeling under such circumstances? I wanted to grasp her hand and embrace her, but she pushed me away and, in terms that still were loving, threatened me with great peril unless I left immediately. "Is there no possibility of my staying with you?" I cried. "Can't you keep me with you?"

My words were spoken in such heart-rending tones and accompanied by such desperate gestures that she seemed touched and after some deliberation finally admitted that a continuation of our life together was not entirely out of the question. Not a man on earth could have been happier than I! I became more and more importunate and at last forced her to speak. She revealed the fact that if I was prepared to become as small as she had been when I had seen her in the casket, I could stay with her in her residence and kingdom and become a member of her family.

I can't say that the idea appealed to me, but at that moment it was quite impossible for me to part from her, and since I had become accustomed to the miraculous some time ago and was in a rash mood, I agreed and told her to do with me what she liked.

Immediately she asked me to stretch out the little finger of my right hand; she put hers against it and, with her left hand, gently slipped the golden ring from her finger onto mine. This had scarcely taken place when I felt a dreadful pain in that finger, the ring shrank and caused my agony. I screamed and reached out for my beautiful love, but she had disappeared, I simply cannot express what I felt at that moment, and there really is nothing to tell except that I very soon found myself a shrunken, tiny figure, standing beside my beloved in a forest of grass. Our joy at finding each other again after such a brief yet strange separation or, if you like a reunion without a parting, defies description. I threw my arms around her, she returned my embrace, and as a tiny couple we were just as happy as we had been when we were big.

We walked up a hill—which was not easy, because the grass meadow had become almost impenetrable forest for us—and finally managed to reach a clearing. To our astonishment, we found there an evenly constructed solid that we soon recognized as the casket. It was still in the condition in which I had set it down.

"Go up to it, my friend," my beloved said. "Knock on it with your ring, and you will see marvelous things."

I did as she told me, and had scarcely knocked when the marvels began to take place. Two ells shot out on either side, and parts of the box fell off like scales or shavings, revealing doors, windows, archways—everything that goes to make up a perfect palace.

Whoever may have seen a trick writing desk made by Röntgen,[32] with springs and secret drawers that can be set in motion, whereupon writing space, paper, letters, pigeonholes, and money compartment are revealed, all at once or one at a time, will have some idea of how this palace unfolded before our eyes. My sweet companion now drew me into it behind her. In the main hall I at once recognized the fireplace I had looked down on and the chair she had sat in, and when I looked up, I thought I could actually see traces of the crack in the dome through which I had peered. I will spare you a detailed description of the rest. Suffice it to say it was roomy, priceless, and in excellent taste. I had scarcely recovered from my amazement when I could hear martial music in the distance. My beautiful lady jumped joyfully to her feet and announced that her father was approaching the palace. We stepped outside and could see a glittering procession emerge from an imposing crevasse in the rocks. Soldiers, servants, household officials, and a whole brilliant court followed, one behind the other. Finally there came a golden multitude, and in its midst, the king himself. When everyone was assembled before the palace, the king stepped forward and approached it with his retinue. His loving daughter hurried to meet him, pulling me along with her; we threw ourselves at his feet, he raised me graciously, and I noticed only when I came to stand next to him that I was better built than anyone else in this little world. We walked up to the palace together, and in a studied speech, the king did me the honor of welcoming me before the entire court. He expressed his astonishment at finding us here, recognized me as his future son-in-law, and set the following day for the wedding.

I can't tell you how horrified I was suddenly to hear mention of a wedding, for I had always been almost more afraid of marriage than of music. Those who make music, I used to say, at least enjoy the illusion that they are in unison and that the over-all effect is harmony, because after they have allowed themselves sufficient time to tune up and have massacred our eardrums with all sorts of discordant sounds, they think that now they are in tune and the various instruments are perfectly suited to one another. The conductor himself suffers from this delusion, and they're off, while the listener's ears are screaming! But in marriage, not even this applies, because although it is nothing but a duet, and one would think that it should be possible to bring two voices— that is to say, two instruments—in harmony, still, it rarely happens. For, if the man gives the pitch, the woman usually wants it higher, then the man raises it again; and this goes on and on, from normal pitch to concert pitch, until in the end even the horns can't follow! And, since I couldn't bear harmonic music, you can't blame me for hating discord even more.

I don't want to speak of the festivities that took place next day; in fact, I can't speak of them because I paid them so little heed. The magnificent food, the priceless wine— nothing tasted right to me. I was considering what I should do. But there wasn't much to consider. I decided to escape and hide somewhere when night fell and actually succeeded in finding my way to a fissure in the rocks and squeezing through it, concealing myself as best I could. My first efforts were bent toward getting that cursed ring off my finger, but I couldn't do it however hard I tried. On the contrary, I could feel it contracting the minute I tried to get it off, causing me great pain which stopped immediately, however, as soon as I desisted in my efforts.

Early in the morning I awoke, the little that was left of me having slept very well, and wanted to move farther away, when something that felt like rain fell on me from above. It was falling through grass, leaves, and flowers, something akin to sand or grit, quantities of it, and I was horrified when everything around me suddenly came to life and a huge army of ants came hurtling down upon me. They saw me and at once attacked from all sides. Although I put up a brave defense, in the end they succeeded in covering, pinching, and tormenting me until I was thankful when someone called out to me to surrender, which I did promptly, whereupon an impressive-looking ant approached me most courteously—I would go so far as to say reverently—and begged for my good will. I learned that the ants were now my father-in-law's allies, that he had called upon them to bring me back, and that they were in duty bound to do so. So there I was, small, in the hands of creatures even smaller than I. There was no escaping the wedding, and I could only thank God that my father-in-law was not angry with me, and my beautiful lady not vexed.

Let me remain silent about the ceremony, let it suffice to say that we were married. I was surrounded by gaiety and mirth, but in spite of this, there were lonely hours that were conducive to thought. And now something took place that had never happened to me before. Let me tell you about it.

Everything around me was perfectly matched to my present size and needs. Flacons and goblets were beautifully proportioned for a tiny drinker—as a matter of fact they were better proportioned than ours. Everything I ate tasted wonderful, my wife's kisses were adorable, and I won't deny that the novelty of the situation made it very enjoyable. Unfortunately, I could not forget my former condition. I discovered within myself; the measure of my former size, and it made me restless and unhappy. For the first time, I could grasp what philosophers mean when they speak of the ideal that is supposed to cause mankind so much suffering. I had an ideal of myself and at times saw myself in my dreams as a giant. In short, wife, wedding ring, the shape of a pixie, and many other constrictions served only to make me utterly miserable, and I began to think seriously about extricating myself.

Since I was sure that the whole spell was contained in the ring, I decided to file it off. Toward this end I stole several files from the court jeweler. Fortunately I was left-handed, and had never done anything with my right hand in my life. I worked hard, but it was not easy, for the little gold band—although it looked thin—had grown thicker in proportion to the amount it had shrunk from its original size. I spent every spare hour on the project and was clever enough to step outdoors when the metal was almost split. And a good thing I did, for the golden band suddenly burst from my finger, and my figure shot up with such velocity that I was afraid it might reach heaven! At any rate, I certainly would have rammed through the dome of the palace and destroyed the whole building with my newborn clumsiness.

So there I stood, alone again, only much bigger and—it seemed to me—much more stupid and awkward, and when I had recovered from my stupor, I saw the casket standing at my side. I lifted it and found that it was heavy as I carried it down the footpath to the station, when I immediately ordered the horses harnessed and drove off. As we drove away, I tried the moneybags on either side. The money seemed to be spent; instead, I found a small key. It belonged to the casket, which contained a considerable replenishment. As long as it lasted, I used the carriage, which I then sold and continued my journey by stagecoach. I rid myself of the casket last because I was always hoping that it might be filled again. And so I finally arrived, although in a roundabout fashion, back in the kitchen where you first met me.

THE FAIRY TALE

Weary from the exertions of the day, the old ferryman lay asleep in his little hut on the banks of the great river which was swollen from a heavy rain and had overflowed its banks. In the middle of the night he was awakened by loud voices. He could hear that they belonged to travelers who wanted to be put across.

He went outside and could see two will-o'-the-wisps hovering over his moored boat. They explained that they were in a great hurry to get to the other side. The old man wasted no time, but pushed off and crossed the stream with his customary skill. Meanwhile the two strangers hissed at each other in a strange language that he could not understand. Every now and then, they laughed loudly. All the time they were jumping back and forth from the edge of the boat to the seats.

"You're rocking the boat!" the old man cried. "If you go on jumping around like that, it will tip over. Sit down, little lights."

They burst into loud, rude laughter at the very thought of such a thing; they jeered at the old man and were wilder than ever. He bore their bad behavior with patience, and soon they had reached the other side.

"This is for your trouble," his passengers cried, shaking themselves, whereupon many shining pieces of gold fell into the dank boat.

"For heaven's sake, what are you doing?" cried the old man. "You will bring disaster upon me. If one of the gold pieces had fallen into the water, it would have reared up and swallowed me and my boat—you, too, perhaps—for it cannot abide metal. Take your gold back!"

"We can never take back anything we have shaken off," said the will-o'-the-wisps.

"So you're going to leave me with the nuisance of picking it up, carrying it on land, and burying it," the old man said, stooping and gathering the gold pieces into his cap.

Meanwhile, the will-o'-the-wisps leaped out of the boat, and the old man called out to them, "What about my fare?"

"He who takes no money must work for naught," they cried.

"But didn't you know that I get paid only with the fruits of the earth?"

"Fruits of the earth? We despise them and have never partaken of any."

"Still, I can't let you go until you have promised to give me three cabbages, three artichokes, and three onions."

The will-o'-the-wisps would have liked to trick the old man by stealing away, but they felt quite incomprehensibly attached to the ground, and it was the most unpleasant experience they had ever had. They promised to fulfill his demand as soon as they could; he let them go and pushed his boat off. He was already quite far away when they shouted to him, "Old man! Listen, old man! We have forgotten the most important thing of all!" But he was too far away and couldn't hear them. He let the boat drift down river, alongshore, intending to bury the dangerous gold in a mountainous region that the water could never reach. When he got there, he spilled it into a great crevasse between high rocks, then he rowed back to his hut.

A beautiful green serpent lived in the crevasse, and the sound of coins clinking awoke her. One look at the tiny discs, and she began to swallow them greedily. She even picked up all the pieces that had fallen among the bushes and into the cracks.

As soon as she had swallowed them, she could feel them melting inside her. It was a very pleasant sensation. They spread through her entire body, and to her delight, she could see that she had become transparent and glowing. She had been promised a long time ago that she would one day look like this, now she began to wonder if the illumination would last. Thus curiosity and assurance for the future drove her out of the rocks to find out who could have scattered all this beautiful gold. She found no one. But she did find it very pleasant to admire herself, slithering between grass and bushes, and the lovely light she shed on the fresh green. Every leaf was an emerald, every blossom magnificently glorified. She roamed the lonely wilderness in vain, but her hopes rose when she came out into the open and, far off, could see a glow that equaled hers. "So I shall find my peers!" she cried and turned in that direction, paying no heed to the difficulties she encountered as she crawled through swamp and reeds. For, although she preferred living in dry, mountain meadows and deep crevasses and was accustomed to quenching her thirst with fresh spring water, she was ready to undertake anything for the sake of the gold and the beautiful light.

When she at last reached the soggy marsh where the will-o'-the-wisps were gamboling she was very weary, but she rushed up to them, greeted them, and was pleased to find herself related to two such pleasant gentlemen. The will-o'-the-wisps brushed against her, hopped over her, and laughed. "Well, dear coz," they said, "even if you are only from the horizontal line of our family, it doesn't really matter. Of course you realize that we are related to one another only because we glow . . . because—look!" and they turned themselves into flames by making themselves as long and pointed as possible. "See how well this narrow shape suits us gentlemen of the vertical lineage. Don't take offense, good friend, but show me another family that can boast the like. Never since the will-o'-the-wisps were created has one of them sat down or reclined."

The serpent began to feel very uncomfortable in the presence of these relatives, because however hard she tried to lift her head, she knew only too well that she would have to put it down on the ground again before she could move away. A little while ago, in her dark glade, she had been very pleased with herself, but here, in the presence of these cousins, she seemed to be glowing less and less by the minute; in fact, she began to fear that she might go out altogether!

It was therefore in a state of embarrassment that she hurriedly asked the gentlemen whether they could give her any information as to where the gold had come from that had tumbled into her crevasse a while ago. She thought it might be a rain of gold straight from heaven. The will-o'-the-wisps laughed and shook themselves.

A huge amount of gold coins fell from them, and the serpent slid forward quickly to swallow them. "Enjoy them, enjoy them, coz!" said the fine gentlemen. "We can let you have plenty more!" And they shook themselves several times with great agility. The snake could scarcely swallow fast enough. Her light grew visibly stronger; now she was really glowing beautifully. The will-o'-the-wisp, however, had grown quite thin and small, yet without losing any of their good humor.

"I shall be forever grateful," said the serpent, when she had caught her breath. "Ask of me what you will. I will do anything within my power for you."

"Very fine!" cried the will-o'-the-wisps. "So tell us—where does the Beautiful Lily live? Lead us as quickly as you can to the palace and garden of the Beautiful Lily. We are dying with impatience to dance at her feet."

The serpent sighed. "I cannot do you this service right away," she said. "The Beautiful Lily lives on the other side of the river."

"On the other side of the river! And we had ourselves ferried across on this stormy night! Oh, what a cruel stream it is that separates us! Do you think we could call the old man back?"

"You wouldn't gain anything by it," said the serpent. "For even if you were to meet him on this side, he wouldn't take you across. He can bring anyone to this shore but take no one to the other side."

"Well, then we've really done it! Is there no other way of getting across the water?"

"There are a few, only not right now. I can put the gentlemen across, but not until noon."

"And that's a time when we don't like to travel."

"Well, then you'll have to cross in the evening, on the shadow of the giant."

"And how do we go about that?"

"The giant, who doesn't live far from here, can do nothing with his great body. His hands can't lift a piece of straw, his shoulders can't bear a bundle of faggots, but his shadow

can do a great deal—in fact, everything. That is why he is
most powerful when the sun rises and sets. All one has to
do is sit down on the neck of his shadow at nightfall. Then
he walks gently toward the shore, and his shadow brings
the traveler across the water. If you want to meet me at
noon in that wooded corner over there where the shrubbery
grows close to the water, I can put you across and introduce
you to the Beautiful Lily, but if you don't like the heat of
noon, all you have to do is seek out the giant toward evening in yonder rocky bay. I am sure he will be pleased to
help you."

With a little bow, the young gentlemen left, and the serpent was quite glad to get away from them, partly because
she wanted to admire her own light, partly to satisfy a curiosity that had been plaguing her strangely for some time.

She had made a most peculiar discovery in the rocky crevasses through which she often crept, for although until now
she had had to crawl through these depths without a light,
she could tell different objects apart very well by feeling
them. She was accustomed to finding herself surrounded by
only the irregular products of nature. Sometimes she slithered past the sharp points of huge crystals or she could feel
the jags and flaws of pure silver; sometimes she brought a
gem out with her to the light. But, to her great astonishment, she had recently stumbled upon some objects in a
hollowed-out cave that betrayed the fact that the hand of
man had formed them. There were smooth walls that she
could not scale, sharp, regular edges, beautifully shaped col-
umns, and—what seemed strangest of all—human figures.
She had wound herself around them several times and come
to the conclusion that they were made of metal or highly
polished marble. Now she wanted to experience all these
things with her eyes and corroborate what until now she
had been able only to surmise; now she thought she could
illuminate this marvelous subterranean cavern with her own
light and hoped to see all these strange objects at once. She
hurried off and on the customary path found the fissure in
the rock through which she usually crept into the sacred
precincts.

When she arrived at the place she looked around her
curiously, and although her light could not illuminate every-

thing in the rotunda, still she could see what was near her clearly enough. With amazement and awe, she looked up into a shining niche that held the statue of a noble king in pure gold. It seemed to be more than lifesize, yet it was shaped like the figure of a slight rather than a big man. He was wearing a simple cloak and a wreath of oak leaves on his hair.

The serpent had scarcely taken in this awesome sight when the king addressed her. "Where have you come from?" he asked.

"Out of the cleft in the rock where the gold lives," said the serpent.

"What is more glorious than gold?" asked the king.

"Light," replied the serpent.

"What is more refreshing than light?" asked the king.

"Conversation," replied the serpent.

As they talked, the serpent caught sight, out of the corner of one eye, of another magnificent statue in the next niche. A silver king sat in it, a tall and slender man. He was ornately clad; crown, belt, and scepter were studded with jewels. The serenity of pride was on his face, and he seemed about to speak when a vein that ran darkly across the marble wall suddenly turned light and spread a pleasant glow through the whole temple. In it the serpent could see a third king, cast mightily in bronze. He sat there leaning on his club. He, too, wore a wreath of oak leaves and looked more like a rock than a man. The serpent was about to look at a fourth king, who was farthest away, when the wall opened and the shining vein disappeared like lightning, and the serpent's attention was now drawn to a man of medium height emerging from the aperture. He was dressed like a peasant and carried a small lamp in his hand. It burned with a quiet flame that was lovely to look into and it illuminated the whole dome in a wonderful fashion without casting a single shadow.

"Why have you come?" asked the golden king. "You can see that we have light."

"And you know that I am not permitted to illuminate darkness."

"Is my kingdom coming to an end?" asked the silver king.

"Late or never," the old man replied.

The bronze king asked in a loud voice, "When shall I arise?"

"Soon," said the old man.

"And with whom shall I ally myself?" asked the king.

"With your older brother," said the old man.

"And what is to become of the youngest?" asked the king.

"He shall sit down," said the old man.

"But I am not tired," the fourth king cried in a hoarse, stammering voice.

While everyone else in the temple had been talking, the serpent had been creeping around admiring everything and now she took a closer look at the fourth king. He was standing, leaning against a column, and his prominent figure was ponderous rather than beautiful. It was not easy to tell in what metal he had been cast. On looking closer it seemed to be a mixture of the three that composed his brothers, but in the casting, the metals had evidently not amalgamated properly; gold and silver veins ran irregularly through bronze, making him a very unpleasant sight.

Meanwhile the gold king said to the old man, "How many mysteries do you know?"

"Three," said the old man.

"Which is the most important?" asked the silver king.

"The manifest one," said the old man.

"Won't you reveal it to us?" asked the bronze king.

"As soon as I know the fourth," said the old man.

"It's no concern of mine," mumbled the composite king.

"I know the fourth," said the serpent, creeping up to the old man and whispering something in his ear, whereupon he cried in a mighty voice, "The time is at hand!"

The temple echoed his words, the metal statues rang with them, the old man vanished toward the west, the snake toward the east, and both hurried as fast as they could through clefts in the rocks.

The walls of every passage traversed by the old man turned to gold behind him, because his lamp had the miraculous power of transforming all stone into gold, all wood into silver, and all dead animals into jewels, and of destroying all metal. But to do all this, it had to shine alone. If another light shone with it, the lamp cast only a lovely glow, and all living things were refreshed by it.

The old man went into his hut, which was built up against the mountain. He found his wife despondent. She was sitting by the fire, weeping, and he could not console her. "How miserable I am!" she cried. "If only I had not let you go out today!"

"What has happened?" the old man asked calmly.

"You had just left," she said, sobbing, "when two blustering travelers came to the door. I was incautious enough to let them in. They seemed to be nice, decent people. They were dressed in bright flames. You could have taken them for will-o'-the-wisps. They barely got into the house when they began to pay me the most shameless compliments and in the end became so impertinent that I am ashamed to even think of it!"

Her husband smiled and said, "I think the gentlemen were only joking, but they really should have been satisfied to remain conventionally polite in consideration of your age."

"My age!" cried his wife. "Why do I have to listen to 'my age' all the time? How old am I, anyway? Conventional politeness! I know what I know. And just have a look round. Look at the walls. Can you see the old stones that we haven't seen for a hundred years? They licked off every bit of gold, and how spryly! And kept assuring me it tasted much better than ordinary gold. And when they had cleaned up the walls, they seemed to be in high spirits—and why not? They had certainly grown taller, broader, and shinier in a very short time. But then they began to be bold again and brushed against me and called me their queen and shook themselves, and a heap of gold coins fell from them and danced all over the place. Look at them shining there under the bench. And what a disaster! Our little pug dog ate some. There he lies by the chimney—dead. The poor thing. I can't get over it. I didn't notice it until they had gone, or I would never have promised to pay their debt to the ferryman."

"What do you owe him?" asked the old man.

"Three cabbages, three artichokes, and three onions," said his wife. "I promised to carry them down to the river as soon as it is light."

"Do them the favor," said the old man, "because they will serve us again someday."

"I don't know about that, but they certainly assured and promised me they would."

In the meantime, the fire in the stove had gone out. The old man spread ashes on the coals and removed the glittering pieces of gold. Now his little lamp shone by itself again, the walls were covered with gold once more, and the little pug dog had been transformed into the most beautiful onyx imaginable. The changeable black and brown of the costly stone made a rare work of art of him.

"Take your basket," said the old man, "and put the onyx in it. Then take three cabbages, three artichokes, and three onions, place them around the onyx and carry all of it down to the river. Let the serpent put you across at noon, and visit the Beautiful Lily. Give her the onyx,. She will bring the dog to life by touching him, just as she kills all living things in the same way. The dog will make her a faithful companion. Tell her not to grieve, her deliverance is nigh. She can look upon the greatest misfortune as good fortune for the time is at hand."

The old woman packed her basket and started out with the dawning day. The rising sun shone brightly on the river glittering in the distance. She walked slowly, because the basket was heavy on her head, yet it was not the onyx that weighed her down. Whatever dead matter she happened to be carrying never burdened her, because then the basket rose and hovered just over her head, but she found carrying fresh vegetables or a small living animal extremely onerous. She had been walking for some time in a dour mood when she suddenly came to a stop, startled. She had almost stepped on the giant's shadow, which stretched out across the ground to where she was walking. Only then did she see the powerful fellow bathing in the river. He left the water, and she didn't know how to get out of his way. As soon as he saw her, he greeted her cheerfully and the hands on his shadow reached for her basket. Nimbly they removed one cabbage, one artichoke, and one onion, and put them into the giant's mouth, after which he wandered on upstream, leaving the woman's path clear.

She wondered whether she should turn back and replace

the missing vegetables from her garden, and walked on beset by this doubt. Soon she had reached the back of the river. There she sat for a long time, waiting for the ferryman, and saw him at last, ferrying a strange traveler across. A young, noble, very handsome man got out of the boat. The woman couldn't take her eyes off him.

"What have you got there?" the old man called out.

"The vegetables that the will-o'-the-wisps owe you," the woman replied, showing him what she had. When the old man found only two of each kind, he was annoyed and assured her that he could not accept them. The woman begged him to take them, explaining that she could not go home again now, and that the basket would be too heavy for her on the way she still had to go. But he stuck to his refusal and explained that it didn't even depend on him. "Whatever I have coming to me," he explained, "must be left together for nine hours, and I can't take any of it until I have given the river a third." After much discussion, the old man finally declared, "We have one more possibility; if you want to give the river a guarantee and acknowledge the fact that you are its debtor, I'll accept the six pieces—but it's dangerous."

"If I keep my word, what can be dangerous about it?"

"Nothing at all," said the old man. "So, put your hand in the river and promise to pay your debt in the next twenty-four hours."

The old woman did and was startled when she drew her hand out of the water coal-black. She scolded the old man, pointing out that her hands had always been the most beautiful part of her. In spite of hard work, she had known how to keep the pretty things white and dainty. She looked at her black hand with chagrin and cried out in her despair, "But that isn't all! It's much worse! My hand is shrunk. Now it's smaller than the other!"

"It only looks that way," said the old man. "But if you don't keep your promise, it may come to pass: your hand will slowly dwindle and in the end disappear entirely—but you won't lose the use of it. You will be able to do anything you wish with it, only no one will be able to see it."

"I'd rather be able to do nothing with it, if only no one can see that anything is wrong," said the old woman. "But it doesn't really matter. I shall keep my word and rid myself of my black hand, and all this vexation." Quickly she picked up her basket, which now rose above the parting in her hair and hovered freely over her head. Then she hurried after the young man who was walking slowly along the river's edge, deep in thought. His marvelous figure and strange attire had made a deep impression on her.

His chest was covered with a coat of mail under which every part of his magnificent body moved freely, and a purple cloak hung from his shoulders. His bare head was covered with brown ringlets, his handsome face was exposed to the rays of the sun and so were his beautifully shaped feet. Anguish seemed to make him impervious to all outer impressions, for he was walking calmly across the hot sand on his bare soles.

The talkative old woman tried to draw him into a conversation but, in curt replies, he gave her little information. In the end, in spite of his beautiful eyes, she grew tired of constantly addressing him in vain. She took leave of him, saying, "I'm afraid you walk too slowly for me, sir. I must not miss the moment to pass across the river on the green serpent and bring my husband's wonderful present to the Beautiful Lily." With these words she hastened on. But the young man came to his senses just as quickly and hurried after her. "You are going to the Beautiful Lily?" he cried. "Then we are going the same way. What is the present you are taking to her?"

"I don't think it is fair, sir," said the woman, "to enquire into my secrets in such a lively fashion after being so taciturn in reply to my questions. But if you would like to strike a bargain with me and tell me your story, then I won't hide mine from you, nor my present." They soon came to an agreement; the woman told him how things stood with her, the story of the dog, and let him have a look at the wonderful gift.

The little pug dog looked so natural lying in the basket. It seemed to be resting. The young man lifted it out and held it in his arms. "Oh, fortunate animal!" he cried. "Her hands will touch you, she will bring you to life—but I who live must flee from her or come to a sad end. But why do I say sad? Is it not far more grievous and frightful to be paralyzed by her presence than it would be to die at her hands? Look at me," he said to the old woman, "how I have to suffer in my youth! This armor that I wore honorably in battle, this purple cloak that I tried to earn by ruling wisely . . . fate let me keep the former unnecessary burden, the latter meaningless adornment. Crown, scepter, and sword are gone, and I am as naked and needy as every other man. For her beautiful eyes have such an unholy effect that she robs all living things of their strength, and those whom her touching hand does not kill are changed into living, wandering shadows."

His lament did not satisfy the old woman's curiosity. She was far more concerned with his material position than with his soul. She didn't find out the name of his father or his kingdom. He stroked the hard little pug dog—who was warmed by the sunlight and the young man's breast as if it were living—and asked a lot of questions about the man with the lamp, and the possible effect of the sacred light on his pitiful condition. He seemed to hope for some benefit from it.

They were still conversing when they could see the majestic span of a bridge in the distance, reaching from one shore to the other and shimmering marvelously in the sun's glowing light. Both were astounded. They had never seen the span so effulgent. "What has happened?" cried the prince. "Wasn't it beautiful enough when it stood before our eyes as if made of jasper and quartz? Shouldn't one fear to cross it now that it seems to consist of emeralds, chrysoprase, and chrysolite?" Neither of them knew of the change that had come over the serpent—for it was the serpent who arched herself every noon across the river in the shape of a bold bridge. The wanderers stepped onto it reverently and crossed it in silence.

As soon as they reached the other side, the bridge began to sway and move. Soon it touched the surface of the water, the serpent, in her proper form, slithered on land and followed the wanderers. They had just finished thanking her for having allowed them to pass across the river on her back, when they noticed that, besides the three of them, others were present whom, however, they could not see; but they could hear a hissing at their sides and the serpent answering in a similar fashion. They listened and could finally make out the following: "We intend to look around the park of the Beautiful Lily first, incognito, and we would appreciate it if you would introduce us to this famous beauty at nightfall, as soon as we are presentable. You will find us at the edge of the big lake."

"Very well," replied the serpent, and a hissing sound was lost in the air.

Now the three travelers discussed in what order they should appear before the Beautiful Lily, for she could receive as many visitors as she liked, but they had to come and go singly or suffer considerable pain.

The woman, with the transformed dog in her basket, approached the garden first and looked for her benefactress, who was easy to find because she was singing to the harp. The lovely tones appeared first as rings on the still surface of the lake, then like zephyrs they set grass and bush in motion. There she sat, in a green enclosure, in the shade of a magnificent group of the most varied trees, enchanting the eyes, ears, and heart of the woman who approached, overjoyed and vowing that during her absence the Beautiful Lily had only grown more lovely. Already from a distance the good woman called out greeting and praise to the lovely girl. "What a blessing it is to look upon you! What heaven is spread by your presence! How charmingly the harp rests on your lap—your arms surround it so gently, it seems to yearn for your breast—and how lovely it sounds under your slender fingers! Oh thrice fortunate man who could take its place!"

With these words, she came closer. The Beautiful Lily raised her eyes, let her hands sink, and said. "Do not distress me with untimely praise. It only makes me feel my misfortune all the more strongly. Look—my poor canary, who used to accompany my singing so prettily, lies dead at my feet. He would perch on my harp and was carefully trained not to touch me. Today, when I awoke refreshed by sleep and raised my voice to sing a tranquil melody to the morn, and my little bird began to sing more harmoniously and brightly than ever before, a hawk swooped down over my head. In its fright, my poor little bird fled to my breast . . . at once, I could feel how the last twitching of life left it. I gave the bird of prey a look . . . you can see him down there, slinking helplessly beside the water. But of what use is his punishment to me? My darling is dead, and his grave will help only to augment the sad hedgerows of my garden."

"Cheer up, Beautiful Lily!" cried the woman, drying the tears the unfortunate girl's tale had caused her to shed. "Do not despair. My old man wants you to know that you are to restrain your grief and look upon the greatest misfortune as a harbinger of good luck, for the time is at hand. And truly, strange things are happening. Just look at my hand, how black it is, and it really is much smaller. I must hurry, or it will disappear completely. Oh why did I promise favors to the will-o'-the-wisps? Why did I have to meet the giant and dip my hand into the river? Could you give me a cabbage, an artichoke, and an onion? I would bring them to the river and my hand would be so white again—I could almost compare it with yours."

"You might possibly still find cabbages and onions, but artichokes you will seek in vain. None of the plants in my garden blossom or bear fruit, but everything I break off and plant on the grave of a beloved greens and shoots up at once. Alas, I have seen all these dales, bushes, and thickets grow. This umbrella of pines, these obelisks of cypresses, these colossal oaks and beeches—all were little sprigs planted by my hand as a sad memorial in otherwise unfruitful earth."

The old woman had paid little heed to this speech. She had been watching her hand, which seemed to grow blacker and smaller from minute to minute in the presence of the Beautiful Lily. The woman wanted to pick up her basket and hurry off, but then she remembered that she had forgotten the best thing of all. She lifted the transformed dog out of the basket and laid him on the grass, not far from the beautiful girl, "My husband sends you this token," she said. "You know that you can bring this precious stone to life by touching it. The good, bright little animal will surely bring you much joy, and my distress over losing him will be dispelled by the thought that you own him."

The Beautiful Lily looked at the little animal with pleasure and, it seemed, with some astonishment. "Many signs come together to give me new hope," she said. "But alas, isn't it natural to delude ourselves by imagining that good things are on the way when much misfortune is heaped upon us?

"What solace can good omen bring to me?
My sweet bird's death, the black hand of my friend,
The jeweled dog—however precious he may be,
Whom Lamp, to comfort me, did send . . .

"Far, far removed from every human pleasure,
My dire grief the only thing I know . . .
Oh, when will temple stand on bank of river?
Oh, when will bridge on shores of river grow?"

This song, which the Beautiful Lily accompanied charmingly on her harp, delighted everyone except the old woman, who listened to it with impatience. She was about to take her departure but was interrupted again, this time by the appearance of the serpent, who had heard the last two lines of the song and it once tried to encourage the Beautiful Lily.

"The prophecy of the bridge had been fulfilled," she cried. "Just ask this good woman here how magnificent the span is. What was formerly jasper and quartz, and let the light gleam through only around the edges, had become transparent gem. Beryl is not so clear nor can emeralds be said to have such beautiful color."

"My congratulations," said the Lily, "and may it bring you good luck, but you will forgive me if I do not consider the prophecy fulfilled yet. People can pass across your bridge only on foot, but we were promised that horse and carriage and all types of passengers would be able to cross back and forth on it at the same time. And didn't the prophecy speak of huge pillars that would rise up out of the river itself?"

The old woman, who hadn't taken her eyes off her shrinking hand, now interrupted the conversation to say farewell. "Stay one moment longer," said the Beautiful Lily, "and take my poor canary with you. Beg the lamp to turn the little thing into a beautiful topaz. Then I will restore him by touching him and, with your dear little pug dog, he will be my favorite playmate. But hurry as fast as you can, for when the sun sets, it will begin to decay horribly, and the lovely unity of its body will be forever destroyed."

The old woman laid the dead bird on some delicate leaves in her basket and hurried off.

"Be that as it may," said the serpent, continuing the interrupted conversation, "the temple has been built."

"But it does not stand on the banks of the river," said the Beautiful Lily.

"It still rests in the deeps of the earth," said the serpent, "but I have seen the kings and spoken to them."

"And when will they arise?" asked the Lily.

The serpent replied, "I heard the words echo through the temple . . . the time is at hand!"

A sweet expression of joy suffused the beautiful girl's features. "So I hear those happy words today for the second time! Oh, when will the day come when I shall hear them spoken thrice?"

She rose, and at once a pretty young girl stepped out of the bushes and took her harp. She was followed by a second girl, who collapsed the carved-ivory outdoor chair on which the Beautiful Lily had been sitting and took away the silver cushion under her arm. A third, carrying a huge parasol embroidered with pearls, appeared next and waited to see if the Beautiful Lily needed her to accompany her on a walk. These three girls were indescribably beautiful; still their beauty served only to heighten the Beautiful Lily's, which everyone had to admit was incomparable.

Meanwhile the Beautiful Lily had been looking down at the wonderful pug dog, and the sight of him seemed to please her. She bent down and touched him—immediately he leaped to his feet, looked about him brightly, ran back and forth, then rushed up to his benefactress and greeted her in the friendliest fashion.

She took the little animal in her arms and pressed him to her. "You are cold," she murmured, "and only half alive, yet you are welcome. I shall love you tenderly, play nicely with you, stroke you with affection, and press you to my heart." Then she let him go, chased him away, called him back, and played on the grass with him so gaily and with such innocence that it was a joy to watch her, and everyone present participated in her pleasure, just as a short while ago her grief had made every heart feel compassion.

Her enchanting play was interrupted by the arrival of the sad young man. He appeared on the scene as we already know him, but the heat of the day seemed to have exhausted him still further, and in the presence of his beloved, he grew paler with every passing minute. He was carrying the hawk on his hand. The bird sat there, quiet as a dove, its wings drooping.

"It is not friendly of you," the Beautiful Lily cried as he approached, "to bring that hateful animal before me, the monster that killed my little songbird."

"Do not rail against this unfortunate bird," replied the youth. "Rail rather against yourself and your fate, and permit me to associate with the companion of my misery."

Meanwhile, the pug dog had never ceased to gambol around his beautiful mistress, and she continued to cater to her little admirer. She clapped her hands to drive him off, then ran after him to bring him back; she tried to catch him when he fled, and chased him off when he came too close. The youth watched their play, taciturn and miserable. But when she took the ugly little thing in her arms—he found the animal repulsive—and pressed it to her heart and kissed its little black nose with her heavenly lips, he lost all patience and cried out in his despair, "Must I see with my own eyes how you may play with such a freak of nature, how it attracts you and enjoys your embrace? I, who by a miserable fate must live in a present that is ever separate from you, perhaps forever? I, who have lost everything through you—even myself—how much longer am I to come and go, pacing off the sad circle that takes me back and forth across the river? No—a spark of the old heroic courage still flickers in my breast. Let it rise up now in one last flame! If stone may rest against your bosom, then may I be turned to stone! If your touch spells death, then let me die at your hands!"

He made a violent gesture, and the hawk flew from his hand as he ran up to the Beautiful Lily. She stretched out her hands to stop him, thus only touching him sooner. He lost consciousness. Horrified, she could feel his dead weight

on her breast. With a scream, she stepped back, and the
youth sank expired from her arms to the ground.

A tragedy had taken place. The Beautiful Lily stood mo-
tionless, staring fixedly at the dead body. It was as if her
heart had stopped beating, and her eyes were void of tears.
The little dog tried in vain to wrest some affection from
her—for her the whole world had died with her friend. In
silent despair she did not look up for help—she knew there
was no help.

But the serpent became more alert than ever. Her mind
seemed bent on salvation and her strange behavior actually
did prevent the most imminent dread effect of the disaster.
With her supple body, she drew a wide circle around the
lifeless form, took her tail between her teeth, and remained
lying there, perfectly still.

Soon one of the Lily's beautiful handmaidens stepped forward, brought back the ivory collapsible chair, and with a
compassionate gesture begged the Beautiful Lily to be
seated. Then the second one came with a fiery-colored
scarf; with it she adorned rather than covered her mistress'
head. The third girl gave her the harp, and she had scarcely
pressed the magnificent instrument to her and played a few
notes, when the first girl came back with a bright, round
mirror and took up a stand opposite the Beautiful Lily,
catching her mistress' glance in the mirror; and presented
her with the most pleasing picture to be found in all nature.
Pain heightened the lovely girl's beauty, the scarf enhanced
her charm, and the harp her grace. Although everyone
hoped to see her unhappy condition changed, they could
not but wish to see her image held fast as it was now.

Looking into the mirror silently, she at first evoked melting tones on the strings, but soon her pain seemed to grow,
and the instrument responded powerfully to her grief. Once
or twice her lips parted as if she would sing, but her voice
failed her. Soon, however, her agony was dissolved in tears,
and two of the girls came to her aid and grasped her under
the arm. The harp sank on her lap. The third girl was just
able to catch it and lay it aside.

"Who will go and get us the man with the lamp before
sundown?" the serpent hissed softly, but quite clearly.
The girls looked at each other, but the Beautiful Lily's

tears only flowed faster. Just then the woman with the basket came back, all out of breath. "I am lost and a cripple!" she cried. "Look how my hand has almost completely disappeared! Neither the ferryman nor the giant will put me across the water because I am still a debtor to the river. I have offered it one hundred cabbages and one hundred onions—in vain. All it wants is the three artichokes—and there isn't an artichoke to be found in the entire region!"

"Forget your troubles," said the serpent, "and try to help us here. Perhaps you will be helped at the same time. Hurry as fast as you can to find the will-o'-the-wisps. It is still too light to see them, but you may be able to hear them laugh and flutter. If you hurry, the giant can still put you across the river, and you can find the man with the lamp and send him to us."

The woman hastened as fast as she could and the serpent seemed to wait for her return with her husband just as impatiently as the Beautiful Lily. Unfortunately the rays of the setting sun were already gliding the crowns of the trees in the glade and long shadows were falling on lake and meadow. The serpent became restless and the Beautiful Lady was again dissolved in tears.

In their dilemma the serpent never ceased looking around her, for she feared that the sun might go down at any moment and that decay would penetrate the magic circle—then nothing would be able to deter its attacking the handsome youth. Suddenly she saw the hawk high up in the sky, its wings purple-red as the last rays of the sun fell on its breast. She shook herself with joy at the good omen and she was not deceived, for soon they could see the man with the lamp gliding across the lake as if on skates.

The serpent didn't change her position, but the Lily rose and cried out to him. "What good spirit sends you to us just at this moment, when we have sent for you and are in such need of your aid?"

"The spirit of my lamp impels me," said the old man, "and the hawk led me here. The lamp sputters when I am needed, and I look for signs only in the air. Birds and meteors show me in what direction to turn. Be calm, beautiful maiden! I don't know if I can help. One man alone doesn't help, but only he who unites with many at the right time.

What we have to do is delay and hope. Keep your circle closed," he went on, turning to the serpent as he sat down beside her on a little hammock and cast the rays of his lamp on the dead body. "Bring the good little canary here, too, and lay him down in the circle." The handmaidens took the little body out of the basket, which the old woman had put down, and obeyed the man.

Meanwhile the sun had set, and as the darkness increased, not only the serpent and the man's lamp glowed, each in its own fashion, but the Lily's scarf gave off a gentle light that colored her pale cheeks and her white garment with infinite loveliness, like the roseate hues of dawn. All of them looked at one another in a silent exchange of contemplation, their anxiety and sorrow eased by certain hope.

The appearance of the old woman, accompanied by the two scintillating lights, was therefore most welcome. The will-o'-the-wisps gave every evidence of having lived extravagantly in the meantime, for they were very thin, but this did not seem to detract in the least from their good behavior toward the princess and the other maidens. They spoke about quite ordinary things with assurance and vivacity and seemed to be particularly fascinated by the enchantment the glowing scarf cast upon the Lily and her girls. The latter lowered their eyes modestly, and the praise of their beauty served only to heighten it. Everyone was pleased and calm except the old woman. Despite the assurances of her husband that her hand could not shrink further as long as his lamp was shining on it, she declared several times that, if things went on like this, her noble limb would have disappeared completely before midnight.

The man with the lamp had been following the conversation of the will-o'-the-wisps attentively and was delighted that the Lily was distracted and cheered by it. And truly, midnight came, no one knew how. The old man looked up at the stars and spoke, "We are assembled here at a most fortunate hour. If everyone stays at his post and does his duty, a universal happiness will resolve our individual pain, just as a universal disaster can destroy individual joy."

When he had spoken these words, there was a miraculous clamor, for everyone present suddenly spoke for himself and expressed what he felt he should do, only the three maidens were silent. One had fallen asleep beside the harp, the second beside the parasol, the third beside the stool, and no one could blame them, for the hour was late. The flaming youths, after having bestowed a few pleasantries on the maidens, had turned all their attention to the most beautiful one of all—the Lily.

"Take the mirror," the old man told the hawk, "light up the sleeping girls with the first rays of morn and awaken them with light reflected from on high."

Now the serpent began to move. She dissolved the circle she had formed and wound her way in great rings to the river. The two will-o'-the-wisps followed her ceremoniously. Anyone might have taken them for very serious little flames. The old woman and her husband picked up the basket—its gentle light had been barely noticeable until now—and came forward, holding it one on each side, and it grew larger and larger and more and more luminous. They lifted the body of the youth into it and laid the canary on his breast. The basket rose and hovered over the head of the old woman as she followed closely behind the will-o'-the-wisps. The Beautiful Lily took the pug dog in her arms and followed the old woman, the man with the lamp brought up the rear of the procession, and the whole region was strangely illumined by the many different lights.

When they came to the river, the little group saw—to their astonishment—a magnificent bridge spanning it. The beneficent serpent had prepared a shimmering path for them. They had already duly admired the translucent gems that formed the bridge in the daylight; now, at night, its brilliance was astounding. At the top, the bright arc stood out sharply against the dark sky, and in the water brilliant rays palpitated toward the center, demonstrating the span's mobile firmness. Slowly the little procession crossed over, and the ferryman, looking out of his hut far away, saw with amazement the glowing circle and the strange lights moving across it.

As soon as they had reached the other side, the span began to sway and undulate down to the water, and soon the serpent was moving across land, the basket set itself down on the earth, and the serpent again described a circle around it. The old man leaned forward and spoke: "What have you decided to do?"

"Sacrifice myself before I am sacrificed," said the serpent, "Promise me not to leave a gem on the ground."

The old man promised, then he said to the Lily, "Touch the serpent with your left hand and your beloved with your right."

The Lily knelt down and touched the serpent and the corpse. At once the youth seemed to come to life. He moved in the basket and sat up. The Lily wanted to embrace him, but the old man held her back. He helped the young man to rise and led him out of the basket and the circle.

The youth was standing, the canary was fluttering on his shoulder, life had been restored to both of them, yet they still lacked spirit. The Lily's handsome friend had his eyes open, but he did not see, or he saw all things without participation, and not until the general astonishment over this had died down, did they notice how strangely the serpent had been transformed. Her beautiful, slender body had fallen apart, forming thousands and thousands of gems. The old woman, who had reached clumsily for the basket, had knocked against the serpent. Now nothing was left of her shape—only a beautiful circle of jewels lay on the ground.

The old man at once began putting the precious stones into the basket, and his wife helped him. Then the two carried the basket to a projection on the banks of the river, and he spilled the jewels into it, not without protest on the part of the beautiful girls and his wife, who would have liked to pick out a few for themselves. The stones swam on the water like glittering, blinking stars, and there was no way of telling whether they were lost in the distance or sank. Then the old man spoke to the will-o'-the-wisps deferentially, "Gentlemen, I shall now show you the path and lead the way. But you will be doing us a great service if you open the portals to the inner sanctum for us. This time we must enter through them, and there are none beside you who can open them."

The will-o'-the-wisps bowed respectfully and remained behind, the old man with the lamp went on ahead into the rock, which opened up before him. The youth followed, still mechanical in his behavior; the Lily kept her distance behind him, silent and uncertain; the old woman, who did not want to be left behind, stretched out her hand so that the light of her husband's lamp would surely shine upon it, and the will-o'-the-wisps brought up the rear. The points of their flames converged, as if they were conversing with each other.

They had not proceeded like this for long, when the procession had to halt in front of a great bronze portal that was sealed with a golden lock. The old man immediately summoned the will-o'-the-wisps, who needed little encouragement and at once consumed lock and bolt with their sharp flames.

The metal resounded loudly as the portal sprang open, and the noble statues of the kings in the temple were illuminated by the lights that now entered. Everyone bowed low before the honorable rulers, especially the will-o'-the-wisps, who couldn't seem to stop their convolutions.

After a slight pause, the golden king asked, "Where do you come from?"

"From the world," replied the old man.

"Where are you going?" asked the silver king.

"Out into the world," said the old man.

"What do you want here with us?" asked the bronze king.

"To accompany you," said the old man.

The composite king was about to speak, but the golden king spoke first to the will-o'-the-wisps, who had come too close, "Get away from me. My gold is not for you," whereupon they turned their attention to the silver king and nuzzled up to him, and his robe glowed with their yellow reflection. "You are welcome," he said, "but I cannot nourish you. Eat your fill outside, then bring me your light." They left him and slunk past the bronze king—who did not seem to notice them—to the composite king.

"Who will rule the world?" the composite king asked, in his stammering voice.

"He who stands on his feet," answered the old man.

"That's me!" cried the composite king.

"It will be revealed," replied the old man, "for the time is at hand!"

The Beautiful Lily threw her arms around the old man's neck and kissed him fervently. "Holy Father," she said, "a thousand thanks, for now I hear the fateful words for a third time." She had scarcely finished speaking when she had to cling to him even more firmly, for the ground began to rock beneath them. The old woman and the youth clung to each other, too. Only the will-o'-the-wisps noticed nothing.

That the whole temple was in motion, like a ship gliding gently out of harbor after the anchor has been raised, was very clearly palpable. The deeps of the earth seemed to open up before it as it passed through them. It bumped into nothing, no rock stood in its way.

For a few moments, what seemed to be a fine rain dripped down through an opening in the dome. The old man held the Lily close and said, "We are under the river. Soon we shall have reached our destination." Then it was as if they were standing still, but they were deceived—the temple was rising upward.

Now there was a strange rumbling above their heads. Boards and beams, in shapeless conglomeration, began to crowd with a crash toward the opening in the dome. The Lily and the old woman sprang to one side, but the man with the lamp took fast hold of the youth and both stood firm. The ferryman's little hut—for that was what the temple had scooped up out of the ground and was swallowing as it rose—sank down slowly, covering the youth and the old man.

The woman screamed, the temple shivered like a ship that has unexpectedly run aground, the women ran around the hut in the confusion of dawn, but the door was closed, and no one answered their knocking. They knocked harder and were greatly astonished when, after a while, the wood began to ring back metallically. The power of the shut-in lamp had turned the wooden hut to silver from the inside out. It wasn't long before it also began to change its shape. The noble metal abandoned the random form of board, post, and beam, and expanded to take on the shape of a magnificent edifice of chased silver, and a beautiful miniature temple stood in the middle of the larger one or, you might say, the temple now included an altar that was worthy of it.

And then the youth could be seen walking up a stairway that rose from the inside of the silver edifice. The man with the lamp was casting his light on the young man and another man seemed to be supporting him; he wore a white garment and held a silver oar in his hand and could be recognized at once as the ferryman, the former inhabitant of the transformed hut.

The Beautiful Lily walked up the steps that led from temple to altar, but she still had to keep her distance from her beloved. The old woman, whose hand had grown ever smaller as long as the lamp had been hidden, cried, "Am I to remain miserable? With so many miracles, is there none to save my hand?" Her husband pointed to the open gate and said, "Look, the day is dawning. Hasten and bathe in the river."

"What sort of advice is that?" she cried. "I suppose you want me to go black all over and disappear completely. I haven't paid my debt yet."

"Go," the old man said. "Obey me. For all debts have been paid."

The old woman hurried off. Just then the light of the rising sun touched the open circle of the dome, the old man stepped between youth and maiden and cried in a loud voice, "Three things there are that rule the earth—wisdom, show, and power."

With the first designation, the gold king stood up; with the second, the silver one; with the third, the bronze king rose slowly to his feet as the composite king suddenly and clumsily sat down.

In spite of the solemnity of the moment, it was difficult not to laugh, because he wasn't sitting, he wasn't reclining, he wasn't leaning against anything—he simply collapsed shapelessly.

The will-o'-the-wisps, who had been hovering around him, were at his side. Although paled by the morning light, they seemed well fed again and in full flame. With their pointed tongues, they had very cleverly licked out the golden veins of the colossal composite king. The irregular spaces thus formed had remained open for a while, and the figure had retained its form, but when the last little vein was hollowed out, the statue had crumbled, unfortunately just in those places that keep their shape when a man sits down. The joints, on the other hand, which should have bent, remained stiff. You either had to laugh or avert your eyes. This in-between thing, neither shape nor lump, was repulsive to behold.

Now the man with the lamp led the handsome youth, who was still staring straight ahead, away from the altar and up to the bronze king. A huge sword in a bronze scabbard lay at the mighty ruler's feet. The youth put it on. "A sword in your left hand and your right hand free!" cried the powerful king, whereupon the old man and the youth moved on to the silver monarch. He held out his scepter to the young man, who grasped it with his left hand. In a benign voice, the silver king said, "Herd the sheep!" When they came to the golden king, he placed his wreath of oak leaves on the youth's head with a fatherly gesture of blessing and said, "Recognize what is highest!"

As they made the round, the old man watched the youth closely. After he put on the sword, his chest expanded, his arms moved, his steps were firmer; when he took the scepter in his hand, a gentleness seemed to enter into his strength, making him more powerful in a rather indescribable way. But when the wreath was placed on his brow, his features came to life, his eyes glowed with incredible spirit, and the first word he spoke was, "Lily!"

"Beloved Lily!" he cried, as he ran up the silver steps to meet her—for she had watched his movements from the top of the altar. "Beloved Lily, what could a man, who is equipped with all things, wish for that is more precious than innocence and the quiet love that your heart feels for me? Oh, my friend," he went on, turning toward the old man, his eyes on the three sacred statues, "magnificent and secure is the kingdom of our fathers, but you forget the fourth power that rules the world before all others, more universally and with greater certainty—the power of love." And with these words, he embraced the beautiful girl. She had cast aside her veil, and her cheeks were delightfully flushed.

Then the old man said, "'Love does not rule, it molds, and that is much more.'"

With all these festivities, this joy and rapture, no one had noticed that the day had dawned. Now quite unexpected objects suddenly attracted the attention of the little group. A large square surrounded by a colonnade formed an imposing courtyard at the end of which they could see a long, marvelous bridge with many lanes across the river. It had been lavishly constructed for the traveler's convenience, with arcades on either side. Thousands of people had already found their way to it and were walking back and forth on it. The broad highway in the middle was alive with herds and mules, riders, and carriages. They moved with the stream of people without getting into one another's way. Everyone seemed to be amazed by the practicality and splendor of the bridge, and the new king and queen were just as enchanted by the motion and liveliness of the people as by their love for each other.

"Think of the serpent and honor her," said the old man with the lamp. "You owe her your life, and your people owe her the bridge through which these neighboring shores are brought to life as countries, and united. Yonder gleaming jewels are the remains of the body she sacrificed; they form the basic pillars of your magnificent bridge. It has erected itself upon them and will support itself on them."

They were about to ask for an explanation of this wonderful and mysterious revelation, when four beautiful girls entered the temple through the portal. Harp, parasol, and chair helped to identify three of them as Lily's companions, but the fourth, who was more beautiful than the others, was unknown to them. She accompanied them gaily and in a sisterly fashion through the temple and up the silver steps.

"Will you believe in me more in the future, dear wife?" the man with the lamp said to the beauty. "Good fortune to you and to every creature who bathes in the river on this morn."

The rejuvenated and beautiful old woman—of whose former shape not a trace was left—embraced the man with the lamp with her revived and youthful arms, and he accepted her affection happily. "If I am too old for you now," he said, smiling, "you may choose another husband today. From today on, no marriage is valid that has not been renewed."

"But don't you know," she cried, "that you have grown young, too?"

"If you see a stalwart youth in me, then I am glad ar

take your hand again and hope to live on into the next millennium with you."

The queen welcomed her new friend and descended into the altar with her and her three playmates, while the king remained standing between the two men, looking across the bridge and watching the crowd of people on it intently. But his satisfaction was short-lived, for he soon saw something that irritated him. The giant, who apparently had not awakened refreshed from his morning sleep, was staggering across the bridge, creating the wildest disorder. He was drowsy, as usual, and seemed intent on bathing in the cove where he always bathed. But instead of the inlet, he found himself on firm ground and was groping his way along the broad pavement of the bridge. He stumbled in the clumsiest fashion between people and cattle, but although his presence astounded everyone, no one could feel him. However, when the sun shone in his eyes and he lifted his hands to rub them, the shadow of his huge fists rammed with such impact and so clumsily into the crowd that man and animals fell in a heap, were hurt, and in danger of being swept into the river.

When the king saw this outrage, he reached for his sword with an involuntary gesture, then seemed to think better of it and looked calmly at his scepter, and at the lamp and oar of his companions. "I can guess your thoughts," said the man with the lamp, "but we are powerless against this powerless creature. Be calm. He does harm for the last time, and fortunately, his shadow is turned away from us."

Meanwhile the giant had drawn closer and let his hands drop in astonishment at what he saw. He did no more damage and entered the open square, his mouth agape. He was approaching the portals of the temple when he was suddenly transfixed, just as he reached the center of the square. There he stood, a mighty colossus made of red, gleaming stone, and his shadow told the time on a circle that was laid out on the ground—not in numbers but in noble, significant symbols.

The king was delighted to see the monster's shadow put to some good use, and the queen was astounded when she emerged from the altar with her handmaidens, attired magnificently, and saw the strange sight that almost completely obstructed the view from temple to bridge.

In the meantime, the populace had crowded behind the giant. When he came to a standstill, they surrounded him and stared in astonishment at his transformation. Then they turned their attention from him to the temple—which they had not seemed aware of until now—and crowded toward the portal. At that moment the hawk soared high above the dome with the mirror and caught the light of the sun in it and poured it down on the group standing on the altar. In the twilit vault of the temple, the king and queen, and their companions, seemed to be illuminated by a heavenly effulgence, and the populace fell on the ground before them. When they had recovered and risen to their feet again, the king had already descended into the altar with his retinue to proceed to the palace through secret passageways, and the people scattered through the temple, anxious to satisfy their curiosity. They stared in awe at the three standing monarchs, but were even more curious to know what could possibly lie hidden under a carpet in the fourth niche, for someone, in well-meaning modesty, had spread a magnificent cover over the collapsed king, which no eye could penetrate and no hand dared to remove.

The people couldn't seem to get their fill of looking and admiring. More and more people crowded into the temple, and they would have crushed themselves to death if their attention had not been drawn again to the square outside where gold coins had suddenly begun to fall out of the air. They clinked on the marble tiles. Those nearest fell upon them. The miracle was repeated—here, there, at random. It is understandable that the will-o'-the-wisps, in parting, wanted to play one more trick and squandered the gold they had extracted from the veins of the collapsed king in this droll fashion. For a while, the people continued to mill around greedily, even after the gold coins had ceased to fall. At last they dispersed, each went his way, but the bridge teems to this day with wanderers, and the temple is more frequently visited than any other in the world.

GLOSSARY OF PERSONS

BATTEUX, Charles. 1713–1780. French critic.

CHODOWIECKI, Daniel. 1726–1801. Engraver in Berlin.

DE PILES, Roger. 1635–1709. Writer, painter, engraver.

ECKERMANN, Johann Peter. 1792–1854. German author.

ERNESTI, Johann August. 1707–1781. German theologian and philologist.

GALL, Franz Joseph. 1758–1828. Anatomist and craniologist.

GESSNER, Salomon. 1730–1788. Swiss painter, etcher, writer.

GOTTER, Friedrich Wilhelm. 1746–1797. Poet. At the embassy in Wetzlar.

HAMANN, Johann Georg. 1730–1788. Philosopher and writer in Königsberg.

HEBEL, Johann Peter. 1760–1826. German poet.

HERDER, Johann Gottfried von. 1744–1803. German philosopher, poet, critic.

HEYNE, Christian Gottlob. 1729–1812. Professor at the University of Göttingen.

KENNICOTT, Benjamin. 1718–1783. English critic of the Old Testament.

KESTNER, Johann Georg. 1741–1800. Charlotte Buff's fiancé.

KLOPSTOCK, Friedrich Gottlieb. 1724–1803. German poet.

LAVATER, Johann Kaspar. 1741–1801. Swiss physiognomist.

LOTTE (CHARLOTTE BUFF), Kestner's betrothed.

MERCK, Johann Heinrich. 1741–1791. Darmstadt. Writer.

MICHAELIS, Johann David. 1717–1791. Göttingham, German Bible critic.

NICOLAI, Christoph Friedrich. 1733–1811. Bookdealer and writer. Berlin.

PEGELOW, David. Russian surgeon from Riga.

SEMLER, Johann Salomo. 1725–1791. Halle. German Bible critic.

SULZER, Johann Georg. 1720–1779. Berlin. Philosopher.

SWIFT, Jonathan. 1667–1745. English satirist.

WEYGAND, Christian. Bookdealer and publisher in Leipzig.

WEYLAND, Friedrich Leopold. Goethe's table companion and friend in Strassburg.

WINCKELMANN, Johann Joachim. 1717–1768. German archaeologist and historian of art.

WOOD, Robert. 1717–1771. Historian of art.

NOTES

THE SORROWS OF YOUNG WERTHER

REFLECTIONS ON WERTHER

had assembled and given each other the names of famous knights.

144 [13] From an anonymous poem of the seventeenth century, *A Satire on the Human Race.*

146 [14] Lodun, God of poetry according to Ossian.

[15] From "Suicide," a poem by Th. Wharton, 1771.

147 [16] Marcus Salvius Otho, Roman emperor, A.D. 69.

153 [17] Zeuxis, a Greek painter.

154 [18] In *Nathan the Wise,* Gotthold Ephraim Lessing (1729–1781), German critic and dramatist, compare three religions with three rings that cannot be told apart—an original and two copies.

GOETHE IN SESENHEIM

175 [19] Now included in Goethe's novel, *Wilhelm Meisters Wanderjahre (Wilhelm Meister's Travels).*

[20] Inserted in Book II of *Dichtung und Wahrheit,* and subtitled "A Boy's Fairy Tale," it is actually an invention of Goethe's maturer years (1811).

176 [21] His theory was that he could tell the character of a man by the shape of his skull

[22] End of *Dichtung und Wahrheit,* Book X. Book XI, published two years later, opens with the famous quotation, "That the trees don't grow up into heaven, has been provided for," and continues the Sesenheim idyl as follows here.

177 [23] Goethe goes into Herder's way of preaching and reading aloud (p. 156, "Goethe in Sesenheim") in order to contrast it tacitly with his own way of communicating with a listening audience.

In a passage at the end of *Dichtung und Wahrheit,* Book X, (pp. 175 and 176 in this volume) Goethe discusses the extraordinary impact of the spoken word on an audience attuned to the speaker. Dwelling on this, he goes so far as to brand writing a misuse of human speech.

There is a curious discrepancy between the passage purporting to give the views of the maturer Goethe on this matter, and the return to the incident in question—his recital of "The New Melusina" at Sesenheim—in the opening pages of

Book XI, published two years later. (This pause
and passage of time is indicated by spacing on
p. 176. See note 22.)

There he tells us that the active response of the
audience was due to their matching of the two
characters of that story with a real couple of their
personal acquaintance. This explanation comes as
an afterthought. Had he inserted his vehement remarks at the end of Book X as reflecting the mind
of the young author at the time of the Sesenheim
idyll, the unity of the mood would have been preserved. But coming forty years later as the reflections of the writer of the memoirs who had
learned the true reason for the extraordinary effect his story had produced, they are out of place.
Obviously, the Goethe who wrote the account at
the end of Book X had not then planned to give
it the peculiar twist that he adds later when he
takes up the situation once more.

Why then did Goethe add this twist in returning
to the matter of the effect of his story upon his
audience? We find the answer in his elaborate reflections on the participation of the reading public
in the case of *Werther,* as told in the following
books of *Dichtung und Wahrheit.* What made the
interest of the public so intense in that instance was
not the pure empathy of sensitive readers with the
fictitious hero and his fate. It was the fact, rather,
that this hero and his fate showed a most striking
resemblance to an actual man and his catastrophic
fate fresh in the memory of the readers. This type
of interest caused the author great annoyance. He
wanted his *Werther* to appeal strictly on its own
merits, as a compelling piece of creative fiction.
Goethe uses the instance of *Werther* to dwell on the
loneliness of the artist and to emphasize the gulf
that separates him from the public that reads him
("Reflections on Werther," p. 154).

In all this, of course, he ignores or minimizes
the fact that in patterning the locale, the circumstances, the time, and the tragic end of *Werther*

on the model of young Jerusalem, he had deliberately invited the type of curiosity that he complains about.—Hermann J. Weigand.

181 24 Goethe here refers to his dancing master's daughter Lucinda, who fell in love with him while he was attracted to her sister, Emilie, a situation he uses in Werther's fist letter to William. In their last encounter, Lucinda kisses him passionately in front of Emilie and says, "Fear my curse! Misfortune upon misfortune shall be heaped forever on her who kisses your lips after me. Just try to approach him again. . . . I know that this time God has heard me." *Dichtung und Wahrheit,* Book IX.

189 25 The bride of the fool in Goethe's farce, *The Fool's Wedding.*

191 26 "Willkommen und Abschied" ("Welcome and Farewell"). "Mailied" ("May Song"). "Mit einem gemalten Band" ("With a Painted Ribbon"). "Erwache Friederike" ("Awaken, Friederike"). "Balde sehe ich Riekchen wieder" ("Soon I Shall See Her Again").

27 "Mit einem gemalten Band" ("With a Painted Ribbon").

197 28 Gretchen (1764), Goethe's first love at the age of fifteen, believed to be partly fictitious and a composite of several figures. *Dichtung und Wahrheit,* Book V.

29 Annette (1766) followed Gretchen in Goethe's affections, when he was a student in Leipzig. She was Anna Katharina Schönkopf, who inspired the only drama left of his youthful days, *Die Laune des Verliebten (The Model of a Man in Love). Dichtung und Wahrheit,* Book VII.

199 30 From Klopstock's ode "Braga."
31 From Klopstock's ode "Skating."

THE NEW MELUSINA

215 32 David R. Röntgen (1745–1807) was a fine cabinet maker in Neuwied, whom Goethe probably met on his Rhine journey with Lavater.

SELECTED BIBLIOGRAPHY

Works by Johann Wolfgang von Goethe

Gedichte (Poems), 1771

Götz von Berlichingen, 1773 Drama

Die Leiden des jungen Werthers (The Sorrows of Young Werther), 1774 Novella (Signet Classic 0451-523032)

Egmont, 1787 Drama

Iphigenie auf Tauris (Iphigenia in Tauris), 1787 Drama

Torquato Tasso, 1790 Drama

Romische Elegien (Roman Elegies), 1795 Poems

Wilhelm Meisters Lehrjahre (Wilhelm Meister's Apprentice-ship), 1795-96 Novel

Hermann und Dorothea (Hermann and Dorothea), 1797 Drama

Faust, Part I, 1808, Part II, 1832 Drama

Die Wahlverwandstchaften (Elective Affinities), 1809 Novel

Dichtung und Wahrheit (Poetry and Truth), 1811-33 Unfinished Autobiography

Die italienische Reise (The Italian Journey), 1816-29 Travel Sketches

Westöstlicher Diwan (West-East Divan), 1819 Poems

Wilhelm Meisters Wanderjahre (Wilhelm Meister's Travels), 1821-29 Novel

Marienbad Elegien (Marienbad Elegies), 1823 Poems

Selected Biography and Criticism

Bielschowsky, Albert. *The Life of Goethe*, 3 vols. Trans. William A. Cooper. New York: Putnam, 1905-08.

Croce, Benedetto. *Goethe*. New York: Knopf, 1923.

Dieckmann, Liselotte. *Johann Wolfgang Goethe*. New York: Twayne, 1974.

Friendenthal, Richard. *Goethe, His Life and Times*. London: Widenfeld and Nicolson, 1965.